she i

"You bought this house from my grandfather," Jed Willetz replied.

"I'm so sorry for your loss."

He made a face, apparently not in the mood for platitudes. She hadn't meant it as a platitude, though. She *was* sorry.

"Have they buried him yet?"

"Who—my grandfather? He was cremated," Jed told her. "I'm up here to bury his ashes."

Well. Wasn't this a fun topic for two people just getting to know each other? "What can I do for you?" she asked, a bit more congenially.

"Put down the damn knife."

"Ah." She climbed back on the porch and balanced the knife on the railing.

"So tell me about the box," he said in an offhand voice.

Wariness overtook her. How had he learned about the box? If he knew of its existence, who else did?

"What box?" she asked with feigned innocence.

"The box you dug out of your garden. Can I have a look at it?"

"I don't know you, Mr. Willetz, and I don't have to show you anything I don't want to show you."

"You do if it's mine...."

Dear Reader,

Writers love playing "what if?" and *Hidden Treasures* is a classic "what if?" book. I'd been doing some mental doodling and found myself wondering, "What if someone unearthed an object of great value hidden in a sleepy little town? How would that discovery change the lives of the people who lived there?"

Rockwell, New Hampshire, is purely fictional (although yes, there is a mountain range in central New Hampshire called the Moose Mountains). I had great fun creating the town and populating it with small-time shop owners, drunks, hustlers, prudes, gossips—and the closest thing Rockwell has to a dynasty: three generations of men named John Edward Willetz.

John Edward III, known as Jed, is an irresistible hero, not quite bad boy but close, not quite a business success but getting there, not scholarly but street-smart, a small-town scamp who found contentment only by leaving the small town behind. When he returns to Rockwell to deal with father Jack and the remains of grandfather John, Jed learns that his hometown is full of surprises, not the least of which is Erica Leitner, a Boston-bred, Harvard-educated schoolteacher who's trying to plant roots—and zucchini—in a place he can't wait to escape.

And then there's that hidden treasure. Is it hers? Is it his? With fame, fortune and a media circus looming on the Moose Mountain–shaped horizon, can Jed and Erica comprehend the true value of what they've found?

Spend a little time in Rockwell and find out!

Judith Arnold

Hidden Treasures
Judith Arnold

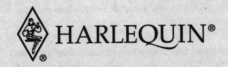

HARLEQUIN®

TORONTO • NEW YORK • LONDON
AMSTERDAM • PARIS • SYDNEY • HAMBURG
STOCKHOLM • ATHENS • TOKYO • MILAN • MADRID
PRAGUE • WARSAW • BUDAPEST • AUCKLAND

ISBN 0-373-71117-4

HIDDEN TREASURES

Hidden Treasures

CHAPTER ONE

ERICA WASN'T THRILLED with Randy's cap. Above the curved visor appeared the words Triple-X—the Sexy Beer. It would have seemed silly enough on an adult, but it seemed even sillier on Randy, who was only eleven years old.

No doubt he'd gotten the cap from his father. Erica had concluded from the few times she'd met Glenn Rideout that the man was a jackass. He ran Rideout's Ride, one of Rockwell's eight bars; maybe the hat was a gift from one of his distributors. He probably thought the thing looked cute on his son.

Even without the hat, Randy didn't qualify as cute. He was skinny and gawky, with an olive-shaped head and a hot-dog–shaped body. He wore his hair in a buzz cut and his two front teeth overlapped. But Erica didn't invite him to her house because she wanted to hang out with a cute little boy. To be sure, she didn't really invite him at all. He just showed on a semiregular basis, foraging for cookies and companionship.

Today, he'd rapped on her screen door when she'd been about to embark on her new project: the garden. "Sure, I'll help," he'd offered when she told her plans. "And after we do your garden, we can have cookies, right?"

"Of course." In an eleven-year-old boy's economic

system, cookies could purchase just about anything—labor, the truth, a new best friend.

Randy had helped her carry the flats of seedlings she'd bought yesterday morning at Tully's Hardware and Garden Center from the rear of her station wagon to the rectangular patch of dirt she'd hacked out of the scruffy tufts of grass that she euphemistically referred to as her lawn. She'd done her best to cultivate the patch yesterday. She'd raked the dirt, sifted out the obvious stones and tossed them into the woods, and felt achy and fulfilled once she'd gone inside to shower. She was a *gardener*—or she would be, once she got all those seedlings into the ground. She would be the sort of woman who connected with the earth, who participated in the cycles of nature and the seasons of life. She would have dirt beneath her nails, and her jeans would fade to white at the knee.

"Pull the tape a little tighter," she instructed Randy, who stood at the far end of the rectangle.

"I don't get why we have to measure it," Randy called back to her. His voice was still high and piping, not much different from its pitch two years ago, when he'd been a student in her class. "Why can't we just plant the plants?"

"I told you, Randy, according to my research, the plants will thrive best if the seedlings start out six to eight inches apart."

"My mom doesn't measure her garden."

"And how are her plants?"

"I don't know. I don't pay attention."

Erica nodded. "I *do* pay attention. And I'm planting my seedlings six inches apart."

Randy obediently stretched the tape measure the length of her garden. Erica used her spade to mark six-inch intervals along the first row. "This is where my tomato plants are going."

"That's an awful lot of tomato plants," he observed, eyeing the plastic frame box of tender green sprouts, which sat beside the garden plot.

"Maybe some of the plants will die. I don't know what my harvest will be like. I'm a novice at gardening. Do you know what a novice is?"

"Something like a priest, I think."

Erica smiled. "It can mean someone who's training for a religious order. In general, it means someone who's new at something. It comes from the Latin *novicius,* meaning *new.*" Aware she was lecturing, she shut up and finished poking indentations in the soil. Randy didn't seem to mind when she veered into pedantic mode. But *she* minded. She'd been living in Rockwell for nearly three years. Surely some of her know-it-all attitude should have atrophied by now.

"Okay," she said once she was sure she'd gotten her didacticism under control. "We'll put the tomatoes in this row, and then we'll measure off a row for cucumbers and peas, and in the last row I'll plant some broccoli and zucchini. What do you think?"

"Broccoli?" Randy wrinkled his nose. "My gramma used to make me eat broccoli when I was bad. It was like a punishment."

"Your grandmother must love you very much," Erica remarked, reeling in the tape measure somewhat and turning it perpendicular so she could get her rows properly distanced.

"My gramma is a statist."

"A statist?"

Randy frowned. "Isn't a statist, like, a mean person?"

"A *sadist*," she corrected him.

"Oh. Whatever. Broccoli sucks. And zucchini…" He shook his head gravely.

"What's wrong with zucchini?"

"If you plant too much of it, it takes over the world."

"The world?"

"Well, your garden, anyway." Randy shook his head at her obvious ignorance. "Nobody plants zucchini."

"Then it's a good thing I'm planting it. Otherwise it might become extinct."

Randy eyed her from beneath his cap. Despite the shadow that obscured the upper half of his face, she could read in his expression a bit of doubt mixed with panic that zucchini might in fact be on the verge of extinction, and only Erica's noble efforts could save it.

The soil she turned with the pointed tip of her trowel smelled malty. It was damp—New Hampshire was just emerging from mud season, the weeks when land frozen through a long New England winter finally thawed. Erica was proud of herself for having learned about things like mud season. She personally knew people who tapped maple trees, and she no longer pictured Bambi and cringed when she saw antlers hanging on the wall of some public establishment. Maybe in another year or two, she'd actually feel she belonged in Rockwell. Meanwhile, it was long past the time she should learn how to garden.

"So when are we gonna start planting this stuff?" Randy asked.

Erica pressed the button to retract her tape measure. Glancing up, she saw him fingering one of the spindly tomato seedlings. He wore shorts even though the temperature couldn't have been much higher than the mid-fifties, and his knobby knees were gray with dirt. The shorts bulged strangely in places; he seemed to have oddly shaped items crammed into most of the pockets.

She surveyed the grid of her garden one more time. "Let's do it," she said, hooking the tape measure over her belt. It had a clip for just that purpose, like for a cell phone or pager. Clipping a tape measure onto her belt made a very different statement from clipping a high-tech gizmo onto her belt. The tape measure said, *I'm competent. I know my tools.* She wished it were true.

She grinned, although she couldn't help gazing warily around her yard, which extended between a fringe of trees on one side and the remnants of a fence on the other. At one time the fence must have stood straight, a row of narrow vertical slats linked by wire, but the wire had rusted, and Erica had demanded that it be removed before she bought the house. All that remained were a collection of rotting slats sprawled between her house and the house where John Willetz used to live.

He'd been her landlord when she'd first moved to Rockwell from Brookline, Massachusetts. Then last year, he'd offered to sell her the cottage she'd been renting from him, and the half acre of land on which it stood—so he could die with money in the bank, he'd told her. Less than six months after the closing, he'd died. She still felt a little guilty about that, as if by agreeing to buy the house she'd somehow hastened his death.

His house had remained empty for more than three months. Every now and then his son, Jack, parked his rust-scabbed pickup in front of the old farmhouse, rambled through its rooms and emerged carrying some object or other. Once he'd taken a skillet, another time a gilt-framed mirror, yet another time a tarnished brass lamp. He never spoke when he showed up. If she was outside, fussing with her property and doing her impression of a proud home owner, he'd nod to her. She'd nod back. That seemed to be all the friendliness he could handle.

She'd peeked into the windows of John's house a few times, but snooping struck her as rude, even if the man she was snooping on was "in a better place," as most people in town tactfully put it. Erica wasn't sure if that meant they believed he'd gone to heaven or just that they considered death an improvement over Rockwell.

"What do you want me to do?" Randy asked.

"We're going to dig the holes now—about three inches deep—and plant a seedling in each. Think you can do that?"

Randy rolled his eyes. Of *course* he could do that, just as he could convert fractions to decimals, recite the entire opening text of *Star Wars* by heart and program a VCR. He often put on a show of exasperation for Erica, but she figured that if she was really that annoying, he wouldn't keep biking up her gravel driveway and sticking around for an hour or two. Her cookies weren't that good, not even the home-baked ones. Especially not the home-baked ones. Baking was right up there with gardening as one of those earthy, rustic skills she had yet to master.

She hoped some sort of synergy would develop around the wholesome north-country crafts she was acquiring. Home owner. Gardener. Baker. Teacher. Put them all together and they'd surely turn her into the earth-mother spirit she'd always dreamed of becoming.

Randy carried a tray of zucchini seedlings over to the row nearest the decrepit fence and dropped to his knees. All her measurements notwithstanding, he wasn't too precise with his planting. He used the claw and his bare hands to shove the moist dirt aside. Before he had the first plant in the ground, he was wearing a streak of dirt on his chin.

Wielding the trowel, she started planting across the garden from him. There was no such thing as too many tomato plants, she reassured herself. If her harvest was too big, she would eat tomatoes for breakfast. She'd stew them into marinara sauce and preserve them— another north-country skill she could add to her repertoire. She'd make tomato sandwiches and tomato omelettes. She'd find a recipe for tomato cookies and bake a few batches.

"You gonna put a fence around the garden?" Randy asked.

"I bought some fencing, yes," she said.

"It better be high enough to keep out deer."

The fence was only two feet tall. "I have yet to see a deer wandering into my yard," she said defensively.

"That's because you didn't have a garden. Now you do."

"Deer go after trees and shrubs, not garden plants," she argued, pretty sure she was on solid ground. "The real pests are raccoons and gophers. The fencing I got ought to keep them out."

"Gophers dig under fences— Hey, wow, there's a huge rock over here."

Erica sat back on her heels and frowned. She'd neglected to calculate huge rocks into her grid. "Can you dig it out?" she asked.

Randy banged the tines of the claw against the rock. It didn't sound like a rock, actually. She couldn't see what he was hitting, but the contact made a dull sound. He pushed some dirt out of his way and banged again.

"What *is* that?" she asked, rising and walking around the garden's circumference. Randy was hunched over his hole, scooping dirt out with his hands. She knelt beside him and applied her spade to the hole. When the metal edge banged against whatever was buried there, she knew the object wasn't a rock. It sounded almost like wood, a hard, rounded surface.

"Keep digging," Randy encouraged them both as he burrowed deeper. Erica was as eager as Randy to find out what lurked under the soil's surface here. "I bet it's a bone," he said.

"A bone?" Erica swallowed hard. What if a body was buried in her backyard? When she'd had the property inspected before signing the final purchase agreement, no one had mentioned anything about a secret cemetery or an Indian burial ground on her land.

What if, instead of a cemetery, the bone belonged to a murder victim? What if John Willetz's previous tenants had met a grisly end? He'd been an ornery old man, crusty and terse, but she'd loved that about him because it had made him seem like an authentic New Hampshire Yankee.

Could he have been a mass murderer in his spare time?

"Like a dinosaur or something," Randy was saying. "Like, maybe we'll find a dinosaur here and we'll wind up on the Discovery Channel."

A dinosaur would be fine with her. In fact, the bone was probably from a dead animal, a species far less exotic than a dinosaur. Like a deer. Maybe this was a deer burial ground, which was why the deer never wandered through her yard. It was sacred territory to them.

Randy was scrabbling away at the dirt, muttering when a mound he'd removed from the hole rolled back in. "There's a shovel in the garage," she said, pointing to the shed at the rear of her property. She didn't think it had been built as a garage, but it stood at the end of the driveway and its doors opened wide enough for her Subaru wagon to squeeze through.

Randy stood and loped to the garage. His feet were too big for him, and at least two times she was sure he'd trip over his own toes, but he made it to the shed and back without incident—and with the shovel. Unfortunately, it was a snow shovel.

"Be careful," she cautioned as he dug the shovel's wide, curved scoop into the soil. "If it's a dinosaur bone, you don't want to damage it."

"Okay." Randy shot her an awed look.

Together they cleared enough dirt to discover that their find was not a dinosaur bone, or any bone at all. It appeared to be the corner of some sort of wooden box with an arched lid.

Please, God, not a coffin, she prayed, although if it was a coffin, the odds were, the remains inside would not have belonged to John Willetz's last tenant. Or if they did, John Willetz would likely not have murdered the tenant. Murderers generally didn't bury their victims in coffins—at least, not in the mystery novels she read.

But it was too small for a coffin. A bit more dirt

clearing revealed the width of the box to be maybe six inches—the distance between two zucchini seedlings.

"Cool!" Randy dug up and flung aside one of the zucchini seedlings he'd planted, a sacrifice Erica wouldn't mind once the remaining zucchini seedlings rose up and overran her property. While he removed dirt from the top of the box, she worked around the sides, loosening the packed dirt that embraced it.

"Be gentle," she warned as Randy scraped the top of the box with the edge of his shovel.

"It's a treasure chest," Randy said, his little-boy voice rising into a squeak. "Like, a pirate's treasure."

"I doubt pirates would bury their treasure in central New Hampshire," she argued. "It's probably something the last resident of this house left behind. Maybe he buried some papers or something."

"Or money. Maybe he buried a million dollars."

As the shape of the box became visible, Erica estimated that a million dollars wouldn't fit inside unless the money was in very large denominations. Who in Rockwell would have accumulated a hundred ten-thousand-dollar bills? And if they had, why would they have buried the money in the yard of a two-bedroom cottage on Old North Road?

Because it was stolen, that was why. Because they couldn't come up with a way to launder the money, so they'd hidden it in the yard with the plan of returning to Rockwell at a later date to retrieve the stash. Which might mean that by exhuming the box, she and Randy were putting themselves in danger, inviting the wrath of whoever had buried the thing.

But no one had come back to get the money in the nearly three years Erica had been living here. Maybe they were in jail. Or dead.

"All right," she said, nudging away the snow

shovel. "We've nearly got the box clear. Help me un-wedge it."

Randy flopped back down onto his knees and worked the opposite side loose. Together they lifted the wood box out of the hole and balanced it on some old fence slats. It felt too heavy to contain money or papers, but the weight might have come from the wooden box itself. Its hinges were rusted, and the front was clasped shut with a delicate brass padlock. Erica brushed off the clods of dirt that clung to it.

"Pop the lock," Randy urged her.

"No!" she exclaimed, then lowered her voice back to normal. "If we pop the lock, we'll break it."

"Well, how else are we going to find out what's inside?"

"We need to handle this box carefully, Randy. It looks like it could be very old."

"Very old? Like, *very* old?"

"Very."

"Like an antique?"

"Older than an antique."

Randy stepped back, his eyes round beneath his cap. He regarded the box as if it was a rare and valuable artifact. Which it well might be.

Then again, it might be junk.

Still, Erica didn't want to mess with their find. On the chance that the box wasn't junk, she would treat it with the proper reverence.

"What do you think we should do?" Randy asked.

Hunkering down, she rested her chin against her knees and studied their breathtaking discovery. Bigger than a shoe box but significantly smaller than a pirate's treasure chest, it had a refined aura to it. It could be a gentleman's caddy, or a container a Colonial-era courier might have used to transport important documents.

Or a lady might have secreted her *billets-doux* in it. Or maybe a few gems. Erica hadn't heard anything rattling around inside, but if it was lined in felt or velvet, that would have muffled the sound.

Or else it was empty. Empty junk.

"What we need," she told Randy, "is an expert."

"For what?"

"To open it."

"Hell, I could get that lock off with one good pop." He considered his words and nibbled his lip. "I mean, heck." He stared at the box, nudging his cap back on his head. "Just one good pop and I could get it open." He brandished the claw to demonstrate his popping technique.

"But if you broke the lock, you might destroy the box's value." She felt like his third-grade teacher again, the wise elder edifying a skeptical student. "If it's really an antique, it could be irreplaceable. If we break the lock—that could destroy its value as an artifact. Do you know what an artifact is?"

"Yeah, there's this computer game that has lots of artifacts in it."

"In this context," she explained, not caring that she was once again sliding into pedantic mode, "the artifact could be of enormous value. A museum might want it. Historians could study it and learn something about the history of this part of New Hampshire. If we break the lock just because we're curious to see what's inside, we could destroy all the knowledge they might extract from this one unique box." Although it *could* be junk, she reminded herself silently. It *could* be worthless.

"Yeah, but…" Randy toed the dirt, kicking a little back into the huge hole they'd dug in her zucchini row. "But it's our box. Like, don't you think we ought to know what's inside? Like, what if it's a bomb or some-thing?''

"I highly doubt it's a bomb." She had more or less concluded that the late John Willetz hadn't murdered his previous tenants. She wasn't going to journey from that conviction to the possibility that he'd instead planted land mines disguised as historical artifacts in her backyard.

"Or maybe there's a ghost or something in it."

"I highly doubt that, too."

"Yeah." Randy tugged off his cap, ran his hand over his hair and put the hat back on. "It would have to be a pretty puny ghost to fit into that box. If you believed in ghosts in the first place."

"Which I don't."

"Me neither."

Silence settled over them for a minute. A crow cawed in the distance, its nasal cry harsh yet wistful. The sun struggled to add warmth to the early-spring air. Erica felt a chill just looking at Randy's exposed pale legs. Next year, or maybe the year after, those calves would be covered with wiry hair. But right now they were still a little boy's legs, and he was still enough of a little boy to entertain, at least for a mo-ment, the possible existence of ghosts.

"I know experts," she finally said.

"What experts?"

"People I studied with in college."

"They're experts in buried boxes?"

"No, but they know how to date artifacts. And maybe how to open an antique padlock without break-ing it."

"But what's inside—that would be, like, ours?"

"If there are old documents in the box, I'd want to pass them along to a museum or a historian—someone who could study them and make use of them. But for all we know, the box could be empty.''

''Who'd lock an empty box?''

Good point. ''Well, whatever is in there, I don't want to break the lock. Let's call one of the experts I know.''

''Okay.'' He peered up at her. ''But I wanna be there when they open it.''

''Absolutely.''

'''Cuz, I mean, we found it together and all.''

''I won't let anyone open the box without you being there,'' she promised.

''So, like, you won't open it when I'm in school or something?''

''When you're in school, Randy, so am I,'' she reminded him.

''Yeah, I guess.'' He stared at the box a moment longer, a deep, hard stare as if willing the lid to become transparent. ''I mean, 'cuz this is cool.''

''It certainly is.''

''And, like, there *could* be money or something in it.''

''We'll find out soon enough.''

He sighed and, after a farewell gaze, turned away from the box. ''I could sure use some cookies right about now,'' he said.

Erica smiled. ''I've got some chocolate chip cookies.''

''Store bought?''

''You bet.''

Randy grinned. ''Great. Let's eat.''

CHAPTER TWO

JED WILLETZ FOLDED a stick of peppermint gum into his mouth and sighed. Gum wasn't a cigarette. Nor were toothpicks, Tic-Tacs, sourballs or candy cigarettes, which looked an awful lot like chalk. Six months after quitting, he ought to have gotten past the craving for nicotine, but he hadn't yet.

That was life, though—the things that ought to get easier in time usually didn't.

So he chewed gum.

Rideout's Ride hadn't changed since the last time he'd been in town. Actually, it hadn't changed much since the first time he'd stepped into the place, when he'd been about three. It had been called Stubby's then, after its owner, Stubby Miller. Jed's dad had asked Jed to wait on the front porch while he went inside to settle a matter with someone, and then the old man had ordered a beer and forgotten that he'd left his young son outside.

Having a father like Jack Willetz had taught Jed to become self-sufficient. At three years of age, he'd had the gumption to shove the door open, march into the dim, salty-smelling tavern and ask the first person he saw, "Is my daddy here?"

After that, people in Rockwell used to say, "That Jed Willetz—he's going places." Prophetic words. The day after Jed had graduated from Rockwell Regional, he'd gone.

He checked to make sure he'd locked the door of his rented Saturn. It was a wussy car, small and lacking muscle in its engine, but the rental had been cheap. That aqua color, though… No car should ever be aqua. It was unnatural, the shade of something that might crawl out of the ocean in a Disney cartoon. Cars ought to be car colored—white, silver, black, red, British racing green or midnight blue. Not the color of bathroom wallpaper.

Grinding his gum between his molars, he strode across the potholed parking lot, up the two crumbling concrete steps and inside.

Same salty smell. Same tacky décor—cloudy mirrors, framed photos of dogs and neon signs advertising beer, one of them shaped like a green windmill even though the Ride had never carried a label as classy as Heineken. Same dusty antlers protruding from the wall above the door. Every bar in Rockwell displayed at least one pair of antlers. Jed wondered whether antlers were a requirement for getting a liquor license in this part of New Hampshire.

Rideout's Ride had the same clientele as last time, too, more or less. At four-thirty on a Sunday afternoon in April, only a certain kind of guy would be hanging out in a gloomy bar, washing away whatever sermon he might have sat through that morning in church—or hiding from church altogether. Jed's father was that kind of guy.

"Well, look what just blew in," Glenn Rideout growled. That was the man's version of a warm welcome, and Jed accepted it as such. Glenn had never quite mastered the art of vocal inflection. Happy, sad, bitter or buoyant, his voice always emerged in a growl, as if the Irish setter in the framed photo behind the bar was a ventriloquist and Glenn was his dummy.

"How's it going, Glenn?" Jed responded with a smile. His eyes had adjusted to the dark, and he surveyed the barroom in search of his father.

"If you're looking for your dad, he ain't here," Glenn told him.

How about if I'm not looking for him? Jed wondered. *Would he be here then?* He didn't say that, though. It would probably skid right past Glenn without leaving rubber. Instead, he shrugged and said, "This is the first place I thought to look."

Glenn apparently took his words as a compliment. He was tall and gangly, his head the shape of a submarine sandwich, his hair like a fringe of curly brown lettuce extending beyond the roll. "What brings you to town?" he asked.

"Gotta bury my grandfather's ashes. Is my dad around?"

"He'll probably be showing up here sooner or later. Take a load off. I'll fix you up with something."

"No, thanks." Beer wouldn't mix well with the peppermint tingling inside his mouth, and Jed rarely drank anything harder. He'd been living in New York long enough that he sometimes found himself drinking bottled water. Embarrassing, but there it was.

Glenn gave Jed a suspicious look. Halfway down the bar, a paunchy guy with hair as gray and fine as cobwebs and a visible hearing aid protruding from his ear shouted, "That the Willetz boy?"

Glenn shouted back, "Yup."

The man gave a wheezy laugh. "Jed Willetz, eh?"

"How's it going?" Jed said in a normal voice, then wondered if he should have shouted, too.

"I hear you're doing pretty damn well for yourself in the big city," the man bellowed.

If he'd heard that, he was deaf. Jed was doing all right, better than he would be doing if he'd stayed in Rockwell, but "pretty damn well" might be a bit of a stretch, depending on how you defined *well* and *damned*. "I can't complain," he said loudly.

"You don't know who I am, do you?" the man hollered.

Jed smiled sheepishly and glanced at Glenn, who continued to glower at him. He'd just driven six hours in an ugly-colored car; did he really have to buy a drink? "Maybe I am a bit thirsty," he said, recognizing that the cost of a soft drink was a small price to pay to stay in Glenn's good graces. "You got any Coke?"

Glenn's face relaxed. "Sure. That's Potter Henley," he added, tilting his elongated head in the man's direction. "Your father's accountant." He bustled a few steps down the bar to a refrigerator and pulled out a bottle of cola for Jed.

Great. His father was entrusting his money—scant though it was—to a deaf fat guy who spent Sunday afternoons drinking in the Ride. Jed forced a smile, ground his teeth into his chewing gum and strode down the bar to shake Potter Henley's hand. "My old man's accountant, huh?"

"I took over his books for him last year. Arithmetic isn't his forte," Henley said, mistakenly giving the word a second syllable.

"If you're his accountant, I hope you're doing more for him than just adding and subtracting."

The man wheezed another laugh. "I'm keepin' him out of jail. You can thank me anytime you want."

Jed wasn't sure thanks were in order. He might prefer if his father *was* in jail, if only because that way he'd be sure the guy was eating three squares and staying out of trouble.

His father wasn't a criminal—at least, no more of one than most of the chumps who called Rockwell home. Given the opportunity, Jack Willetz would cut a corner or two, fudge a little, sweet-talk his way past a cop. But who wouldn't? A man didn't survive by saying, "Yes, Officer, you're right, I really was driving ten miles above the posted speed limit," or, "You're right, Officer—that song and dance I gave you about having split all that wood myself was of questionable veracity. The truth is, I helped myself to some firewood from the stash the Kelbys keep under their back porch. You'd better just go ahead and arrest me. Please don't make the handcuffs too tight."

Jed didn't know if his father was still song-and-dancing his way through life. It wasn't his business, though. He was not his father's keeper.

Just thinking about having to deal with the old man made Jed sigh. Glenn Rideout had poured him a beer mug full of cola, and he reached for it and took a sip. It fizzed around his chewing gum and stung a path down his throat.

"So, life is expensive down in New York, is it?" Glenn asked.

Jed shrugged. "More expensive than here. Why do you ask?"

"Just wondering how come you've been avoiding a barber. I'm guessing all they've got down there is *stylists,* huh."

Jed smiled with forced patience. They had barbers in New York, and he made use of them, paying maybe twice as much for a decent haircut as what a really bad haircut in Rockwell would cost. But he hadn't been to a barber in a month, and he wasn't going to apologize. His hair wasn't that long. Nobody gave it a second look in the city.

Damn. He really wanted a smoke. The last time he'd survived a full twenty-four hours in Rockwell without a cigarette, he'd been about ten. "You have any idea when my father might be rolling in?" he asked Glenn.

"He's probably on his way over now," Glenn snarled. "May as well take a load off and enjoy that soda." He gestured toward one of the empty stools on Jed's side of the bar.

Sitting would mean accepting an obligation to make small talk with these clowns—and any of the other clowns who might wander over to the bar from where they were seated at the rear of the narrow room. Two gaunt, grizzled guys in plaid shirts huddled across from each other at one of the tables, and a man no older than Jed occupied a table by himself. He had a dark, scraggly beard, and a glass half-full of something and ice stood at his elbow. His eyes were closed.

If Jed wandered back there, he'd recognize the guy. A classmate of his, no doubt. The regional high school had been small enough for everyone to know everyone. None of his classmates would have changed much in the twelve years since graduation. Even he hadn't changed that much. He might have added a final inch to his height after his departure, and yeah, his hair was longer. But other than that, he was still Jed Willetz. A happier version, but not much different.

One of the reasons he'd left town was that he'd

known everyone. If he'd wanted to spend the rest of his life getting drunk at places like the Ride with people like—Sleeping Beauty back there *could* be Matty Blancher, Jed realized—getting drunk with guys like Matty and Stuart Farnham and JoAnn Meese—man, she used to get wild after a couple of wine coolers... Well, he'd wanted something more.

The door swung open and hope geysered inside Jed. It subsided when he saw not his father but a skinny squirt of a boy bounding into the bar. "Hey, Dad!" the boy chirped, a baseball cap shoved back on his narrow head. Glimpsing his face, Jed scowled. The poor kid looked like a miniature version of Glenn.

"What are you doing here?" Glenn asked none too graciously.

The kid seemed undeterred by his father's surly greeting. "Dad, guess what? This is, like, so cool you won't believe it!"

"I already don't believe it," Glenn grumbled.

"I was over at Erica's house? And we found this treasure chest."

"A treasure chest?" Glenn snorted. So did Potter Henley, who punctuated his skepticism with an indulgent shake of the head.

Unlike them, Jed was intrigued. One of the ironies of Rockwell was that the people who lived here were exposed to very little yet acted as if they'd seen everything, whereas in New York City, where people *did* see everything, sometimes several times in one day, they didn't seem anywhere near as jaded. But neither central New Hampshire nor Manhattan struck him as locales where one would ordinarily stumble upon a treasure chest.

"Where'd you find it?" he asked.

The kid turned to him, gratitude augmenting the excitement that lit up his eyes. "At Erica's house."

"I told you to call her Miss Leitner," his father scolded. "And I don't know why you spend so much time there, anyway."

Glenn's son ignored him and talked only to Jed. "It was buried in her garden, where she was going to put her zucchini. You wouldn't believe how many zucchini she was planning to plant, but I think I set her straight on that."

"That's a big favor you did her," Jed praised him, trying not to smile.

"So we were digging, and we dug up this treasure chest. It's real old. Like *real* old. Erica—Miss Leitner—she says we can't open the lock because we'd break it, so she's going to get this expert to open it and then we can find out what's inside. Like, maybe it's full of secret talismans or something. Or jewelry. Or a million dollars."

Glenn Rideout perked up at the possibility the chest could contain something of value. So did Potter Henley. So, even, did the two codgers and Matty Blancher, who stirred lazily in his chair and blinked his bleary eyes open. "A million dollars, you think?" Glenn asked, dropping the damp cloth he'd been using to wipe down the scarred pine surface of the bar. "Where'd you find this thing again?"

"In Erica's garden, where the zucchini were supposed to go."

"Who's Erica?" Jed asked. The name Erica Leitner rang a vague bell. She must have moved into town after he'd left, although he had trouble believing anyone would ever voluntarily move *into* Rockwell.

"She's this lady," the boy explained. "She was my third-grade teacher."

A new third-grade teacher. Jed wondered where they'd recruited her from. The potato fields of Maine, maybe; or one of the Canadian provinces where unemployment was in the double digits. People didn't move to Rockwell unless they were moving out of somewhere worse.

"She's real nice," the boy continued. "She gives me cookies."

Glenn broke in, sounding like a Doberman growling and sniffing at the invasion of a stranger. "So, what about this treasure chest? You think it's full of valuables? How big is it?"

"I don't know," his son replied. "Like a shoe box, maybe? A big shoe box. The kind boots would come in. Work boots. Not real high boots, waders or something like that, but, like, ankle-high work boots—"

Potter Henley cut him off with a laugh that caused his spare chin to vibrate. "Can't fit much treasure in a box that small."

"You sure as hell can," Glenn argued. "A shoe box full of money? I wouldn't turn it down."

"We don't know what's in it," the boy reminded his father. "Erica doesn't want to break the lock."

"What is she, nuts? Yeah, she's nuts," Glenn answered his own question. "Hanging around with a twerp like you proves as much. She worries me, that woman."

"She's nice," the kid argued.

"I'll bet." His father rubbed his long chin, looking as if thought required a great effort on his part. "The thing to do is find out what's in the shoe box, Randy.

If your teacher can't figure out how to open a damn shoe box, I can help her there.''

"It's not a shoe box," the boy reminded him. "All I said was, it's like about that size. But it's real old, with rusty hinges." The boy ruminated for a moment. "I bet it was real pretty when it was new."

"A box is a box," his father muttered. "How pretty does it have to be?"

The kid lifted his eyes to Jed again, as if seeking an ally. He was refreshingly unstylish, compared with the precociously fashionable children who lived in Jed's Manhattan neighborhood.

"So, when is Miss Leitner going to open the damn box?" Glenn asked.

"I don't know. She said she was going to bring an expert in to open it."

"An expert?" Glenn snorted again. "Where's she gonna find an expert?"

"Harvard," Randy told him.

"Harvard?" Jed blurted out in surprise. Rockwell wasn't the sort of community that drew experts from Harvard, although if some academic hotshot wanted to do research on a down-at-the-heels quarry town clinging desperately to its mediocrity, this would be the place to set up shop.

"Oh, that gal," Potter Henley boomed. "Harvard. Isn't she's something."

"She's cool," Randy insisted, obviously smitten with his former teacher.

"Okay, wait." Glenn leaned forward on his elbows, his narrow body hunched over the bar. "Let me get this straight. You found a shoe box in her garden—a box the size of a shoe box," he corrected himself when

Randy appeared ready to interrupt. "And she wants to find someone from Harvard to open it."

"Yeah."

"I told you she was a little off," Glenn muttered, also eyeing Jed in search of support. Jed shrugged.

"Who dug up this box?" Potter Henley shouted. "You or her?"

"We both did," Randy said. "It was, like, I was digging over by the zucchini part of the garden, and I felt what I thought was this big rock, and then we both dug it up."

"He found the box," Potter pointed out to Glenn. "You know what I'm saying?"

"You found the box?" Glenn grilled Randy.

Jed swallowed some Coke to keep from laughing out loud. The idea of the Rideout family staking a claim on some old box that likely held the remains of someone's beloved pet cat was ludicrous. But Glenn's eyes were unnaturally bright. He was no doubt visualizing a major haul for whoever could stake a valid claim.

Randy evidently didn't catch his father's angle. "I found it, and we both dug it up."

"Maybe we need an expert of our own," Glenn muttered to Potter.

Potter frowned, leaned forward and cupped a hand behind his ear. "Huh?"

Before Glenn could repeat his statement at the proper decibel level, Jed turned to Randy and asked, "Where does Miss Leitner live?" If she was new in town, someone ought to warn her that Glenn Rideout's eyes were glowing with a greed as dangerous as UV rays in July. If she thought experts from Harvard were all she needed, she had a lot to learn. People like Glenn Rideout—hell, people like liquor-dimmed Matty

Blancher—could knock a Harvard expert flat around here. This was Rockwell. Fancy degrees and lofty credentials didn't count for much in these parts.

"She lives on Old North Road," Randy informed him. "Over by the old Willetz farm."

"Your grandpa used to rent to her," Potter yelled. "Know that farmhand cottage sitting on the edge of the property? Your grandpa made himself a nice little profit selling it to the schoolteacher."

That was why her name had sounded familiar. Jed remembered his grandfather telling him he'd sold that old wreck of a building. To a schoolteacher, he recalled. She'd been renting the place, and then she'd bought it. But the few times Jed had visited in the past couple of years, he'd never met his grandfather's neighbor. She must have been over at the school, teaching earnest third-graders.

So now this small-town schoolmarm was living on land adjacent to the farm Jed had inherited, and a box—*a treasure chest*—had been found on her land. Was it actually on her land? How clearly had the property lines been drawn?

Sure, she ought to be warned about Glenn Rideout's greed. But if Jed was going to do her this good deed by warning her, well, it wouldn't hurt to find out exactly where the box was when she and the Rideout kid had dug it up. Property lines could be a tricky thing.

Yeah, he'd like to have himself a look at exactly where this box was when she and Randy had unearthed it. On the slim chance they were talking about something of real value here—and if anyone knew the difference between junk and something of real value, it was Jed—he decided he'd better check out this new lady and her old box.

CHAPTER THREE

ERICA'S HOUSE WAS NOT designed for a cordless telephone. Her cordless required a phone outlet and an electric outlet so the handset battery could be recharged when the cordless wasn't in use, but her house had only two phone jacks and neither was near an electric outlet. She'd called the phone company to see if they could install a new jack for her, but the price they quoted—just for showing up...she'd have to pay extra if she actually wanted them to *do* anything—had deterred her. She was responsible for a mortgage now. She couldn't afford such extravagances as paying phone company employees to ring her doorbell.

So she'd set up her cordless on a kitchen counter, with one wire stretching to connect to the wall-phone jack and the other stretching in the opposite direction to share a double socket with her toaster oven. Having wires snaking across the counter looked messy, but it wasn't as if the kitchen was a *House and Garden* showcase to begin with. The counters were gray linoleum with black-and-white speckles running through it, and the cabinets were metal layered with white enamel paint that was chipped along the edges, as if a tiny rodent had been gnawing on them. The sink was a porcelain basin with a few indeterminate yellow stains that no amount of scouring and bleaching could obliterate. The floor was also linoleum—green agitated by spumes of black and white that reminded her of *The Perfect Storm.* It was truly an ugly kitchen, not the sort of environment she'd fantasized as a place for kneading bread, whipping up wholesome casseroles and baking cookies.

Maybe that was why cookies were as far as she'd gotten in her culinary aspirations. By the end of the summer, if Randy was right, she'd be whipping up lots of zucchini casseroles. And kneading lots of zucchini bread.

At least her oven no longer chirped. When she'd first moved in, it chirped every time she turned it on. She'd complained to her landlord: "I think there's a cricket living inside my oven, and the heat makes it screech."

John Willetz had marched over the flattened fence to her house, poked around inside her oven with a flashlight and pronounced it cricket free. Then she'd turned on the oven and he'd heard the chirp. He'd slid the oven away from the wall and tipped it at an angle. A cricket had scampered out from underneath. John had mercilessly crushed the bug under his heel, abandoned its smashed carcass on her seasick floor and taken his leave.

As landlords went, he hadn't been bad. Despite his advanced age, he'd been strong and tall, his shoulders barely hunched and his skin stained a weak-tea brown by sunshine and time. The lines in his face had had a permanence about them and the backs of his hands had been blotchy with age spots, but the only thing that had really marked him as old was his temperament: taciturn bordering on grouchy. Erica had liked to think he was the epitome of a true New England Yankee, but as she'd gotten to know other Rockwell residents, she'd realized they didn't all grunt and drop their *R*s.

Randy Rideout had spent his entire life in Rockwell, and sometimes she couldn't get him to shut up.

John had been fine, though, not just as a landlord but as a neighbor. When she'd needed something he'd supplied it. Otherwise he'd stayed out of her way and expected the same from her.

Sometimes she got lonely, occupying her small stretch of Old North Road with John as her only close neighbor, but her loneliness hadn't been his fault. Any newcomer moving into a small New England town would feel a little isolated, especially if she'd come from an urban area, carrying with her a different way of talking and moving, different experiences, a different worldview. Erica had made great progress in adapting to the Rockwell way, though. People seemed a little more accepting of her now than when she'd first arrived.

Buying her house also helped her to feel a kinship with her fellow Rockwellians. Paying property taxes in New Hampshire was like joining a club with extremely pricey dues, and as soon as she'd taken title to the charmingly ramshackle cottage adjacent to John Willetz's land, she'd become a full member. He had sold her the property for eighty-nine thousand dollars, which in her hometown of Brookline, just outside Boston, might buy a person an upscale doghouse, but she was billed a staggering amount in property taxes on her modest little home. Amazing that property taxes could be so high but teacher salaries—paid for out of property taxes—could be so low.

She carried her phone handset with her into the living room and listened while, on the other end, Avery Gilman babbled about the box she and Randy had dug up. "Can you identify the wood? And the hinge ma-

terial. Is it really brass?'' he was asking. ''I'd have to
see the piece, of course, but whether the hinges are
actually brass could impact significantly on the process
of evaluating its provenance.''

Erica remembered why she used to doodle in his
class. He was a brilliant man, but he could also be
boring.

''Well, you know, I'm not an expert—''

''You're a highly educated individual,'' Avery
countered. ''I ought to know. I highly educated you.''

He'd been only one of the many professors who
could take credit for that, but he was an expert in Colonial-era artifacts. He consulted for museums, gave
lectures before historical societies up and down the
eastern seaboard and earned spare change advising his-
torical-reenactment clubs on the proper technique a
minuteman might have employed to fill his rifle with
gunpowder or shape his tricorn hat after a downpour.
He'd also made himself unusually available to his students, hosting coffees at his Concord Avenue apartment and handing out his home phone number to anyone who asked. He hadn't seemed at all surprised that
a former student would call him on a Sunday evening
five years after she'd taken his history class on eigh-
teenth-century New England and ask him about a very
old-looking box that she'd just happened to dig up in
her backyard garden.

Generous though he was, Avery Gilman did tend to
run on. It was the price one paid for his expertise, and
she didn't begrudge him. She simply listened, trying
to snag every third word or so, wondering whether his
bushy black beard had begun to go gray yet and
whether he still used a pocket watch—a cute affecta-
tion, she recalled. He used to make quite a production

of sliding the watch out of his pocket midway through his class lecture, flicking open the cover and checking the time.

As his voice melted into a soothing drone in her ear, she gazed out her living-room window—something she could do because she was on her cordless phone. The evening sky was a pale lilac, and the horizon rose in the looming gray curves of the Moose Mountains. In another month, they'd be lush with spring foliage, but winter took its time letting go of the central New Hampshire hills. At least the lower-elevation flora— like her scraggly lawn and her soon-to-be garden— showed encouraging signs of life. Next door at the old Willetz place, the field behind the farmhouse had gone fallow, but it was slowly transforming from beige to green. She wondered what he used to grow there. Zucchini?

While Avery blathered on about the accuracy of dating techniques, she ambled from her living room to the dining room. It contained an old oak table and a sideboard in need of refinishing, but she used the room mostly as a study. The table held neat piles: math work sheets, book reports, spelling tests. She hated having to teach spelling—it seemed like such an idiot-savant skill—but the curriculum required it, so she drilled her kids once a week on twenty spelling words. One of her students, Cammie Merton, had not yet misspelled a single word this year. She gave Erica the creeps.

The dining-room windows overlooked the broken fence and the abandoned Willetz farmhouse. Only, it wasn't abandoned tonight. Lights were on in several windows.

She circled the table and peered outside. One upstairs window was aglow, as were two adjacent downstairs windows, one of which held the silhouette of a man.

It took her a moment to shake off her big-city panic. This was Rockwell. There was no such thing as a stranger here—at least, theoretically. The silhouette probably belonged to John Willetz's son, even though he never came to the house at night…and his shoulders weren't as broad as that man's, and his hair wasn't that thick.

"Erica?" Avery's voice droned through the line. "I asked if the lock appears to be the same metal as the hinges."

She spun away from the window and tried to pretend the house next door was empty. "Um, yeah, looks the same. But it's really dirty. The keyhole is clogged with dirt. I tried to clean it out with a toothpick—"

"No, you mustn't do that. The tip of the toothpick could snap off and get lodged inside the lock. Wait until I get up there. I'll bring the proper tools."

"So, you're going to come here?"

"Well, you said you couldn't bring the box down to Cambridge."

Had she said that? She couldn't really remember anything she'd said before she'd spotted the stranger in the house next door. "I can't," she confirmed. "Not until the weekend at the earliest."

"I could get there Thursday evening, if you'd be so good as to find me a place to stay."

Curiosity got the better of her. She peeked over her shoulder. The silhouette looked larger; he must have moved closer to the window. Was he watching her? Should she turn off the dining-room light?

"You could stay here," she offered. "I've got a spare bedroom."

"I think it would be better if I stayed elsewhere. I'm a difficult houseguest."

Erica appreciated the warning. Most difficult houseguests would simply show up and be difficult. "I'll reserve a room for you. We've got some motels and bed-and-breakfasts in town. I'd recommend one of the bed-and-breakfasts."

"By all means, then." The man in the window across the way seemed to be shrugging something over his shoulders. A shirt. Had he been shirtless? Standing in the window seminaked? While she was trying to decide whether to be afraid or offended, Avery broke in again. "So you'll let me know what arrangements have been made?"

"Yes, of course. I appreciate your coming, Dr. Gilman."

"And I appreciate your letting me get first crack at this treasure," he said.

"Assuming it's a treasure."

"I taught you well, Erica. You wouldn't lure me up to that godforsaken hamlet if you didn't think your find had value."

She considered objecting to his description of Rockwell, then decided not to.

"Don't let any museum sneak in ahead of me," he reminded her. "I want to be the first."

"You will be," Erica assured him. "I won't let anyone else look at it until you get here." The silhouette shook his head briskly, like a dog shaking off water. His hair spiked out from his scalp. "I'll call you after I've reserved a room for you. I've got to go now." She really did. The silhouetted man had vanished from the window. He could have gone anywhere. He could be doing anything. With or without a shirt on.

"Very well, then. I'll see you Thursday evening. I suggest you refer to me as Avery at this point," he added. "I'm not grading you anymore."

Five years after graduating from Harvard, Erica ought to stop viewing her former professors with awe. Randy Rideout was only two years out of her class, and he didn't treat her with awe. Even so, she felt funny saying, "Goodbye, Avery."

She disconnected the phone, returned to the kitchen to hang up the handset and peeked out the back-door window. The man was standing near the fallen fence, staring at her half-planted garden. He was still a silhouette in the gray twilight, but he was a full-length one now, tall and long limbed and definitely better built than Jack Willetz.

And he was crossing the fence onto her land. What were the rules about trespassing in Rockwell? Either she was supposed to be neighborly or she was supposed to haul out a shotgun and aim it at him. She didn't own a shotgun, but she wasn't sure she wanted to be neighborly to a man who stood a good six feet tall and had to outweigh her by at least fifty pounds.

She shouldn't have ended her phone call with Dr. Gilman—*Avery,* she mentally corrected herself. If the stranger continued to approach, she could have told Avery and he could have…well, he couldn't have done much from Concord Avenue in Cambridge, Massachusetts. But he could have dialed 911 for her.

She could dial 911 for herself—except that Rockwell didn't have a 911 system. Grabbing a knife, she nudged her kitchen door open.

She flicked on the porch light, and as he approached, the jaundiced glow from the yellow bulb spilled light across his features. He had a wide forehead, a sharp nose and, as best she could see in the rapidly dying evening, pale, intense eyes. His face was framed by shaggy hair that could either be dark blond or light brown. He wore black jeans and a dark wool shirt over a snug-fitting T-shirt, which implied that he hadn't been topless when she'd seen him in Mr. Willetz's window. She wasn't sure if she was relieved or disappointed by that.

He arrived at her back porch, and more light bathed his face. He looked familiar, but she wasn't sure where she'd seen him before. At a school function? On a Most Wanted poster in the post office? She clutched her knife more tightly and asked, "Can I help you?"

"I'd consider it a big help if you'd put down your knife," he said. His voice had a raspy edge to it, as if he'd spent the past few weeks screaming. Where had she seen him? Maybe he was a movie star. He was certainly that handsome. Then again, she'd been living long enough in Rockwell that any new male face would dazzle her. One thing Rockwell didn't have in abundance was gorgeous men.

"I'm Jed Willetz," he said, extending his right hand. He still kept his distance—her knife must have spooked him—so if she wanted to shake his hand, she was going to have to descend from the porch.

She could bring the knife with her, just in case. But he was a Willetz—and then she remembered where she'd seen him before: at John Willetz's memorial service back in January. His hair had been a lot neater then, and he hadn't had a day-old growth of hair smudging his jaw and upper lip, but yes, he was the fellow her friend Fern had pointed out to her after nudging an elbow into her ribs with enough force to leave a bruise. "That's the grandson," Fern had whispered. "John Edward Willetz III. He was two years behind me in school. Every girl at Rockwell Regional would have dropped her panties for him when he was there."

"Including you?" Erica had asked.

"If he'd asked? You bet," Fern had said fervently. "I probably would even today. Look at him."

Erica had looked. She wasn't sure she'd drop her panties for him, but admiring his rough-hewn face and honey-blond hair had been the highlight of John Willetz's funeral.

Actually, it had been just a church service not a funeral. The ground had been too frozen for a burial. As Erica had learned, no one got buried in central New Hampshire in January. People stored their loved ones' remains until mud season, when the ground was soft enough to enable the digging of graves. Erica found this tradition morbid, but it was what Mother Nature demanded.

Jed Willetz remained where he was, a few paces back from the foot of the porch stairs, with his hand still outstretched. She shifted her knife to her left hand, marched down the steps and shook his hand. His palm was as smooth and hard as finely sanded pine. "Erica Leitner," she introduced herself.

"You bought this house from my grandfather."

"I'm so sorry for your loss."

He made a face, apparently not in the mood for platitudes. She hadn't meant it as a platitude, though. She *was* sorry.

"Have they buried him yet?"

"Who, my grandfather? He was cremated," Jed Willetz said. "I'm up here to bury his ashes."

Well. Wasn't this a fun topic for two people just

getting to know each other? "What can I do for you?" she asked a bit more congenially.

"Put down the damn knife."

"Ah." She climbed back onto the porch and balanced the knife on the railing. After considering her options, she decided to remain on the porch. Jed Willetz was too tall. When she'd briefly stood next to him, she had felt small enough to need the knife. From the top step, she loomed an inch taller than him.

"Can I ask you a question?" he inquired, his gaze drifting to the knife perched on the railing and then back to her empty hands.

"Of course."

"Has anyone been in my grandfather's house since he died?"

"I don't know. I'm not here during the day. I have seen your—I guess he's your father, or your uncle? Jack Willetz. He's been in and out a few times."

"My father." Jed nodded, his forehead creasing into a frown. "So, he's been around?"

"I don't keep tabs on him," she said, a bit irked. His father's comings and goings weren't her business.

Jed scruffed a hand through his hair, an easy, casual move that made her think his father's occasional visits to his grandfather's house didn't matter much to him, either. She liked the way his shoulder rolled when he lifted his arm and then lowered it.

"So, tell me about the box," he said in an offhand voice.

She stopped thinking about his shoulder as wariness overtook her. How had he learned about the box? If he knew of its existence, who else did? She didn't want the entire town of Rockwell badgering her about her possible archaeological find.

"What box?" she asked with feigned innocence.

"The box you dug out of your garden."

"Where did you hear that?"

He chuckled without smiling. "By tomorrow morning everyone'll know about it."

"Why? It's just a box."

"Can I have a look at it?"

She hesitated. She didn't want him to see it, partly because, for all she knew, it could be extremely valuable, but mostly because she'd promised Avery she wouldn't show it to anyone else before he arrived in town. "I've put it away for safekeeping," she said.

"If it's just a box, why does it need safekeeping?"

Jed Willetz was a lot pushier than his grandfather had been. With shoulders like his, and those hard, cool eyes, he probably thought he could persuade anyone to bow to his will. But she wasn't about to drop her panties for him. No way. "Look, Mr. Willetz. I don't know you, and I don't have to show you anything I don't want to show you."

"You do if it's mine."

"Yours?" She drew herself taller and gave him her sternest look. It usually cowed her third-graders. He seemed unmoved.

"You dug it out from over there, right?" He gestured toward the edge of her garden, near the collapsed fence. "That's my property."

"Your property? What are you talking about?"

"My grandfather left me his house and land."

"Be that as it may…" God, she sounded pompous. She took a deep breath and strove for plainer words. "I own the property east of the fence line. Your grandfather sold it to me. It's mine."

"I'm not so sure where that property line lies. The

fence was crooked, and now it's broken. I'm thinking maybe you were digging on land that's legally mine.''

"That's ridiculous! We had a surveyor come out here and review the property lines before the sale went through. You can check in town hall. Everything's on file there.''

"So this box is worth nothing," he said, knocking her thoughts askew. What was he getting at? Why had he changed the subject back to the box if he was so worried about where his property ended and hers began? "Makes me wonder why you're fighting so hard to keep me from having a look at it.''

"Because I made a promise," she said, figuring that if he was going to be her new next-door neighbor—a ghastly thought; she didn't think she could bear to have him rolling his shoulders just a few yards from her dining-room windows—she'd be wise to avoid quarreling with him. "I've got an expert coming up to evaluate the box, and I promised I wouldn't let anyone mess with it until he got here. Why do you think everyone's going to hear about it, anyway? I haven't told anyone about it.''

"You told your expert. From Harvard, right?''

That took her even more aback. "How did you know that?''

"Same way I knew about the box. Randy Rideout has a big mouth.''

Damn. Randy *did* have a big mouth. She usually was amused by what came out of it. But not this. Discretion would have been the prudent course, at least until she'd found out exactly how valuable the box was.

The crunch of tires against loose gravel jolted her and Jed Willetz both. She turned in time to see twin shafts of light shoot up her driveway, followed by the rumble of a large engine. "You expecting someone?" he asked her.

She'd showered and changed after her gardening adventure that afternoon, but she was wearing old jeans, a Sierra Club sweatshirt and her L.L. Bean clogs. Her hair was pulled back into a ragged ponytail, held in place with a green ribbon. She was quite obviously not dressed for company. "I wasn't even expecting you," she said.

"Nobody ever expects me," he commented, then turned back toward the driveway as the loud *kachunk* of a heavy door slamming resonated through the night. The knife was within easy reach, she noticed. One swift move and she could tuck it against her palm. Jed Willetz might thank her for her foresight.

Good grief. She'd moved to Rockwell to escape from big-city paranoia. She'd come here so she could join a community where people dropped in on one another and trusted one another, where a person didn't have to reach for the nearest knife whenever a strange vehicle coasted up the driveway.

Maybe she wouldn't need the knife if she had Jed Willetz to protect her. Yeah, right, as if she was prepared to turn her back on a lifetime of feminism and let a big, unshaven guy protect her. Especially him. He was planning to give her a hard time about her property lines. She couldn't depend on him at all.

Footsteps rattled the gravel, and a small, round-faced woman emerged from behind the SUV. Her hair, styled in a rigorous pageboy with bangs stretching across her forehead, made her face look even rounder. Recognizing her, Erica let out her breath and smiled. See? This small-town living was all it was cracked up to be. She *did* know just about everyone.

"Meryl," she said pleasantly, even though Meryl Hummer was not her favorite person. The chief reporter for the *Rockwell Gazette,* Meryl had a way of turning every conversation into an interview. Her sense of her own importance was grossly inflated. The *Rockwell Gazette* was a flimsy weekly with so little news to report that it had to pad its pages with articles about every varsity, junior varsity and intramural sport at the high school. Senior Shot-Putter Sets His Sights on Plymouth State College, a headline might scream, or Outing Club Plans Annual Hike Up Mount Washington. Meryl favored large, bubble-shaped earrings that echoed the roundness of her face, and she always poked her curved chin outward as if it were a weapon, even though it was about as deadly as the edge of a teaspoon.

"I hope you don't mind my stopping by like this," Meryl said, striding across the back lawn as purposefully as her short, stocky legs would allow. She carried a tweedy bag on a strap over her shoulder, and her cardigan was textured with pills and pulls. As she neared the back-porch light, Erica could see that she'd slathered her face with makeup that gave her complexion a uniformly dull peach hue. The effect, ironically, was to make her look much older than her thirty-something years.

Before Erica could say whether she minded, Meryl had reached the steps, barely sparing Jed Willetz a glance. "Jed, I heard you were home," she said as she brushed past him.

"I'm not home," he argued. "This isn't home."

"If you say so." Evidently, she wasn't among the Rockwell womenfolk willing to drop her panties for him. According to Fern, Meryl was married to seventy-year-old Dunc Hummer, who'd earned his fortune years ago when the granite quarry north of town was more productive than it currently was, and used said fortune to shore up the *Gazette* so his child bride could continue to accumulate bylines. Jed Willetz apparently couldn't compete with a sugar daddy like Dunc.

Meryl's gaze and her oddly artificial smile zeroed in on Erica as she dug into her bag. "I'm doing a story on the box. Where is it?"

Erica suppressed a groan. Jed had warned that her that everyone would know about the box by tomorrow. Obviously, he'd missed his estimate by a few hours, but that minor error didn't keep him from grinning smugly. He had a remarkably sexy grin, she noticed with some annoyance.

She turned back to Meryl. "I'm sorry," she said, "but the box isn't for public consumption."

Meryl smiled. "No one wants to *consume* the box, Erica. The people of Rockwell just want an accurate report about what it looks like. I've already interviewed Glenn Rideout—"

"Randy's father? What does he have to do with it?"

"He's Randy's father," Meryl explained. She pulled a camera from her bag. "I'd like your side of the story, as well as a photo. This is page-one stuff."

"My side of the story?" Erica would have laughed if she didn't feel so uneasy. "There's no *side* of the story."

Erica slung the camera around her neck on its strap, then plucked a notepad and pen from a side pocket of her bag. She flipped open the pad and skimmed her jottings. "What I have is that Randy found the box—"

"We found it together," Erica muttered, aware that

perhaps there *was* more than one side of the story after all.

"You're disputing the Rideout version?" Meryl's eyes sparkled.

"There *is* no Rideout version. Glenn wasn't here. He has no idea what happened." Erica sighed. "Randy and I were planting my garden. Right where the zucchini were going to go—"

"According to Glenn, you were planning to plant too many zucchini."

"Glenn wasn't here," Erica repeated. "That was Randy's opinion, about too many zucchini plants. But I did research, and I believe I selected the correct number of zucchini plants." She heard a chuckle rising from the foot of the steps but chose to ignore it. "While digging in the area of the zucchini plants, Randy and I unearthed the box. I've put it in a safe place, and it's going to stay there until an expert evaluates it."

"From Harvard," Jed added quietly. "There's a question about whether they found the box on my land."

Meryl glanced at him, then turned back to Erica, her eyes even brighter. "Really? You were poaching on his property?"

"Of course not." Erica bristled. Why was Jed stirring Meryl up? "The garden is on my land. I bought this land from his grandfather. Mr. Willetz has nothing to do with it."

"But I'm here," he said cheerfully, climbing the steps to join her and Meryl on the porch. "Let's go have a look at the box."

"Who's this expert from Harvard?" Meryl asked, clicking her pen. "Do you have a name?"

Erica sighed. It wasn't as if she had anything to hide.

Avery Gilman was highly esteemed in his field. Maybe
if people reading the *Gazette* realized that she had connections to one of the nation's foremost authorities on
Colonial artifacts, they wouldn't railroad her the way
she felt she was being railroaded right now.

"Avery Gilman," she said. "*Dr.* Avery Gilman.
One L."

Meryl jotted down the name and gave Erica another
watermelon smile. "Now, how about let's have a look
at this box and get some photos taken?"

"Yeah, how about it?" Jed chimed in.

Erica sighed again. She really wanted to protect the
box—from publicity, from prying eyes, from the sort
of attention that could put it at risk. If it was a genuine
artifact, it could be priceless. If it was a piece of junk,
hyping it in any way would be ridiculous.

But, as Jed had pointed out, everyone in town knew
about the box already. And maybe if she played along,
if she let Meryl write a story about it, complete with
a front-page photo, Rockwell would embrace Erica
even more completely, letting her feel like a genuine
part of the town. When in Rockwell, do as the Rockwellians do—even if what they did was go nuts over
a dirty old box.

"Okay," she said, allowing herself one final sigh
before she scooped up the knife and opened the kitchen
door. "I'll show you."

CHAPTER FOUR

"CHECK IT OUT," Fern said, jerking her chin toward her desk. She was over at the sink, filling a paper cup with water for the small, wan child standing beside her. "Front page."

Erica drew in a deep breath and entered the nurse's office, a glum little room tucked behind the bigger, brighter janitorial-staff room at Rockwell Regional Primary School. Fern had tried to perk the room up by adorning the walls with posters. The most prominent one featured a tooth with a cartoon face drawn onto its crown and its roots extended to resemble feet. It appeared to be dancing with a toothbrush that had a face superimposed on its bristles and tiny arms and legs protruding from its handle. The tooth and the toothbrush looked as if they were having a grander time than the girl at the sink, who had apparently just lost a tooth and was not in the mood to dance. "It's bleeding," she whined. "It's bleeding in my *mouf*."

"Rinse your mouth out," Fern instructed her as she handed her the cup of water. "One rinse ought to do it."

"It's bleeding," the girl moaned, as if her condition was critical. "Don't lose my *toof*."

"I won't," Fern assured her.

"I need it." The child took some water into her

mouth, coughed and sputtered it out into the sink. "I need it for the *toof* fairy. Don't lose it."

"I won't lose it," Fern said with admirable patience, thrusting her cupped palm under the girl's nose. "See? I've got it right here in my hand."

Erica was glad she wasn't a school nurse. She wouldn't want a job that included holding saliva-slick milk teeth that had popped out of the gums of six-year-olds. Fern Bernard's other professional responsibilities included scrubbing bloody knees, placing compresses on bloody lips, inspecting scalps for lice and cleaning up vomit. How she managed to maintain a sense of humor Erica didn't know.

Come to think of it, Fern's sense of humor was a sometime thing. A person could laugh about stomach-flu epidemics only so much. "By my fourth puke of the morning, I've pretty well had it," she occasionally lamented to Erica when they met for lunch on those days that Erica didn't have cafeteria duty. After a few minutes of that sort of conversation with Fern, Erica's appetite generally disappeared.

A first-grader losing a tooth wasn't going to steal Erica's appetite today. But the sight that greeted her on Fern's desk might. It was that day's edition of the *Rockwell Gazette,* which Erica hadn't yet seen because it always arrived at her house after she'd already left for school. Most of the page was occupied by a large photo of her, Jed Willetz and the box beneath the headline Could This Find Be Worth Millions?

If there hadn't been a student in the nurse's office, Erica would have cursed. Instead, she gritted her teeth so tightly her jaws ached. Bad enough Meryl Hummer had written the damn story—did she have to give it such a sensationalist headline?

She tried to focus on the column of small print running along the right edge of the photo, but her gaze veered back to the picture itself. It was a color shot, oddly mushy, as if the printer's hues hadn't quite lined up. In it she looked tired, her sweatshirt fresher than her face, which was framed by squiggling strands of dark hair that had unraveled from her ponytail. She needed to do something with her hair, but she had yet to find a salon she trusted within a fifteen-mile radius of Rockwell. The last time she'd gotten her locks professionally trimmed had been during the school's winter break, when she'd driven down to Brookline to visit her family. Her mother had taken one look at her, shrieked, ''You resemble an escapee from an asylum,'' and made an emergency appointment for her at Armand's for the morning after Christmas. The unlucky young stylist who'd gotten stuck having to work over the holiday week had obeyed Erica's directive to leave her hair long—the style was more in keeping with the earth-mother image she was trying to cultivate—but he'd added some desultory layers and treated the whole thing with a relaxer that had sapped the life out of the curls. After she'd returned to Rockwell, Fern had evened out the layers for her, and eventually the curls returned.

All right, so her hair looked wild and disheveled in the photo. It hardly mattered, when her skin was so pale, her smile so grim and forced. Next to her, Jed Willetz appeared positively glorious. His hair was a mess, too, but on him the unkempt look worked. His eyes seemed brooding, unlike hers, which were wide and startled, as if the flash had stunned her, and he wasn't smiling at all. After this photo made the rounds,

Erica was certain more women than ever would be volunteering to bare their bottoms for him.

Positioned in front of them in the photo, the box seemed much too mundane to warrant the headline Meryl had written. Squat and decrepit, a dull brown container with a curving lid and a dirt-caked padlock that photographed a grayish-beige rather than brassy yellow, it sat on her dining-room table where she'd cleared away the spelling tests.

Erica circled Fern's desk, appropriated the nurse's chair and lifted the article to read. It stated that the box was found by "Erica Leitner, a third-grade teacher at the primary school, and Randy Rideout, eleven years old, a former student of Leitner's, while they were planting zucchini in Leitner's garden, which abuts the Willetz property." Well, that covered everyone's claims, she thought. The bulk of the article hypothesized on the box's age and value—a perfunctory mention of "Professor Abraham Gallen of Harvard University" was included—and what it might contain. Among the possibilities, Meryl listed diamonds, Confederate scrip, emeralds, snuff, rubies and a deed that could throw the entire ownership of both Jed Willetz's grandfather's land and Erica's property into question.

She waited as calmly as she could while Fern placed the child's tooth in a blue plastic container shaped like a miniature pirate's chest and snapped it shut. "Take good care of that," she cautioned the child, "and maybe the tooth fairy will visit you tonight."

"She better," the girl muttered menacingly.

Fern continued smiling until the girl had departed from the office. Then she closed the door, sank against it and groaned. "One of these days I'm going to knock out some kid's teeth with my fists. I'll go down in history as the youngest victim of menopause meltdown in New Hampshire history."

"You're not that young," Erica muttered.

Fern pulled a face and scraped her hand wearily through her loud orange hair. It was not a shade designed by nature, and Fern clearly didn't mean for anyone to think it was. Erica liked it. It added a touch of vibrancy to a community that tended to be as gray as the granite hacked out of the quarry on the western edge of town.

"I'm at least ten years away from menopause," Fern argued, shoving away from the door and returning to the sink, where she washed her hands. "Probably at least fifteen years," she added as she crossed to her desk, yanked open a drawer and pulled out an insulated lunch bag. "I only *feel* about a hundred years old. If you had to spend your days dealing with whiny snots who can't even pronounce the word *tooth,* you'd feel old, too." She ceded her chair to Erica and dragged a folding metal chair over to the desk. "Now, tell me about this," she demanded, jabbing a finger at the newspaper. "I can't believe something so important happened to you and you didn't call me."

"Well…" Fern was Erica's closest friend in Rockwell. She really should have called. "I didn't think it was such a big thing."

"Standing that close to Jed Willetz? Of *course* it's a big thing. How did he smell?"

"Smell?" Erica removed a cup of yogurt and a plastic spoon from her oversize purse. "What do you mean, how did he smell?"

"I mean, are we talking Old Spice? Calvin Klein? Polo? The guy lives in Manhattan. It looks as if the city has been treating him very nicely.'' She gazed at the photo and sighed.

"I don't know. He smelled kind of pepperminty,'' Erica said. She'd bet the "very nicely'' aspect of his appearance in the photo had less to do with Manhattan than with his genes. He could live in a shack up in Coos County with three mangy retrievers and no indoor plumbing and he'd still look great. He might not smell so good, though.

"He's so…'' Fern concluded that thought with an erotic-sounding grunt. "How can you act so blasé about him?''

"I'm not blasé,'' Erica argued. She'd certainly noticed Jed's attributes, especially once they'd entered her house and she could see him in real light. Yes, indeed, she'd noticed. She'd noticed the way he seemed to fill every room he entered, so tall and male and vibrant. She'd noticed the way the fluorescent ceiling light in the kitchen had captured the blond highlights in his tawny hair. She'd noticed the cool, misty gray of his eyes, and his large, blunt-tipped fingers, fingers that had closed as snugly as leather straps around her hand for an instant outside.

She'd also noticed that he, like Meryl, had been more interested in the box than in her. She'd noticed that he moved around her house as if he was more familiar with the layout than she was—and he probably was, since his grandfather used to own the place. She'd noticed that he stopped making small talk the moment she carried the box into the dining room from the closet in her bedroom, unwrapped the towel she'd swaddled it in and set it on the table. He'd zeroed in on the box, no doubt recognizing that it was an antique and trying to figure out how he was going to claim a portion of its value for himself.

Questionable property lines? That wasn't going to fly.

"So, what do you think is in the box?" Fern asked after swallowing a mouthful of her sandwich.

"I have no idea. Probably not diamonds, rubies or emeralds. I don't know where Meryl came up with all that."

"Meryl," Fern said with a sniff, as if no further explanation was necessary.

"Maybe it's got somebody's baby teeth in it," Erica said, remembering the tiny plastic treasure chest Fern had given the girl to hold her tooth.

"That's gross." Fern took another lusty bite of her sandwich, chewed and swallowed. "The thing is, life as you know it is going to change. This million-dollar find of yours is the biggest thing to come through town since Joey Binnick almost made the U.S. Olympics snowboarding team five years ago."

"It's not a million-dollar find," Erica insisted. "And it's not such a big thing."

"When you live in a town where nothing happens for five years, an old box in a zucchini patch is a big thing."

"Uh-huh."

"Everyone will want to talk to you about the box and nothing but. Are you a teacher? Who cares? Did you bake cookies for the summer-sports fund-raiser? Irrelevant. *Everyone* bakes cookies, but not everyone has an old box that they dug up in their backyard."

And not everyone baked cookies as tasteless as Erica's. But boy, would she blow them away when she baked zucchini cookies for the fall-sports fund-raiser, after her crop came in.

"So, what did you think of Jed?" Fern asked.

"We've already discussed his smell."

"There's more to him than his smell." Fern leaned back in her chair, which squeaked plaintively, and regarded Erica.

She realized she'd eaten barely half her yogurt. Thoughts about her box and Jed Willetz were enough to shut down her digestive system.

Fern might be her closest friend in town, but Erica wasn't prepared to admit to anyone that Jed Willetz could interfere with her appetite. Just because he looked gorgeous and currently occupied the house next door to hers—and smelled like peppermint—didn't mean she intended to get into a state over him. He certainly wasn't in a state over her. As soon as Meryl left last night, he'd departed, too. His final words, tossed casually over his shoulder as he'd headed out her back door, were, "I'm going to check those property lines at town hall tomorrow."

"He's only in Rockwell to bury his grandfather's ashes."

"So how did he wind up in your house? That *is* your dining room, isn't it?" Fern spun the newspaper toward her and studied the photo.

"He invited himself."

"You didn't invite him?"

"I didn't invite Meryl, either. I didn't want anyone to know about this." She gestured toward the photo.

"Welcome to Rockwell," Fern said with a grin. "Life travels slow and word travels fast. Don't look so gloomy, Erica. This is exciting!"

Erica didn't think so. Back in Brookline, *exciting*

used to mean the president was in town for a fund-raiser, or the new Almodóvar movie was playing at the Coolidge Corner Theater or a Degas exhibit was opening at the Museum of Fine Arts. It meant driving to Hanscom Air Force Base to see the Blue Angels fly in formation, or riding the T into Boston to hear Yo-Yo Ma at Symphony Hall or Dave Matthews at the Fleet Center, or the Boston Pops at the Esplanade. It meant the Red Sox beating the Yankees, and club-hopping after dark, and finding the perfect little something on sale on Newbury Street.

In Rockwell, exciting meant a fresh shipment of Ben & Jerry's ice cream at Hackett's Superette.

And Erica liked that; she really did. She appreciated the peaceful, modest rhythms of small-town life. Really.

She just hadn't expected her old box to rank up there with Ben & Jerry's ice cream.

The phone on Fern's desk erupted in a shrill ring. Erica handed her the receiver, then snapped the lid onto her half-full cup of yogurt and slipped it and her spoon back into the bag she'd brought them in. Maybe she'd be hungry later. She'd get another break at two-fifteen, when her class had art.

"Okay," Fern was saying. "No, I haven't. Please assure her I haven't... Look, Burt, she's a little obsessive, okay? But just because she doesn't trust me doesn't mean... Okay. I promise I won't." She passed the receiver to Erica, who hung it up and then let out a breath. "Someone's going to have to die."

"More of that early menopause?" Erica joked.

"That was Burt." Fern gestured toward the phone. Burt Johnson was the school's principal, an innocuous blob who favored plaid sportjackets and didn't believe in curriculum workshops or educational theory. "He keeps getting calls from Hazel Nagy. She thinks I'm teaching sex in my health classes."

"Hazel Nagy?" Erica scowled. Hazel Nagy ran the stationery store in town. She had to be at least seventy years old, which would place her safely beyond the range of people who had children attending Rockwell Regional Primary School. "Why should she care what you're teaching?"

"She's got morals," Fern said sourly. "She doesn't want our students learning anything dirty. According to her, discussing menstruation is dirty."

"Some of the fifth-graders—"

"Some of the fourth-graders, too," Fern pointed out. "I'll damn well teach those kids about menstruation, and Hazel Nagy can stand at the gates to hell and greet me when my time comes." She sighed melodramatically. "Why on earth did you move here, Erica? This place is insane."

"You're here."

"And I'm insane." Fern laughed. "I'm here because I grew up here and I figured, what the hell. You should have known better."

"I like it here," Erica told her, which made Fern laugh harder. Erica cracked a smile, too, although she meant what she'd said. "Lunch is almost over. I'd better get back to the classroom."

"Make sure you don't use the word *period* unless you're teaching punctuation," Fern warned her. "And seriously, Erica, brace yourself. You're a celebrity now." She waved at the photo of Erica grinning woodenly at them from the ghastly front page of the newspaper. "Not only are you a celeb, but you've been photographed with Jed Willetz. The gossip could get very interesting.''

The gossip could stand on its head, for all Erica cared. Jed Willetz was only in town to deliver his grandfather's ashes to their final resting place, and then he'd be gone. And she'd be here—with her box, her classroom and her zucchini, assuming they flourished the way Randy had predicted. She'd have lots of zucchini, and Jed Willetz would be back in New York City, and people in town would find something more interesting to gossip about.

JED POPPED a cherry sourball into his mouth and sucked hard. It didn't clear his head the way a cigarette might have, but it gave him something to do with his tongue.

April had settled another sunny day on central New Hampshire, and today he could actually enjoy the weather, instead of spending most of the daylight hours cruising various interstates in his rental car. He'd spent most of today indoors, inventorying his grandfather's possessions so he could get an idea of what his father had filched, but at least he was able to take occasional breaks and breathe some fresh air from his grandfather's front porch.

He'd immediately noticed, when he'd stepped inside the house last night, that certain items were missing. His grandfather's cast-iron fry pan, which had always sat on the stove whether or not anything was cooking in it, was gone, and the stove looked strangely naked without it. Jed had rummaged through the rest of the kitchen, discovered a few more cooking utensils unaccounted for, then proceeded through the house, searching for what wasn't there. The matching lamps from the living room—those were worth some real money, which probably explained why his father had taken them. The portable TV—although Jack had left the cable box behind, a forlorn black wire looking for a screen to hook up to. The toaster oven. The Weed Whacker. The police scanner Jed had given his grandfather for his birthday a couple of years ago.

John Willetz had left his grandson the house and its contents because he hadn't trusted his son with them. "Jack will get my money when I die, but my property is going to you. Your dad doesn't know manure from mulch," John had told Jed. "You know what's valuable and what's junk. Your dad still hasn't figured that out."

Unfortunately, Jed realized, his father had figured out how to help himself to whatever he wanted, even if it didn't belong to him.

Jed was annoyed. So annoyed, he still hadn't contacted his father, let alone made a plan regarding the old man's ashes. He'd gone to Hackett's and stocked up on edibles, missing New York City more with each item he tossed into his cart, and then he'd devoted the rest of the morning and much of the afternoon to writing a list of everything his father hadn't already lifted from the house. So what if the ashes didn't get buried immediately? He had pressing business to attend to.

As he sat on the creaky swing on the broad farmer's porch that extended the length of his grandfather's house, he acknowledged that his business entailed more than just taking care of what was left of his grandfather's life. There was that other matter. The matter of Erica Leitner.

Everyone at the Superette had been buzzing about her when he'd gone in to buy a few days' worth of food. Of course, once he'd stepped inside the glaringly lit shop, everyone had started buzzing about her and *him.* "I see you're making friends with that schoolteacher," Harriet Ettman had remarked, a dangerous glint in her eyes. "You sure know how to work fast. Barely back home, and you're already cozy with that lovely young lady."

"You'd be the first," Pop Hackett had commented from his post at the cashier counter. "Not that others haven't tried with her."

"I hope *you* haven't tried with her," Harriet had clucked, wagging a bony finger at Pop. "Elaine wouldn't be too happy with you. Besides, you're old enough to be Erica's father."

"You're old enough to be her grandmother," Pop had retorted.

"Well, who cares how old I am? I think it's lovely that she came here all the way from Boston just to teach our children. That shows true dedication. Not too many young people would be happy settling in a sleepy little town like Rockwell. Isn't that right, Jed?"

"She's Jewish," Toad Regan had commented to no one in particular as he emerged from behind a rack of potato chips. Toad Regan had a way of addressing the air molecules around him rather than actual people. Much of what he said made no sense, and a goodly portion of the rest of it was irritating or offensive.

"What's her being Jewish got to do with anything?" Harriet had inquired, her voice as prickly as a porcupine.

Toad had glanced up, as if startled to discover human beings within hearing distance of him. "Well, we ain't got no Hebrew National here, if you get my meaning," he'd muttered before shuffling out of the store, a wrinkled paper bag shaped suspiciously like a whiskey bottle tucked under his arm.

Jed hadn't gotten his meaning, but that was nothing new. The last time he'd seen Toad was a few years ago, when he'd been visiting town and had spent the night at his father's place. In the morning, he'd discovered Toad passed out on the living-room sofa. Jed had awakened Toad and asked him what the hell he was doing, and Toad had answered, "I'm sleepin'." He'd launched into a monologue about having seen a UFO the night before and Jack Willetz's house was the closest, and he'd had to find cover, and by the way, where did Jack keep his blankets, because it was as cold as a witch's tit in the living room and he hadn't been able to find a blanket anywhere. Besides which, what the hell was Jed doing there, anyway?

Jed supposed every small town had its version of Toad Regan, a skinny, underemployed fellow in baggy, stale-smelling clothes, who alternated between two states: drunk and hungover. Toad was generally harmless, and because front doors were left unlocked, he never went wanting for a place to sleep if UFOs were in the vicinity and he was too crocked to find his way home. New York City was crawling with guys like Toad, but unfortunately people kept their front doors locked in the city, so all its Toads wound up sleeping on sidewalks and park benches.

Jed had managed to pay for his purchases at the Superette without too much more needling over his having gotten up close and personal with Erica Leitner. He'd driven home, reminding himself that one of the particular joys of Rockwell was that everyone felt entitled to comment and conjecture on everyone else's affairs—even when those affairs didn't exist.

Yet, for some reason, Pop Hackett's words resonated inside him: *You'd be the first. Not that others haven't tried with her.* Who'd tried? Why hadn't they succeeded? What was her story?

Jed shouldn't even be thinking about it. He didn't have time for her, even if her lips were the color of a cherry sourball and her hands were strong—especially when she was aiming a carving knife at him—and her hair was as thick and lush as the tresses in a Renaissance painting of Eve or Venus or any of those other mythical women who were always depicted in artwork as naked and sexy and worthy of worship. Erica was thinner than the fine-art Eves and Venuses he'd seen, but not skinny. Hard to tell with the baggy sweatshirt she'd had on last night, but he was reasonably sure she had some nice curves going on under her clothes. And beautiful eyes, dark and soulful, full of worry even when she was trying to smile.

He didn't have time for her.

Still, there he was, sitting on his grandfather's porch swing, gazing out at Old North Road and wondering when she'd be rolling home from her job at the primary school. According to Meryl Hummer's article in the *Gazette,* Erica taught third grade. Jed didn't remember his own third grade teacher, but he'd probably hated the woman. He'd hated pretty much all his teachers.

He heard the spit of tires on gravel and straightened up. A Subaru wagon braked by her roadside mailbox. Erica reached through the car window to retrieve her mail, then proceeded up the driveway.

He crunched his teeth into the remains of his candy and watched as she pulled to a halt and climbed out of her car. Her curves were better displayed by the outfit she had on today—tailored navy-blue slacks and a soft, silky-looking beige blouse. Her hair was clipped back from her face, emphasizing her cheekbones.

She crossed her backyard, pausing briefly to study her half-planted garden, then pursed her lips and scaled the steps to the back porch. She carried a bulging leather tote, the kind very busy women in New York seemed to favor. Maybe they liked those leather totes in Boston, too. Wasn't that where Harriet Ettman said Erica was from?

God, he really didn't have time for this.

"Hey," he called over to her.

She glanced in the direction of his voice, then squinted, then frowned. His grandfather's front porch and her back porch were maybe two hundred feet apart, and nearly on the same latitude, since her house was much closer to the road than his grandfather's.

His house. He owned this place now. He ought to start thinking of it as his so he could figure out what to do with it. And what to do about the items his father had stolen from *him,* not from his grandfather.

She was still standing on her back porch, staring at him. He shoved himself to his feet and strode across the grass to the broken fence that separated their property. She wasn't exactly frowning, which he took as encouragement to step over the fence slats. "How was school?"

"Awful," she told him. "Have you seen today's *Rockwell Gazette?*"

He noticed an edition of the newspaper protruding from her tote. "I saw it," he said with a smile. "We're famous."

"I don't want to be famous," she announced, then pulled a key from her pocket and unlocked the back door. "I can't believe how Meryl mangled Dr. Gilman's name. He's going to be upset about that."

"As if he actually reads the *Rockwell Gazette*."

He couldn't tell if his sarcasm annoyed her until she glanced over her shoulder at him. Yeah, it annoyed her, but her eyes had laughter in them. "Maybe it would be best if I don't mention the article to him."

"That would be my strategy."

She shoved open the door, which stuck a little around the molding—his grandfather should have taken care of that when he'd sold her the place—and didn't try to prevent him from following her inside. A frantic beeping came from the telephone sitting on a counter. She tossed her tote onto a chair beside the small pine table near the window, crossed to the phone and pressed a button on the console. He realized it was an answering machine, and all those beeps—he lost count after five—were messages.

"Hello, this is Doug Brezinski from the *Boston Globe*. I'm writing a piece about your archaeological find. I've already spoken with a Mr. Rideout, and I'd like to speak with you, too. My phone number…"

"This is Sandy Bradburn from Channel 3 News in Manchester. I'm heading up to Rockwell today, and I'm hoping we can talk. I'll call again when I get into town…"

"I'm trying to reach a Ms. Leet-ner. My name is Malcolm Moody, and I'm a historian with the Minuteman Historical Society…"

"Jeez Louise, Erica! How'd you get so friendly with Jed Willetz?"

Erica slammed the off button to silence her messages.

"Hey, who was that?" he asked, pretending enormous interest. "It sounded a little like Janelle Dickerson." He'd gone to high school with Janelle. He'd gone the distance with her, too. She'd been quite the party girl back then. Last he heard, she was working behind the counter at Rockwell Rx, keeping tabs on who in town was taking which drug.

"It wasn't," Erica said swiftly. Then she sighed. "She's Janelle Mondo now."

"No kidding? She married Danny Mondo?" He flipped a chair around and straddled it. "When did that happen?"

"It was rather sudden. She was pregnant." She bit her lip and turned away, her cheeks flushing pink. "I shouldn't have said that. It's only gossip."

He grinned. He liked her qualms, even though they were misplaced. Everyone knew everything about everyone in Rockwell. The only reason he hadn't known about Janelle was that he no longer lived in town.

She turned back to Jed, her cheeks still bright with color but her eyes steady. "Did you get lots of calls like these?" she asked, gesturing toward her answering machine.

He shook his head. "I haven't got a phone. Well, I've got my cell phone with me, but nothing hooked up at my grandfather's house. No number people from the *Boston Globe* could look up in the directory." He pondered the other messages he'd overheard, even though he'd much rather contemplate Janelle's insinuation about him and Erica getting friendly. "It looks like you really *are* famous."

"It's ridiculous. Why would the *Globe* want to write a story about an old box I dug out of my garden?"

"Maybe because you're from Boston?"

She frowned. "I'm not. Technically. I'm from Brookline, which is a large suburb of Boston."

"And that makes all the difference, doesn't it?" He shrugged. "That Harvard-professor pal of yours is interested in your box. Why wouldn't the *Globe* be?"

"Well...the box could have historical import."

"It could be worth millions," Jed noted, pulling her copy of the *Gazette* from her tote and holding it up so she could see the banner headline.

She sagged against the counter, unclipped one of her barrettes and smoothed her hair back before refastening the barrette. It was such a thoughtlessly graceful gesture his mouth went dry. He wanted to smooth her hair back from her face, kiss her cheek, kiss her jaw, work a path to her lips. He lived in Manhattan, he knew women there, he was mature and seasoned...but at that moment, when her fingers nimbly worked the barrette into place, he felt a surge of lust almost adolescent in its irrationality.

He definitely did not have time for this.

"If it's worth millions," she was saying, "everybody's going to want a piece of me."

Especially him, but he didn't tell her that. The thought made him uneasy. He had to bury his grandfather's ashes and go home, escape from this smothering little town before it made him crazy. Twenty-four hours inside its borders, and he was already feeling slightly deranged.

More than slightly. If he were sane, he never would have said, "So, I went down to town hall today and looked at the records, and I think that million-dollar box was at least fifty percent on my land."

CHAPTER FIVE

DERRICK MESSINGER wouldn't have come to a crummy little hole-in-the-wall like Rockwell if his career depended on it—except that his career *did* depend on it, and here he was.

Another man might have been stirred by the greening humps of the mountains surrounding the town, so damn pretty they looked like something a set designer might have painted for a summer-stock production of *The Sound of Music*. Another man might have swooned at the tangy pine scent and the stunningly blue New England sky. Derrick wasn't another man, though, and pretty mountains and pine trees didn't do it for him. He'd seen the underbelly of life, the squalor, the tragedy. He'd witnessed grief, loss, despair—not just witnessed it but reported on it. He'd reported on toxic dumps in Tennessee, airplane disasters in Arkansas, neo-Nazis in Nebraska. He'd been reviled by environmental radicals, stalwart racists, politicians, animal rights activists and even fellow journalists. He'd gone undercover in a prison—or it would have been undercover if a few of the cons hadn't immediately recognized him and started blabbing their guts out, drowning him in their hard-luck stories—and he'd once talked a potential jumper down from the Tappan Zee Bridge, on the air, live and unedited.

And now he was supposed to do a story about the

opening of a box? In this half-dead town, where every fourth storefront seemed to be a bar? Had he really come to this?

"I'm telling you," Sonya, his producer, honked in her profound Bronx accent, "this is gonna be a great show." She was seated shotgun in front, and Mookie, Derrick's good-natured lunkhead of a cameraman, was behind the wheel. Derrick liked to sit in back. These days, it was as close as he got to riding in a limo.

Like doing this stupid story was going to get him any closer to his limo days.

"Big ratings," Sonya insisted. "Double digits, I'm telling you." Nowadays, with all the cable channels vying for eyeballs, if a show broke into double-digit ratings it was a big deal. "What I'm thinking is, we'll capture the entire atmosphere of this town—"

"What atmosphere?" Derrick snapped. "There's a bar on every corner."

"That kinda makes the place, if you ask me," Mookie said.

Sonya shoved her hair back behind her ears. If her hair had been long, the gesture would have been dramatic, but she'd recently hacked her tresses to chin length, and the grand hand flourish seemed like overkill. "I was thinking about the mountains. The forests. The small-town charm. Look—there's a crafts store— I mean, a *crafts* store! And a pharmacy—"

"This is special?" Derrick muttered.

"And a *general store!*"

"What do they sell there?" Mookie wondered aloud. "Generals?" He let out a snorting laugh.

Derrick wished he could be anywhere else. But Sonya was right. She always was. She had a nose for news, as the saying went. Derrick used to have a nose for news, but then he'd gone through that long stretch when his ratings had been way down, not just single digit but in the two range. Maybe he'd lost his nose for news literally because his nose had been fractured during a scuffle on his show a few years back, when two professional wrestlers had started taking swings at each other and Derrick had stepped between them. Now, *that* show had gotten double-digit ratings.

A plastic surgeon had reshaped Derrick's busted nose to resemble his old nose pretty closely, and he didn't think his appearance had suffered. His ratings, though...

So he relied on Sonya. Despite all her annoying tics, she knew what she was doing. She would package this show about the damn box in the teacher's garden and turn it into a phenomenon. Hadn't she worked miracles with his last special, "The Search for Jimmy Hoffa"? Of course, Jimmy Hoffa was a newsworthy name, even though Derrick's search for him was no more successful than any of the other searches for him over the past thirty years. Finding Hoffa or not finding him wasn't the point. The show had been good TV.

Sonya seemed to believe that the opening of an antique, possibly valuable, wooden box would also be good TV. The instant she'd spotted the story on the wires about some mousy schoolmarm in a central New Hampshire granite-quarry town digging up an ancient relic in her garden, she'd been on the phone to Derrick, telling him to pack some sweaters and meet her at LaGuardia. "We've got to get to the teacher first," she said. "I'm telling you, Rockwell is going to be overrun by the media in two days. That's why we've got to get there in one day. Mookie'll drive up tonight with his gear and meet us at the airport in Lebanon tomorrow."

Derrick highly doubted that the media would over-run this dead-end burg, but he knew better than to ar-gue with Sonya. She'd pulled him out of the Valley of Oblivion, where he'd fallen after the network honchos had axed him for questioning a Supreme Court justice on live TV about his rumored sexual predilections. Af-ter that debacle, Sonya had agreed to produce him, putting together independent reports and selling them into syndication. She'd saved his butt. She'd turned his show, *I'm Just the Messinger,* into a nationally known brand name.

So when she told him they were going to Rockwell, New Hampshire, to do a story on a mysterious old box that might contain millions of dollars, he'd packed his sweaters.

A freaking box, though… This was still a long way down from an exclusive interview with a Supreme Court justice.

Mookie pulled into a parking space that angled back from the curb in front of a place called Hackett's Superette. "You want the usual?" he hollered over his shoulder.

"They're not going to have the usual here." Derrick eyed the sign above the store suspiciously. "Super-ette" sounded like the name of a sixties girl group, not a store that would carry Chivas Regal.

"You're the one who pointed out that there's a bar on every corner," Sonya reminded him. "This is ob-viously a community that takes its booze seriously."

Derrick folded his arms across his chest and scowled at her. He liked to have a bottle of Chivas on hand for a shoot. All he needed was a couple of nips in the evening to unwind—in his own room, in privacy. No way was he going to sit on a bar stool in one of those seedy-looking joints, swapping yarns with crusty cow farmers and unemployed quarry workers while he enjoyed his nightcap. None of the bars in town looked as if they'd carry Chivas, either. He should have brought his own supply with him. But Sonya had been in such a big hurry to get to Rockwell ahead of everyone else in the media, he hadn't thought to toss a bottle into his bag. He was lucky he remembered to pack his toothbrush and his good-luck rubber band.

Mookie got out of the car and loped into the Superette. Sonya pulled some papers out of her leather briefcase and shuffled them importantly. "I'm figuring we'll contact the schoolteacher as soon as we get checked in," she told him.

"Where are we staying?" Once upon a time, Derrick stayed only in three-star or better hotels. During his long climb from hellhole ratings to syndication, he'd learned to be content in chain motels. But if the motels he'd noticed on the outskirts of Rockwell belonged to any chain, it was the "Quickie Adultery" chain.

"I got us rooms in a bed-and-breakfast right in town," Sonya told him without looking up from her papers. "The Hope Street Inn. I checked it out on the Internet. It looked cute."

Just what he needed—a cute place to stay. "The Hope Street Inn sounds like a halfway house. Maybe a battered women's shelter."

"They've got private bathrooms, and fresh coffee and pastries in the morning. And the price fit into our budget. So—" she jotted something on one of the papers "—we'll check in and then we'll set things up with the teacher. I wanna get first crack at her, see if we can get her to agree to an exclusive."

"Is she pretty?" Derrick asked. His curiosity was strictly professional; her appearance would influence how he approached her and how they filmed the story.

Sonya fished a file folder from her briefcase and pulled out some papers. "Here's a photocopy of the original story in the *Rockwell Gazette,*" she said, handing him one sheet. "From other sources, I got that she's twenty-seven, grew up in Brookline—not Brook-*lyn,* Brookline. It's a suburb of Boston."

"What am I, an idiot?"

Sonya didn't bother to answer that question. "She earned her undergraduate degree in English at Harvard, then got a masters of arts in teaching at Brown. *Veddy veddy* Ivy."

"And she wound up in this rat hole. I'm glad I didn't waste all that money getting a Harvard education."

"Single, no kids, no pets. In high school she was the captain of the girls' volleyball team, she served on the student senate and she did debate. While at Harvard, she coordinated a bunch of community-service stuff—a literacy project, a program that got uninsured city kids vaccinated. She sounds like a do-gooder."

Nodding, Derrick glanced at the picture of her from the *Rockwell Gazette* story. If she was nice-looking, he sure couldn't tell from the photo. It was smudgy and blurry. About all he could say with certainty was that she had dark hair.

When it came to interviewing women, he approached the beautiful ones in a flattering way. They knew they were gorgeous, and if he conveyed that *he* knew it, too, they believed he shared their worldview and were happy to open up to him. With plain-looking women, his strategy was different. He had to be more businesslike, less personable. If he flattered too much, they'd think he was a phony and refuse to open up.

In the case of Erica Leitner, he couldn't be too hard-hitting. She was an overeducated bleeding heart. If he went at her aggressively, she'd shut him out. He had to approach her like a fellow Good Samaritan, interested in helping poor, uninoculated children and solving the mystery of the incredible box she'd dug out of her garden.

"The most important thing," Sonya went on, "is to make sure she opens the box on camera—for us alone. If there's a million dollars in there, I want the exclusive. You up for that, Derrick?"

"Do you even have to ask?"

Mookie emerged from the store, carrying a paper bag. Derrick's spirits improved marginally. "Any luck?" he asked as Mookie slid behind the wheel.

"They had Johnny Walker, Derrick. Sorry."

"Red or Black?"

"Red."

Derrick let out a disgusted breath. Johnny Walker Red. Not even Black. The sooner they got this story and left, the happier he would be.

FERN HAD CLAIMED she wanted to see the box, but Erica suspected that she might have another agenda.

"We'll make pasta," she'd suggested when she'd cornered Erica in the faculty parking lot at three-thirty. "Pasta primavera and garlic bread. I'll buy the ingredients if you'll supply the wine."

"I'd love to have dinner with you," Erica had said, adjusting her sunglasses in the afternoon glare. "But isn't this kind of sudden?"

Fern's wounded look failed to convince Erica. "I

didn't know I had to book you weeks in advance. Come on. Where's your sense of spontaneity?"

"Spontaneity is take-out pizza. It's not pasta primavera and garlic bread."

Fern laughed. "Pasta primavera is the easiest thing to prepare. Easier than phoning Jimbo's Pizza. I'll bring all the ingredients. All you have to do is pick up a bottle of wine."

"I've got wine. Why do you really want to get together for dinner?"

Fern again attempted to look offended, then grinned sheepishly. "I want to see the box, okay? You've already shown it to the whole world, thanks to that photo Meryl Hummer ran in the *Gazette,* and I'm your best friend, and I haven't seen it. Except in the newspaper."

Erica had decided she'd enjoy Fern's company for dinner enough to let her see the box. She was right, after all—it had already been photographed and publicized. As long as Fern didn't tamper with it—and she wouldn't—where was the harm in showing it to her?

Besides, how often did Erica have the opportunity to learn how to make pasta primavera? Maybe if she mastered the recipe and her garden came through for her, she could prepare the dish with homegrown vegetables next fall. She could use up some of her overabundant crop of zucchini that way—if she ever got around to planting the rest of her zucchini seedlings.

She'd managed to listen to the day's phone messages before Fern arrived at her house. Her answering machine stopped recording after fifteen messages, which was just as well. Today's batch was all nonsense—a newspaper in Camden, Maine; a disc jockey from a radio station in Worcester, hoping to interview her live on his show; a professor from a college she'd never heard of, questioning the identity of "Abraham Gallen"; someone inquiring about licensing miniature reproductions of the box, to be sold in airport gift shops; an attorney who claimed to be representing the Rideout family; and a lot of calls from people she knew in town, reminding her what good friends they were. Obviously, they assumed the box contained great riches.

None of the messages was from Jed Willetz. She had no reason to expect a call from him, but yesterday she'd made him promise to return to town hall and double-check the property line between her house and his grandfather's. She was sure the records would back up her claim of where the line was located, and it would have been courteous of him to apologize for implying that her garden had encroached on his land.

But he hadn't done the courteous thing. Big deal, she'd thought as she'd changed from her school clothes into khakis and a cotton sweater. She and Fern would have a lovely dinner. She would learn how to cook something new and she'd show Fern the box, and who cared about Jed Willetz?

Once Fern arrived at her house, though, she had seemed less than eager to view the box. She emptied an array of ingredients from a couple of paper bags onto the kitchen table: a box of dry rigatoni, broccoli florets, carrots, plum tomatoes, a single green zucchini, a bulb of garlic, a bottle of olive oil, a long, skinny loaf of bread and a pale-yellow wedge of Romano. As she folded the bags flat along their creases, her gaze drifted to the window.

"Do you want to see where I found the box?" Erica asked, pulling her apron from the hook inside the broom-closet door and offering it to Fern.

"In your vegetable garden, right?" Fern answered as she took the apron. "Your backyard."

But she was staring at the side yard. Beyond the side yard, actually. She was staring at the Willetz front porch.

"You came here to check out Jed Willetz," Erica accused her.

Fern spun around and laughed guiltily. "I came here to make you a feast. You should be worshiping me. And pouring me a glass of wine. And getting me a cutting board and a sharp knife."

"You want to drink wine while you're using a sharp knife?"

"Okay, give me a dull knife." Fern looped the neck strap of the apron over her head and tied the belt around her waist. "There. Do I look like someone from the Food Channel?"

"No. You look like a ninny who'd drop her panties for my next-door neighbor."

"Is he your neighbor? Really? As in, he's planning to stay in town for a while?" Fern peered eagerly out the window again.

"I have no idea how long he's planning to stay."

"I wish I had a neighbor like Jed Willetz. Fill a big pot with water and get it boiling, okay? I wish," she said, breaking off a couple of cloves of garlic, "I had a neighbor as handsome as him, anyway. Do you know what it's like to go down to my mailbox to pick up my newspaper every morning and come face-to-face with Angus Murray?"

"Angus is a nice man," Erica called over from the sink, where she was filling her largest pot with water.

"He looks like a squid. I don't know how Norma

can stay married to him. I mean, *ugh.* She goes to bed
every night with a man who looks like a squid.''

"I'm sure that in her eyes he's gorgeous. Love is
blind.''

"Well, I'm not in love *or* blind, and seeing Angus
first thing in the morning is awful. I'd much rather see
Jed Willetz.''

Erica had to admit that seeing him first thing in the
morning wouldn't be the most unpleasant experience
in the world. Seeing him any time of day was a treat.

Yesterday, when she'd gotten home from school,
he'd almost seemed to be waiting for her. She'd actually suffered a little pang of disappointment that he
hadn't been out on his grandfather's porch when she'd
come home today. Which was stupid, of course. She
wasn't going to make herself silly over the guy. He
was her temporary neighbor; that was all. And possibly
her adversary, if he decided to contest the property
line.

The scent of the raw garlic Fern was mincing filled
the room, so heavenly she nearly forgot all about Jed
and the box and all the annoying phone messages that
had been jamming her machine. She cranked a corkscrew into the bottle of Chianti Classico, one of several
bottles of wine she'd brought back from Brookline during her last visit home, because none of the stores in
Rockwell carried decent vintages. Erica wasn't a wine
snob, but the stuff sold in Hackett's had screw tops.
For the rare occasions when she desired a glass of
wine, she thought it best to import the stuff.

Her phone rang and she cursed. Fern eyed her cu-
riously. "Expecting someone?''

"You don't know what it's been like here.'' She
pressed down the metal levers to raise the cork and

filled two goblets with wine while the phone rang a
second and a third time. "The calls never end. I had
fifteen messages when I got home today, all about the
box."

The machine clicked on. Through the speaker, Erica
heard a familiar voice: "Erica? Darling? It's your
mother. I just called to say hello, nothing urgent,
Daddy and I are both fine, thank God. So give me a
call when you've got a minute." She hung up and the
machine clicked off.

"She doesn't know about the box," Fern commented.

"How would she know? She doesn't subscribe to
the *Rockwell Gazette*."

"I thought mothers knew everything. If I ever have
kids, I intend to know everything."

A knock on the back door startled them. Erica
glanced wistfully at the knife Fern had in her hand; as
a Rockwell native, it probably wouldn't occur to Fern
to remain armed until the identity of the visitor was
known. In another year or three or seven, Erica promised herself, she would no longer want to have a knife
with her when a stranger showed up at her door.

Her visitor was no stranger, though. Through the
window in the top half of the door, she recognized Jed
Willetz's silhouette.

So did Fern. "Well, look who's here!" Before Erica
could answer her own door, Fern was turning the knob
and pulling the door open. "Jed Willetz!" she greeted
him heartily. "I heard you were back in town."

He made her day by recognizing her. "Fern...
Bernard? Or is it Fern Something-Else now?"

"Still Bernard," she told him, her eyes glittering as
if someone had lit sparklers in them. "Still available."

Smiling vaguely, Jed turned to Erica. She hoped her eyes weren't glittering the way Fern's were. Just because the man deserved his own gallery in the Museum of Hunky Guys didn't mean she wanted to turn into a silly, simpering flirt in his presence. "Hi," she said curtly, then took a sip of wine.

"Okay," he said. "I checked the records. The property lines are kind of iffy, but I'm not going to push it."

A begrudging admission at best, lacking the proper contrition. She took another sip of wine to keep herself from thanking him.

He dug his hands into the pockets of a pair of well-worn jeans. He had on another snug T-shirt, topped by an unbuttoned flannel shirt. Didn't he know that grunge had gone out of style years ago? Why the hell did grunge look so good on him, anyway?

"So…you ladies are cooking up a feast, huh," he observed.

"A big feast," said Fern, sending Erica a pleading gaze. "More than enough for two."

Erica relented. Inviting Jed to join them for dinner wasn't the same thing as throwing herself at him. And she wasn't about to throw herself at him, anyway. Fern would be in charge of that part of the evening's entertainment. "Do you want to have dinner with us?" she asked.

He eyed the food on the table and drew in a deep breath. The air vibrated with the scent of garlic. "Well, I was planning on having a peanut butter sandwich for dinner," he said, shooting Erica a grin. "Let me think about it." His smile was almost as good as an apology. Damn it, it was *better* than an apology. She turned her back on him and reached into the cabinet for a third wine goblet.

Fern's energy level kicked up a few notches. "How's that water coming?" she asked. "Are you watching it?"

"If I watch it, it won't boil," Erica said, filling the glass and handing it to Jed. He took it and his smile grew gentle. She sensed an apology in it. Or *something,* some intangible message—she wasn't sure what. She ought to forgive him for the property-line misunderstanding and cheer up. She ought to forget about all the phone messages, including the one from the Rideouts' attorney, and especially her mother's call. She knew what would happen when she phoned her mother back, as she eventually would. Her mother would tell her that Rockwell was a ghastly place and she'd list all the reasons why. Her mother had visited Rockwell only once in the three years Erica had lived here. One time had been enough. "This place gives me the willies," she'd declared. "It's too quiet and small. It makes me claustrophobic. And you can't buy a good bagel anywhere. I'm not talking about those doughnut-shaped things they were selling at that supermarket—well, it's hardly a supermarket, they carry only two brands of toilet tissue—but *real* bagels. I don't know how you survive up here."

"The water's boiling," she informed Fern.

Beaming, Fern launched into high gear. She emptied the box of rigatoni into the pot, then dug through Erica's cabinets until she found a skillet and set it on another burner. Stepping out of her way, Erica glanced toward Jed and found him gazing at her.

"She's a better cook than I am," she explained.

"I'm glad she's doing the cooking, then," he said

before taking a sip of his wine. "Are you still getting lots of calls?"

She sighed. It wasn't his problem, but he appeared sympathetic, so she said, "Glenn Rideout seems to have hired an attorney."

Jed choked on his wine, coughed a few times and let out a laugh. "What does he need an attorney for?"

"To intimidate me, I guess. To make me share my newfound wealth with Randy."

"What newfound wealth?" Fern called from the stove, where she was sautéing vegetables in garlic and oil. "Erica, would you slice the bread? Inch-thick slices. Thanks. Anyway, if you're wealthy, I think you ought to share the wealth with me, not with Randy. I'm a much better friend."

"Hire a lawyer and take a number." Erica found another knife and settled in at the kitchen table with the loaf of bread. "There's no million dollars in the box. If it turns out to be a historical artifact, I'm going to donate it to a museum. I don't know why Glenn Rideout is dragging lawyers into this."

Jed took another sip of wine and shrugged. "If the box is worth something and you donate it to a museum, Rideout'll demand half the tax credit."

Erica sighed. She didn't want to think about tax credits. She didn't even want to think about the box. She wished it had been found in someone else's backyard. "Fern, do you know any lawyers?"

"Around here?" Fern snorted. "You'd be better off finding someone from Boston. Don't you agree, Jed?" she asked, peering over her shoulder at him.

"I haven't lived here for twelve years. What would I know?"

"Does your dad have a lawyer?"

"No. He could probably use one, though," Jed muttered.

"Is your father in legal trouble?" Erica asked. She pictured the thin, silent man she'd seen wandering in and out of John Willetz's house. What might he need a lawyer for?

Jed snorted, then strode to the table with his wine and slumped into the chair across from her. "When it comes to my father, you never know."

She waited for him to elaborate, and when he didn't, she asked, "Have you and he made arrangements for your grandfather's ashes?" As soon as the words were out of her mouth, she regretted them. Once Jed and his father had made arrangements, he would bury his grandfather's ashes and leave town. Which really shouldn't matter to her, one way or another—as long as he didn't sell his grandfather's house to someone who looked like a squid.

Jed ran his index finger around the rim of his glass. His fingers were thick and blunt, callused. From what? she wondered. Manual labor? What did he do in New York City? She knew nothing about him.

Well, she had a knife. So did Fern. As long as she was armed, she could enjoy having a gorgeous guy drinking wine in her kitchen, even if he was practically a stranger.

THE LAST PERSON he wanted to talk about was his father. After a quick, cursory stop at town hall that morning, where popcorn-brained Myrna Gilhooley forgot she was the town clerk for ten whole minutes so she could badger him about when he'd gotten to town and what his business was with Erica Leitner—"You think there's money in that box? Is that why you're being so neighborly?''—he'd decided to skip checking the deeds on Erica's and his grandfather's houses and instead headed over to the Moosehead, where he'd found his father enjoying a belated breakfast of orange juice, scrambled eggs and Ice House beer.

"Oh, so here's my famous son," Jack had greeted him with phony enthusiasm as he shook a sluggish stream of ketchup onto his eggs. "You want something to eat? Order it at the counter. They don't have a waitress here till afternoon."

"I'm not hungry," Jed said, taking the seat across from his father and sighing. After fifty-three years of hard living, his father's skin looked like scuffed shoe leather and his fingers had deep creases scoring them, like frets on a guitar. Jed had reminded himself that the old man was what he was, and he wasn't going to change. Even so, he didn't have the right to filch stuff John Willetz had left to his grandson.

"Get a cuppa coffee, at least," Jack insisted. "I don't want to eat alone."

"You were all set to eat alone before I walked in. Dad—"

"Now, don't you go 'Dad'-ing me. You've been in town how long? Talkin' to Meryl Hummer, talkin' to that snooty teacher, and you don't even let your father know you're here?"

"I came up here to bury Grandpa's ashes." Jed kept his tone level so the anger wouldn't spill out. "And I go into his house—*my* house—and discover you've been stealing things from it."

"Haven't been *stealin'* them. Just took a few items that the old man said should be mine."

"The old man left you all his money. I'm sure his will didn't say his fry pan should be yours."

"I need a pan," his father had argued before shoveling a forkful of ketchup-covered eggs into his mouth. "What's the big deal?"

"The big deal is that you went through the house and took things. Things Grandpa left to me."

"Don't be greedy, Jed. What the hell were you going to do with that old pan, anyway? I need a pan."

"Why? You never cook anything." At least, Jed couldn't recall his father ever cooking anything for him. His mother used to cook, and after the divorce, Jed had spent most of his time between her house and his grandfather's.

"I do so cook, sometimes. Maybe now that I've got a pan I'll cook more. Look, Jed, don't tell me you traveled all the way up from the big city to fight with me over a pan."

"No, I told you, I came up here to bury Grandpa's ashes. But when I got here, I found that you'd taken things from his house. Those things weren't yours to take."

"Get over it," Jack said before gulping down some beer. "No big deal."

The things themselves weren't a big deal. It was his father who was the big deal. If his mother had still lived in town, she would have given Jack an earful for taking stuff from John's house, but she'd moved to upstate New York with Jed's stepfather a few years ago, and without anyone to keep an eye on him, Jed's father did whatever the hell he wanted. A fun way to live, probably—until whatever the hell you wanted crossed into someone else's territory.

Jed shouldn't let his father irritate him so much. He should just bury his grandfather's ashes and go back to New York. But after he'd left the Moosehead, all he'd been able to think about was talking to Erica, venting to her. As if she'd understand. As if she'd be sympathetic.

She just might be. She was an outsider in Rockwell, and although Jed was a native, he felt like an outsider, too.

He'd spent the rest of the day cataloging what his father hadn't filched from the rambling farmhouse and watching for her car. From one of the upstairs windows, he'd seen the Subaru wagon roll to a stop at her mailbox around three forty-five, and then bump up her unpaved driveway. Then he'd seen her duck into her house.

Instead of chasing her inside, he'd decided to wait. He'd drop by around five and ask her to have dinner with him. They could go somewhere, or fix something at home, if they wanted to avoid town gossip, which was as irritating as his father's attitude. Talk to an unmarried woman in Rockwell and folks assumed you were enjoying a steamy romance with her.

He hadn't expected to find Fern Bernard in Erica's house. He remembered Fern from high school. Her hair wasn't so red then, but she'd been sassy and smart, and he was surprised to learn that she was still in Rockwell. If she was friends with Erica, it probably said good things about Erica.

Fern remained at the stove, babbling about her job as a nurse at the primary school. "You don't know this current principal," she was saying. "Burt Johnson. He lives in fear of every tight-ass in town. I'm not allowed to use the word *tampon* in front of the fifth-graders. I'm supposed to call it a *feminine hygiene product*."

Well, this was real exciting: discussing tampons with two members of the primary school faculty. Jed met

Erica's eyes and a quiet laugh escaped her. He laughed, too. She immediately bent over the bread she was slicing, concentrating hard on that simple task, measuring the width of each slice as if it had to be calibrated to the nearest millimeter.

"So, how about you, Jed?" Fern called from the stove. "You doing exciting things in New York City?"

"I'm living there. I don't know how exciting that is."

"Well, compared with living here…" Fern sent him a knowing look. He grinned. "What kind of work are you doing there?"

"I guess you could say I'm in the family business."

"What family business?" She hooted. "Your dad runs a junkyard."

Jed shrugged. Erica gave him a hard look. "You run a junkyard in New York City?"

"I run a resale business," he said. "Same thing."

"What do you mean, a resale business?"

He quoted the old line: "'I buy junk. I sell antiques.'"

"You buy junk?" Fern shouted at the same moment Erica asked, "You sell antiques?"

"Something like that." He didn't want to go into it, not if Fern was going to draw connections between his father and him. It wasn't as if he'd deliberately pursued his father's trade. It was just that he'd needed to make some money and he'd stumbled onto something he could do. Unlike Jed, his father might buy junk, but he also sold junk.

Erica's phone rang. She kept gazing at him, as if trying to figure out how much like his father he was. *Not much,* he wanted to assure her. When the phone rang a second time, she resumed sawing away at the loaf of bread.

"Aren't you going to answer it?" he asked.

"No. It's probably someone else's lawyer, planning to sue me for a share of my abundant wealth."

"Or else it's her mother," Fern called from the stove.

It rang a third time. He was impressed by Erica's refusal to answer the phone. That took genuine willpower. "What do you want me to do with this bread?" she asked, gathering up the slices.

"Have you got a cookie sheet? They need to be spread on a cookie sheet," Fern instructed her.

"Okay." Erica pushed to her feet as the answering machine clicked on.

"Erica Leitner?" a smooth male voice purred through the speaker. "This is Derrick Messinger. I'm in town, and I'd really like to talk to you."

Erica stared at her answering machine as if unsure whether to pick up the receiver. It was probably a good thing she didn't, because talking to Derrick Messinger, the oily TV journalist, would have been impossible with Fern screaming at the top of her lungs. "Derrick Messinger? Derrick Messinger's in town? And he wants to talk to you? *Erica!*"

"About what?" Erica asked stupidly. "What on earth would he want to talk to me about?"

"Your box!" Fern shrieked, swooping down on Erica and giving her a hug, nearly smacking her with the spoon she'd been using to stir the vegetables. "Derrick Messinger! Oh my God! Erica, you're *famous* now! You're going to be on TV, on *I'm Just the Messinger!* Oh! My! God!"

Jed recalled the artifact she'd shown him and Meryl

on Sunday evening. It had been a musty, chipped, faded chunk of wood, its hardware tarnished and crusted with dirt. A box. Why Derrick Messinger would want to talk to Erica about it was beyond him.

Of course, folks got carried away over junk all the time. If they didn't, he'd be out of business.

People were weird, that was all. Some people had taste, some had credentials, some had serenity. Some danced around the room, cheering and hooting at the mere thought that a reporter as famous as Derrick Messinger had come to their boring little town. Some drank wine to take the edge off the lingering craving for nicotine. Some had beer for breakfast.

And some, like Erica, looked utterly bewildered, overwhelmed by what life had thrown at her, or, more accurately, laid beneath her shovel in her garden.

Lawyers. TV reporters. Erica was in for it, all right.

And Rockwell suddenly seemed more interesting to him than it ever had before.

CHAPTER SIX

AS EAGER AS FERN had been to have dinner with Erica, she seemed just as eager to leave once she'd swallowed the last limp coil of rigatoni from her plate. The box from Erica's garden had apparently slipped her mind.

Well, she hadn't come to see the box. She'd come to see Jed Willetz. Erica refused to feel exploited because, after all, she'd gotten a delicious dinner out of the deal. The thing she couldn't figure out, though, was why, with Jed sitting right in the same room, right at the same table, Fern had decided to depart so abruptly. She'd said something about having work to do, work tonight, work tomorrow, busy-busy-busy, and off she'd flown, leaving behind enough leftovers for two more pasta primavera dinners—or one more pasta primavera dinner for two, if Erica happened to find someone to have dinner with in the next several days.

She eyed Jed, then glanced away. She wasn't going to be having dinner with him on a regular basis.

To be sure, she expected him to leave when Fern did. But he stuck around, carrying the dishes in from the dining room and lingering in the kitchen while she cleaned them. He didn't say much, and neither did she. It was as if Fern had been the only one among them who knew how to sustain a conversation, and now that she'd abandoned them, Erica and Jed were floundering.

They'd had conversations before, though. They'd

had conversations during which Erica had been holding a knife, and other conversations during which she'd been unarmed. She wasn't sure whether scrubbing the stickiness from a knife under a stream of steamy water counted as being armed, but while she washed the dishes Jed wandered lazily around the kitchen, scrutinizing the streaked enamel paint on the cabinet doors, studying the awkward arrangement of wires snaking out from the console of her cordless phone, peering through the dingy window in the back door, roaming the place as if it were his.

She liked having him in her kitchen. She didn't object to his poking around, scanning the contents of her cabinets, resetting the clock on her cooking range so it was no longer three minutes slow. His presence made the room feel...different. The proximity of testosterone seemed to rearrange the air molecules in an exhilarating way.

She shook the excess water from the final plate and stacked it in the dish rack to dry. Now what? she wondered as she dried her hands on a paper towel. Was she supposed to entertain him? She couldn't regale him the way Fern had, with updates on Stuart Farnham—"Remember how he sounded like an asthmatic horse when he laughed? Well, he still does"—or Cynthia Conklin—"She's always getting brought in on traffic violations, and then the charges are dropped. She's sleeping with the entire police force. Marty Nichols—he's a sergeant now—says the joke around the station house is that she's a case of 'arrested development.' I guess if you saw her bosom, you'd get the joke."

True, Cynthia was well endowed, and she did seem to run red lights and stop signs with impunity. And Erica had heard Stuart Farnham snort and wheeze when he laughed too hard. But she didn't know these people the way Fern and Jed did, the way someone who was truly a Rockwellian would.

"So," he said when the silence deepened with her shutting off the water, "I see there's still some wine in that bottle."

Great. He was hanging around to drink her wine. Given what a sterling conversationalist she'd been, why else would he have stayed so long?

"It's kind of warm out," he went on. "For April, anyway. We could refill our glasses and sit on the porch."

"I haven't got a porch," she said. "The back porch is really just a couple of steps."

"I meant my porch."

He had a huge porch. And there was enough wine left to top off both their glasses. If they sat outside, the night air would dilute his testosterone effect. In all honesty, she wasn't ready to say good-night to him, even if she'd had trouble thinking of anything else to say to him.

They'd find things to talk about on his porch. She wanted to hear more about his junk business. She'd driven past his father's junkyard a few times; it seemed to be little more than a huge lot enclosed by a chain-link fence and filled with wrecked cars, rusting refrigerators and other large appliances from which salvageable parts could be harvested. What Jed did had to be different from what his father did, which, as best Erica could tell, amounted to sitting on a bench in the doorway of a small, ramshackle shed near the gate, listening to talk radio and waiting to make a profit off someone's desperate need for a gasket from an old Whirlpool dishwasher.

Jed bought junk; he sold antiques. His father didn't sell antiques. For that matter, he didn't buy junk. As Erica understood it, people paid him a fee to truck their old appliances or tow their wrecked cars away. So he made money on that end, and on the other end, when he cannibalized his acquisitions and sold the parts. In theory it sounded like a pretty shrewd arrangement. But Jack didn't appear to be raking in the big bucks with his junk trade.

Neither did his son. But what did she know?

Not much, she acknowledged as she slipped her arms through the sleeves of her field jacket. Late-April warmth in Rockwell was not the same thing as late-April warmth in Miami. Without the jacket, she'd be too cold outside to enjoy her wine, let alone Jed's company.

He grabbed the bottle and both glasses and preceded her out the back door. Walking behind him afforded her an interesting view of his narrow hips and long legs, his relaxed gait and solid shoulders. For a junk-dealing son of a junk dealer, he was damn nice eye candy.

The porch of his grandfather's house was furnished with a swing and several deeply sloping Adirondack chairs. The swing looked more comfortable, and she'd be able to burn off her nervous energy by swinging. Not that she was nervous, but sitting in the peace of a half-moon evening, drinking wine with Jed, was just romantic enough to make her edgy.

As soon as she was seated, she realized her mistake. If she'd sat in one of the Adirondack chairs, he wouldn't have been able to plant himself right beside her. But the swing was wide enough for two, and his legs, being much longer than hers, got to dictate whether they swung, and how fast.

And it wasn't a very big swing. Once he'd settled his large frame next to her, she realized he was awfully close.

He refilled their glasses, set the empty bottle on the porch planks and said, "So, what do you think about Derrick Messinger?"

She didn't want to think about him at all. That a TV tabloid journalist had phoned her was preposterous. "I think he wears a toupee," she said.

"Nah. That's real."

"No way."

Jed eyed her, not quite smiling. "Fifty bucks says it's real."

"Fifty bucks?" She scowled. Even if she were a wagering woman, fifty dollars was a lot of money.

"Okay. Ten bucks."

"I'm not going to bet on something like that!"

His smile widened into something mischievous, challenging her. "What would you bet on, then?"

"Absolutely nothing."

He laughed. "Not a risk taker, are you?"

She bristled defensively. She'd taken a huge risk by moving to Rockwell, hadn't she? Not a life-and-death risk, not a major financial risk, but she'd moved to a tiny village in the shadow of the Moose Mountains, where she knew no one. She'd defied her parents' expectations by choosing to settle in a place where Clinique facial cleansers and the *New Yorker* were unavailable in the local stores. She'd bought a house and planted a garden—or at least gotten a start on that. She considered herself rather daring, all things considered.

"I don't wager money," she explained.

"What do you wager?"

She couldn't tell if he was mocking her or coming on to her. She decided to change the subject. "I have no idea why Derrick Messinger would want to see me. Maybe it's not about the box. Maybe it's about something else, although I can't imagine what." She took a sip of her wine, carefully, because Jed was nudging the swing back and forth with his toe and she didn't want to slosh any Chianti on her jacket. "Doesn't Messinger usually do shows on gangsters and missing people?"

"He does shows on anything he thinks will attract an audience. The guy's slick. He's into ratings."

"As if a show about an old box with a dirt-clogged lock is going to get high ratings," she said.

"If the box is filled with a million dollars, it is."

"It's not," Erica said with a certainty she didn't feel. Actually, she didn't feel certain about anything. The air seemed to fluctuate between mild and cool. Her wine tasted more tart than it had inside. Scattered clouds drifted across the sky, pale gray against dark blue like a Magritte painting. And Jed was so *warm*. He hadn't bothered with a jacket, and he clearly didn't need one. He radiated heat like someone with a fever; only, he was obviously healthy. Big and hot and healthy.

She lowered her gaze to his left hand, which dwarfed his wineglass. She was used to eight-year-old hands, soft and small, with dirty nails or pencil smudges on them.

"How do you know it's not?"

It took her a moment to remember what they'd been discussing: the estimated value of the box's contents.

"I don't know," she admitted. "I just hope it's not filled with money."

"You don't want a million dollars?"

"Even if the box contained a million dollars, I couldn't claim the money as mine."

He shifted slightly to look at her, and the swing rocked from his motion. She saw mischief in his eyes. When was the last time she'd sat alone at night with someone like him? "In other words, you admit half the money is mine?" he asked.

That was why he was being nice to her, she realized—if jostling her on the swing so she had to keep flexing her wrist to keep the wine level in her glass, and giving her grins just a bit too tricky for her to interpret, constituted being nice. He wanted half of whatever was in the box. She hoped it was pebbles and pine needles. She'd gladly give him half of that, and it would serve him right for being so greedy.

Then again, he might just be teasing her. She couldn't tell.

She straightened her back. For God's sake, she wasn't a ditz. She was a Harvard graduate in charge of her own life. She'd taken on fabulous-looking guys before. Maybe no one quite as fabulous-looking as Jed, but honestly. He was a junk dealer. A Rockwell native. She had the brains to handle him. "Tell me about your business," she said.

His gaze softened, his smile losing its taunting edge. "It's a shop in New York," he told her. "City Re-sale."

"You really buy junk and sell antiques?"

He chuckled, shook his head and twisted back on the swing's bench so he was facing the porch railing. He propped one foot up on it and used it to rock them.

JUDITH ARNOLD   99

His foot was big, too, encased in a thick-soled work boot. Big feet, big hands. She wondered what else about him was big, then shut that thought down before it could get her into trouble.

"I don't buy junk," he told her, "and I don't sell antiques."

"I see." Actually, she didn't.

"When I went to New York, I had nothing. A few bucks saved from summer jobs and working on my grandfather's farm—" he gestured toward the fallow field that extended back from the house "—but that was it. I was fresh out of high school and I didn't own a pot to...well..."

"Piss in," she said helpfully, so he'd know she wasn't a prig.

"Yeah. I got a job as a night janitor in a midtown office building, and when I'd leave work around six in the morning, I'd see all this stuff people would discard on the sidewalk. I guess the trash collectors were supposed to pick it up, but it was just out there—tables, lamps, rugs, all kinds of stuff. I couldn't afford furniture, so I'd pick up whatever I could use and bring it home with me. I'd clean it, repair it—the lamps usually just needed rewiring or some other easy fix—and that was how I furnished my apartment. You wouldn't believe what some people throw out. Really good stuff."

Erica nodded, remembering with a twinge all the really good stuff her family had thrown out over the years, simply because they could afford better stuff. When the old stuff was in decent shape, they donated it to Goodwill, but if it needed repair, they'd just pay their trash-removal service to haul it away.

"When people came to visit they'd be blown away by some lamp I'd rewired, or a chest of drawers I'd refinished, and they'd tell me I could make money selling it. So I decided to give it a try."

"Just like that?"

He nodded. "After a while, I was making enough money to quit the janitor job."

"That's amazing."

"No, it's not." He bent his knee and straightened it, pushing the swing in a gentle rhythm. "Most people have no idea of the value of things. They want to get rid of something, so they toss it. They don't stop to think about what they've got." He drank some wine, then glanced at her. "I don't scavenge on the street anymore. I've got my store and workshop downtown, in SoHo. People sell their old stuff to us. Or someone dies, and the survivors just want grandma's apartment closed up fast, so they take a lump sum for everything in it. Then I figure out what's worth working on. We've got a shop upstairs from the store, where we do the repairs and refinishing. And then these chic artsy customers come in and drop a bundle to buy the old tea cart or sling chair someone else thought was garbage."

It was Erica's turn to shift in the swing, not to stare at him but just because she felt she needed a new position. There she was, an Ivy Leaguer who had grown up in affluence, seated next to a high school–educated almost-junk dealer who'd created a business successful enough to occupy two floors of a building in SoHo, where he catered to the frivolous tastes of chichi New York connoisseurs. Who would have thought Rockwell—and in particular, Jack Willetz—could have produced such a person?

"You're very enterprising," she remarked, then

cringed at the possibility that she sounded condescending.

He only laughed. "Oh, yeah, that's me. Mr. Enter-
prise." He drained his glass and leaned forward to set
it on the floorboards. The motion unbalanced her phys-
ically as much as his nearness unbalanced her mentally, and she pitched forward, then sideways into him
to keep from tumbling off the swing.

"Sorry," he said, catching her and settling her back
in the seat. He wrapped one arm around her shoulders
to steady her and curved his fingers around her upper
arm. The heat of his hand seeped through the sleeves
of her jacket and sweater to spread through her arm.
How could he be so warm? They were in central New
Hampshire at night, just barely out of mud season. And
he wasn't even wearing a jacket.

The swing stabilized, but he didn't remove his hand.
His arm was also warm, radiating heat down her spine.
His chest was warm. The swing was too tiny, the air
molecules surrounding her were in a hormone-fed
frenzy and Jed Willetz, the guy every female classmate—and perhaps a few male classmates, too—had
lusted after in high school was leaning in, drawing her
closer, lowering his face until his strong, sturdy features blurred before her eyes. And then he kissed her.

Jed Willetz. The heartthrob of Rockwell Regional.
The junkyard owner's son. The man who'd fled this
town, which Erica was trying very hard to make her
new home.

Oh, God. She was in trouble.

She tried to remember the last time she'd been
kissed like this, and realized the answer was never.
She'd dated a fellow from Manchester for a while, an
insurance adjuster who'd moved his jaw too much

when he talked, enunciating his words as if he were hoping to win an elocution contest. And when she'd been in Brookline during the school's winter break, she'd run into an old boyfriend in the cheese aisle of Stop-and-Shop and learned that in the years since she'd last seen him he'd gotten married and divorced. They'd gone out for dinner, necked a little for old time's sake, and then went their separate ways.

This was different, even though Erica knew it would end with her and Jed going their separate ways. He'd turned his back on Rockwell. He'd rejected everything she'd longed for: the small-town charm, the coziness, the tight community. He was going to bury his grandfather's ashes and disappear.

But damn, he could kiss.

It occurred to her that most men did not know what to do with their tongues. Not that she'd kissed enough men in her life to make generalizations, but Jed... Jed definitely knew what to do. He didn't poke at her teeth and jab inside her mouth. Instead, he used sweeping motions, licking motions, taking motions that sent her temperature soaring. Maybe that was why he was so warm: his tongue was a source of heat and he had it inside his mouth all the time. Now it was inside hers, and she was burning up.

She felt cheap and silly, kissing this man for whom so many women in town would allegedly drop their panties. She didn't love him, she hardly knew him, and she was behaving in a way her mother always told her nice girls did not behave. She was being kissed by a near stranger, being kissed hard, being kissed so wantonly that even though their mouths were the only parts of their bodies involved, it felt like the most erotic act she'd ever engaged in.

She tried to kiss him back, but he was definitely the dominant one, determining the pressure, the speed, the depth. That felt strange to her, too, because she was by nature used to being on top of things. Jed was on top of things now, and when she closed her eyes her body shuddered at the thought of how heavenly it would be to have him on top of her.

His arm was still around her, and he lifted his free hand to cup her cheek. His fingers dug into her hair, and his palm covered half her face. The warmth made her jaw go slack, giving him access to even more of her mouth. Either the swing was moving or his kiss was making her dizzy.

After a minute—actually, it could have been two or ten minutes, or maybe just a few seconds—he pulled back and sighed. He let his hand slide down to the side of her neck where it rested, so hot it might be giving her a second-degree burn. She started breathing again, and when he rested his forehead against hers she felt, for reasons she couldn't fathom, like crying.

"We'd better stop," she whispered. That must be why she was near tears. She didn't want to stop, but the nice girl was wresting control back from the silly, cheap lady inside her.

"Why?"

She drew in a deep breath. The air had grown cooler. Her lungs felt colder than the side of her neck where his hand lingered. "I have no idea where we're going with this," she said.

He laughed softly. "I think it's pretty obvious where we're going." His thumb stroked the underside of her chin, sending ripples of heat down into her.

She wished he'd move back a little so she could see him, but she couldn't bring herself to push him away.

"Maybe where we're going is someplace we shouldn't go."

"Why not?"

"Because…" Because she was a nice girl again, and he was going to leave, and while a little just-for-the-hell-of-it making out was fun, something told her that going any further with Jed was not going to be a just-for-the-hell-of-it experience. She'd likely wind up scorched inside and out. The man was just too…*hot*.

"How do I know you're not kissing me because you think there's a million dollars in my box?" she asked when no better argument presented itself.

He laughed again. "You figured me out," he joked, his lips brushing hers with each word. "I'm just after your money."

"I haven't got any money," she warned, hearing her voice waver. Maybe he *was* after her money. Maybe he was a low-down creep. It didn't seem fair that someone so vile should be able to kiss the way he did, but whoever said life was fair?

"You haven't opened the box yet. You don't know what you have."

"You might be really wasting your time with me."

"Yeah. I might." But he kissed her again, a brush of his lips, just enough to remind her of what an all-out kiss from him was like. "If I was smart—" kiss "—and *enterprising*—" kiss "—I'd set my sights on genuine millionaires. Heiresses—" kiss "—and rich divorcées, and gallery owners on Madison Avenue." He gave her one final kiss, lightly sucking on her lower lip, and her hips twitched from the heat rushing through her. "Guess I'm not so enterprising after all."

"I guess you're not," she said. Her voice sounded choked and raspy. She was in big trouble here. She was about ten seconds away from begging him to go back to her house with her, to her bedroom, to do to the rest of her body what he was doing to her mouth.

But how could she know this wasn't about her box? He hadn't denied it. He'd joked about it, but he hadn't assured her that she was what mattered, her box and its contents were of no interest to him, he loved her and intended to remain in Rockwell forever and the hell with his New York City resale business.

He wasn't going to say any of that, because it wasn't true.

"I'd better go," she said, pressing as far back into the swing as she could.

With apparent reluctance he withdrew, letting his hand drop and sliding his arm out from behind her. At last she could see his face. He looked bemused but not devoid of hope. Even when he was no longer touching her he seemed to exude heat. She tried to guess its source. His eyes, maybe. They glowed in the dim light. "I'll walk you back," he offered, moving to stand.

She nudged him down as she rose, and said, "No, that's all right." If he walked her to her house, he'd wind up at her door, and then it would be too easy for him to follow her inside, and then she'd be in big trouble again, much bigger trouble than she was in now.

He peered up at her as she gathered their empty glasses and strode to the porch steps. Lifting his leg to the railing again, he pushed himself in a calm rhythm, his gaze remaining on her as she descended to the dead, scraggly lawn that extended out to the road. She was almost clear of his house when he called after her, "Say hi to Derrick Messinger for me."

CHAPTER SEVEN

Ah, THE CITY.

Through the soft haze that marked the halfway point between asleep and awake, Jed heard the rumble of a car engine, the distant honk of a horn, the tinny squawk of a man's voice somewhere below his window. Pressing his head deeper into his pillow, he listened for the familiar clank of the radiator kicking on, the faint rumble of a subway passing beneath the street a block away.

Thank God he was home, miles from his father and his smothering little hometown and that woman…that woman who…God, *that woman.*

His legs kicked reflexively at the sheets. He heard a horn again and his eyes blinked open. He wasn't in the city. He was in Rockwell, and *that woman*—the one who had hijacked his dreams and kept him aroused all night, who'd caused him to wake up as hard as a fresh-picked zucchini, damn it—was right next door.

A schoolteacher, of all things. An overeducated teacher who seemed actually to like Rockwell, which proved that for all her intelligence and Ivy League pedigree, she had no sense. Why was he even thinking about her?

So he'd made a move on her last night. Big deal. He'd enjoyed their dinner with Fern Bernard, and he'd enjoyed every other time he'd been with Erica—especially those times when she wasn't pointing a knife at him—and the night had been balmy. The wine had been smooth and potent and Erica had been sitting so close to him, her big, dark eyes glowing with laughter and generosity and who the hell knew what else. Her eyes were amazing.

He'd figured the worst that could happen was she'd shoot him down. He'd been shot down before and it hadn't killed him. So he'd gone ahead and kissed her.

He hadn't expected her mouth to be like a ripe peach, all sweet, juicy texture. He'd wanted to devour it—to devour *her*. He'd wanted to haul her into his lap and feel her weight on him. He'd wanted to close his arms around her and open her legs around him and do all kinds of fun, dirty things with her.

All night long he'd dreamed about her, about kissing her, the smooth, cool surface of her cheek, her hair sliding through his fingers and all the fun, dirty things he wanted to do with her. Now here he was, wide awake in the bedroom he used to use when he stayed with his grandfather, still thinking about her and feeling as horny as a fifteen-year-old locked in a bathroom with the latest edition of *Penthouse*.

With Erica living in the house next door, he just might find remaining in Rockwell bearable, at least until he'd taken care of his grandfather's ashes and figured out what to do with the house and its contents. Even if he never got further with Erica than he'd gotten last night, he'd like to stick around long enough to find out what was inside her box.

The hell with her box. He wanted her. He hardly even knew her, but he wanted her the way a kid wants an ice-cream cone on a scorching August day. For a few creamy licks of that rich peach-flavored ice cream—sure, he could put up with Rockwell for a little while.

He heard the drone of a car idling somewhere near his house. Traffic? On Old North Road? Then he heard the man's voice again, scratchy and unintelligible as he shouted to someone. Jed sat up, pinched the bridge of his nose to squeeze his eyes into focus, swung out of bed and crossed to the window. He lifted the corner of the curtain and frowned.

Two vans, a car and a pickup truck lined the road outside his and Erica's houses. He didn't recognize the vans or the car, but he knew the truck, dusty gray with scabs of rust and a funky dent twisting the rear bumper below the tailgate.

Letting the curtain drop back across the window, he grabbed his jeans from the chair where he'd tossed them last night and yanked them on. He flung his arms through the sleeves of his flannel shirt and stormed out the bedroom and down the stairs, ignoring the cold floor against the soles of his feet. He kept on through the hall to the front door and out onto the porch, which was even colder, clammy from the layer of early-morning mist that hovered just above the ground. The sky was pearly; the sun, not yet up. What time was it, anyway? He'd forgotten to grab his watch before barreling down the stairs.

He heard a muffled voice again, and then his father appeared from the far side of one of the vans. He must have spotted Jed on the porch, because he ambled over, more energetic than anyone deserved to be this early in the morning. Dressed in his plaid wool jacket and a pair of corduroy slacks that billowed around his skinny legs, he appeared uncharacteristically cheerful.

"Big happenings, eh?" he said, his voice emerging on puffs of vapor in the chilly air.

"What the hell is going on? What are you doing here?"

"Well, these newsfolks needed to know where the teacher lived. I was happy to show them."

"I'll bet you were." Actually, Jed bet his father had been paid to lead them here. He was always happy to help out if someone waved a few crisp bills under his nose. "Newspeople?"

His father glanced over his shoulder and pointed proudly at all the vehicles but his banged-up truck. "There's a news team outta Manchester, one outta Boston, and that guy, Derrick Messinger, the one that does all those TV specials on Mafia crime and the like."

"I know who he is," Jed muttered, wondering if Erica was awake yet, if she was aware of what was going on right outside her front door.

His father patted his chest as if in search of something, then asked, "You got a smoke on you?"

"I quit," Jed said, his scowl deepening. He never missed cigarettes more than when he uttered those two words.

His announcement seemed to vex his father. "Quit, eh? What, you're trying to get healthy or something?"

"Yeah, something like that."

Jack shook his head, clearly disappointed. "Well, maybe one of them newspeople's got one." He turned and sauntered over to the caravan of vehicles.

Swearing quietly, Jed marched back into his house and slammed the door. His chest was damp from the morning fog, and he belatedly buttoned his shirt. Then he dug into his jeans pocket for his cell phone, flipped it open and stalked down the hall. His grandfather kept important phone numbers on scraps of paper taped to the inner surfaces of his kitchen cabinets. Jed hoped he'd find Erica's among them. She'd been the old man's tenant for a while, so he probably would have wanted to keep her number handy.

There she was, alongside the number of the pharmacy and just above the number of the National Weather Service on the door of the cabinet where Jed's grandfather had stored his cooking spices. Jed punched her number into his phone, then moved to the window above the sink and adjusted the blind slats so he could see her house. It looked dark.

She answered halfway through the third ring: "H'lo?"

He'd awakened her. A glance at the wall clock told him it was six-forty, and he experienced a fleeting stab of guilt about having roused her from sleep. But the guilt faded, replaced by a much deeper stab of lust at the thick, dazed sound of her voice. She was in bed, he realized, all warm and soft and tousled. Did she sleep nude? Or in something lacy, maybe?

"It's Jed Willetz," he remembered to say. His voice came out a little raspy, but she was probably too drowsy to care.

"Jed?"

His abdominal muscles tightened. He'd like to hear her say his name that way when he was lying beside her, waking up with her. She'd smile, remembering the previous night, and murmur his name, and he'd proceed to replace those last-night memories with some new ones. Yeah, that would work.

He pinched the bridge of his nose again, as if he

could squeeze out all those distracting images. "So you're answering your phone now?"

"Only when I'm half asleep and not thinking straight."

He tried not to take her words as an insult. "There's a bunch of media people in your front yard," he told her.

"What?" She sounded more alert now.

"TV journalists," he repeated. "Derrick Messinger and some others. My helpful father brought them here."

"In my front yard?"

"Look out your window."

She sighed, a wavering whisper of breath. "Hang on a second," she said, followed by a muffled thud as she put down the receiver, and then the rustle of sheets as she got out of bed. Her sheets might be dark—midnight blue, or chocolate brown. Or maybe something pastel and flowery.

Like he'd even notice her sheets if he was in bed with her.

While he waited for her to return, he tackled the challenging task of preparing a pot of coffee with only one hand. The stove still looked strangely barren to him without his grandfather's skillet sitting on a rear burner. It had always sat there, like a part of the range. He wanted to get the pan back from his father, but he wasn't sure it was worth fighting over.

To silence his cravings for a cigarette, he rummaged through the drawers until he found a toothpick. After wedging it between his teeth, he sucked on the tip.

A rattle on the other end of the phone signaled that Erica was back. "My God."

"They're from Manchester and Boston, as well as

your good buddy Derrick Messinger." The toothpick bobbed up and down as he spoke.

"My God." She sounded bewildered and resigned. "This can't just be about the box."

"No?" He felt his eyebrows rise. "Have you got some other newsworthy stuff going on in your life? Are you having an affair with a congressman or something?"

"I am the most unnewsworthy person in the world," she said dryly.

"Then it's about the box." The aroma of brewing coffee somehow warmed his bare toes. "Open the thing up and those people will disappear."

"Unless it's got a million dollars inside."

"But you don't think it does," he reminded her.

After a minute, she said, "I'm not going to open it. Not until Professor Gilman gets here. I'm not going to risk breaking something that could be a priceless artifact."

"Even if it's priceless, it's not going to be worth as much as the million dollars inside it," Jed pointed out. The toothpick snapped and he tossed it into the trash. He still wanted a cigarette, but at least he hadn't caught a splinter in his tongue.

"I mean, this is Rockwell." Her voice took on a slightly hysterical edge. "I came here because it's a peaceful, quiet place."

A dead place, he thought.

"It isn't overrun with people intoxicated with their own importance."

No, just people intoxicated the old-fashioned way.

"I mean, Meryl Hummer. She's the sum and substance of the media around here."

And she'd gone and written a story about Erica's

box and plastered it across the front page of her newspaper, and now look. *I'm Just the Messinger* and those news outlets from Manchester and Boston were crawling all over Erica's front yard at six-forty in the morning.

Not that Jed cared one way or the other. It was her box from her garden, on her property, and it was her headache. He would have helped shoulder the burden if she'd been more open-minded about the property line, but she didn't want to share the box and its bounty with him, so he wasn't going to share her hassles with her. Let her keep her million dollars—if Glenn Rideout didn't figure out a way to get his greedy paws on it. What would Jed do with half a million dollars, anyway?

Lots of things, he admitted, pulling a mug from the cabinet that contained the phone numbers of the police station, Ostronkowicz's garage and Reena Keefer, a plump, taciturn widow who ran a small maple syrup operation west of town. Jed's grandfather had never come right out and said so, but Jed had always suspected there was something going on between those two. Reena hadn't shed a single tear at the church service after old John died, and that was just the kind of thing John would have admired in a woman. He'd been about as sentimental as a block of granite. Reena was that way, too.

Half a million dollars. Jed filled the mug with fresh coffee and contemplated what he'd do with that much cash. He could buy his apartment, do away with having to budget according to the whims of his landlord. Or maybe he'd invest the money—some in the store, some in stocks. His accountant kept saying he should set up a retirement fund.

Half a million dollars could pay for some useful things. One thing it couldn't pay for was a cure to nicotine addiction. He considered whether to mangle another toothpick with his teeth and decided that drinking coffee was just as effective. He sipped it slowly, peering out the window again, across the collapsed fence that separated his house from Erica's. He could see her back door and her garden from where he stood. Right now, she would be at the opposite end of her house, where her bedroom was located.

He wondered what she'd do with a million dollars. Or even half a million, if she was forced over to fork the rest to Glenn Rideout.

In her position, Jed would leave Rockwell. But he'd done that already. You didn't need a lot of money to get out of a town like this.

He turned from the kitchen window and wandered back down the hall to the front door. "Look," he said into the phone, "I'm sorry I woke you up, but I thought you could use a little warning."

"Thank you," she said.

Closing his eyes, he pictured her one more time in bed. He pictured her hair mussed and her legs extended, her toenails painted red. She didn't strike him as the type to paint her toenails, but this was his fantasy and he could make them any damn color he wanted. He pictured her lips slightly parted, the way they'd been last night just before he'd kissed her, and his jeans suddenly felt snug.

She could keep her money, whatever it turned out to be. She could keep her front-page fame, her tabloid celebrity, her Harvard-professor buddy, her priceless artifact and all the rest.

He knew what he wanted from her, and it had noth-

ing to do with what she'd dug out of her garden patch
a few days ago.

AFTER SHE HUNG UP, she berated herself for having
failed to bring up the subject of last night's kiss.

She wasn't sure what she should have said, but she
should have said *something*. "Jed, you shouldn't have
kissed me," she might have declared. "It's made
things awkward between us. You're just passing
through town, and I've planted my roots here, and
there's no reason for us to start something we have no
intention of finishing."

A hot shudder rippled through her as she considered
finishing what she and Jed had started last night. The
real finish wouldn't be having sex with him, though.
It would be saying goodbye and waving him off as he
returned to New York City.

In principle, she saw nothing wrong with recrea-
tional sex, as long as both participants recognized the
situation for what it was. But she didn't think she was
cut out for that kind of recreation. She hadn't even
mastered gardening or baking bread. No-strings-
attached sex seemed far more challenging. She knew
her limitations.

Perhaps it was just as well that she hadn't brought
up the subject of last night's kiss. Jed hadn't said anything about it. He'd probably forgotten it already. Just
because she'd been restless most of the night, remembering the seductive pressure of his mouth on hers,
didn't mean her mouth had left any impression on him.

That restlessness was taking its toll on her now.
Waking up twenty minutes before her alarm sounded
would have left her groggy, anyway, but the previous
night's insomnia staggered her with fatigue. She'd

need strength and lucidity to face the small army of reporters outside her house, and right now she had neither.

Maybe she should avoid the reporters altogether. She could duck out the back door, race to the shed, dive into her car and leave rubber speeding past them—as if she had something to hide. She didn't, unless you counted the box, which she wasn't hiding so much as protecting.

The thing was, she had nothing to say to the reporters other than "Good morning," or "Isn't Rockwell a charming town?"

She took her time getting dressed, donning a plain brown corduroy jumper and a plaid blouse, then headed for the kitchen to eat breakfast. Maybe they would go away if she ignored them. Starvation might drive them down to Main Street for breakfast. The Eatzeria opened early. They could all clog their arteries with omelettes, bacon and home fries, and then they could have heart attacks and flee to the hospital in Manchester, because as charming a town as Rockwell was, its residents couldn't count on receiving state-of-the-art medical care within its borders.

She filled a bowl with cereal and skim milk and carried it to the living-room doorway, from which vantage she could see through the windows to the front yard and the road. Either she hadn't counted correctly when she'd peeked out earlier, or another car had arrived. Various news-media types milled about on her lawn, sipping coffee from travel mugs, checking their watches and conferring with one another. Some carried videocams with large microphones attached to them, and others were coiffed with alarming precision. It wasn't hard to guess who the on-air talent was.

She spooned some cereal into her mouth and shook her head. This was really stupid. The box couldn't possibly be that fascinating to people in Manchester and Boston, to say nothing of Derrick Messinger's national audience. People in Miami and Dallas and Los Angeles were surely not perched on the edges of their seats, dying to hear about some antique wooden box a third-grade teacher and her former student had excavated from her backyard garden.

Granted, they might be lured to the edges of their seats by the prospect that the box contained a bounty of stunning magnitude. But Erica wasn't going to open the box until Avery arrived, which would be tomorrow evening. The reporters would just have to cool their heels until then.

She decided not to sneak out of the house like a coward, especially since the reporters would surely spot her making a break for her car, and they'd chase her with their cameras bouncing and their mikes thrust at her like tilting lances, and she'd look like a racketeer or a corrupt politician trying to dodge an interview on *Sixty Minutes*.

Emboldened, she donned her lined raincoat, grabbed her leather tote and swung open the front door. The horde on her front lawn immediately launched their strike, charging across the grass and shouting at her.

She recognized one—a perky blond woman in a pink wool suit—from a network affiliate in Boston. On TV, the woman had always looked normal, but in person she seemed like an escapee from an anorexia treatment center. Her suit had to be a size zero, unless there was a smaller size than that. She was short, too, a sprite in pastel pink. The thought amused Erica, but only for a moment, because her vision soon filled with the sight of Derrick Messinger.

No, that was *not* a hairpiece. It couldn't be. The ruler-straight part slicing through his lush strawberry-blond mane appeared to be cut right down to his scalp. Had he been wearing a toupee, he wouldn't have parted his hair like that.

They were all yammering at her: "Ms. Leitner! Ms. Leitner!"—some of them pronounced it "Leet-ner" instead of "Lite-ner"—"Have you opened the box yet? Where's the box?"

The sprite from Boston was wearing bright-red lipstick. The other female reporter wore a parka, as if she thought April in New Hampshire was still ski season, which, Erica supposed, it was. The male reporter who wasn't Derrick Messinger was almost as carefully polished and made-up as the females. A conservative beige plaid scarf shaped a V below his chin, and even as he peppered her with questions his voice remained stentorian.

Erica suppressed a laugh. The idea of reporters primping and researching and traveling all the way to Rockwell to interview her about her box was so goofy. Still, she wondered whether she should have added a little blush to her cheeks and a layer of gloss to her lips. Given the dreary morning light, she was going to look wan on TV.

No, she wasn't. She wasn't going to appear on TV at all, at least not based on this encounter. She had nothing to say to these people. Perhaps, once they realized that, they'd pack up their equipment and leave.

She held up a hand to silence them, and tried to ignore the huge microphones aimed at her. "I haven't opened the box," she announced.

"Where is it?" the sprite demanded.

"It's in a safe place."

"Why are you hiding it? What else are you hiding?" The questions buzzed around her like black flies.

Mentally swatting them away, she searched within herself for her calm, earth-mother soul. She ought to be annoyed at the intrusion of the reporters, but they were too silly to be annoying. In the grand scheme of things, her celebrity—even if it lasted only her Warhol-allotted fifteen minutes—was far less significant than the historical import of the box.

"The box is in a safe place," she repeated. "And that's where it's going to stay for now. If you'll excuse me, I have a class to teach." With what she considered crushing dignity, she nodded a farewell to the reporters and strode around her house to the garage. She heard them swarming after her, but she refused to acknowledge them.

She ought to be involved in a scandal sometime, she thought. She handled the press so well.

She started to drag open the garage door, but Derrick Messinger practically shoved her out of the way in his quest to assist her. She doubted that his motives were pure, but she gave him a grateful smile and said, "Thank you."

She got into her car, revved the engine, checked her mirror to make sure she wasn't going to hit any of the reporters and backed slowly along the driveway. One last check in the mirror, and she slammed on the brakes. There he was again, her knight in hair spray. Derrick Messinger stood squarely in the center of the driveway, a hulking teddy bear of a cameraman at his side.

As soon as she stopped the car, Messinger glided

around to the driver's side, his cameraman trailing him. Messinger waved a business card at her, and she reluctantly rolled down her window.

"I want an exclusive, Ms. Leitner," he murmured, so quickly the words would have blurred into babble if his diction hadn't been so precise. He'd pronounced her name correctly, she noted. "I'm staying at the Hope Street Inn, right here in town. We can arrange the terms. I want what you want, Ms. Leitner—a responsible, respectful report. I know we can work together." He pressed his card against her palm and backed up, presenting her with an enigmatic smile.

Responsible and respectful, huh. His report on Jimmy Hoffa had been inane and sensationalistic. Perhaps he had more respect for a dirt-encrusted box than for a mysteriously vanished labor leader.

She conceded that Messinger had shown more resourcefulness than his competitors. He'd phoned her last night, so his appearance at her house this morning, while unwelcome, wasn't exactly unexpected. And unlike the others, he would go national with the story. If she gave him his exclusive, the entire country could learn what was inside her box.

The laughter she'd been stifling bubbled up and out of her. She wished Jed were here so they could laugh together. No, she shouldn't be wishing that.

"I'll think about it," she promised Derrick Messinger, giving his hair one more furtive look. It sure was thick. Probably real, but suspiciously thick.

By the time she'd backed out to the street and pointed her Subaru in the direction of the school, she was no longer thinking about Messinger's hair. She was thinking about Jed Willetz's hair, and his silver-gray eyes, and his amazing mouth. She really didn't want to be thinking about him, but she couldn't help herself.

WALKING OUT of the old shingled house where Sewell McCormick had his office, Jed sensed that something was out of whack.

The day had stayed overcast, fat gray clouds trudging across the sky, but down below, on Main Street, windows glistened as if they were reflecting a diamond-bright sun. Jed ordinarily didn't pay much attention to the cleanliness of windows, but this was noticeable.

Sewell had mastered multitasking long before anyone had coined the term. He was the Rockwell town manager—which was different from the mayor in that he wasn't elected and he did all the work—as well as a podiatrist and also the overseer of the town cemetery. Jed's feet were fine, and he couldn't care less how Rockwell was managed, but he did need to make arrangements to bury his grandfather's remains.

"He was a fine man, your grandfather," Sewell had said with practiced solemnity, patting his white medical coat in the vicinity of his heart. He'd occupied his swivel stool, leaving Jed no choice but to sit on the special podiatrist examining table, a cross between a dentist's chair and a sectional couch, covered with a strip of sterile white paper. It wasn't uncomfortable, but it didn't seem like an appropriate place to discuss John Willetz's ashes.

"He was a son of a bitch," Jed argued mildly, "but other than that, yeah, he was a good guy."

"This town is poorer in his absence."

It wouldn't be poorer once Jed paid the damn property tax on his grandfather's land. He supposed that overdue tax bill would have been even greater if his grandfather hadn't sold off a chunk of his estate to Erica Leitner.

Whom Jed was not going to think about anymore today.

"Maybe you never knew this about him," Sewell confided, leaning toward Jed and staring through his horn-rimmed eyeglasses, "but he had a real stubborn toenail fungus in '99. I attacked that beast with every weapon in my arsenal. Got to the point where he looked like he had cauliflower growing out of the cuticle."

This was more than Jed needed to know. "I want to lay his ashes to rest, Sewell. Just tell me when I can get that done."

"Will you be having a ceremony? Have you talked to Reverend Pith about it?"

Jed hadn't talked to Reverend Pith because he hadn't decided yet whether to have a ceremony. Whom would he invite? His father? The Widow Keefer? Or would it be like the memorial service they'd had in church right after his grandfather died, when just about everyone in town had crammed into the church? Not because they all loved John Willetz so much, but because nothing else had been going on that day. January in Rockwell was pretty slow.

April in Rockwell was pretty slow, too. Every month in Rockwell was slow. Maybe a graveside ceremony would give folks some desperately needed entertainment—Jed's gift to his hometown.

But as he gazed down Main Street, he wondered if April already had something going on. At least one thing had happened here: a massive downtown window washing.

It was more than windows. The obligatory American
flags were out, hanging limply in the damp midday air,
but some stores had put decorative flags on display,
too. Dangling from a pole beside the door of Harriet
Ettman's crafts shop was a bright-blue pennant featuring a nauseatingly cute bunny. The Eat-zeria's door
was flanked by two flags, one depicting a bottle of soda
and the other two sunny-side-up eggs frying in a pan
that reminded Jed of the skillet his father had stolen
from his grandfather's kitchen. Potter Henley's ac-
counting office, on the second floor above the Moosehead, flew a flag in the shape of a large dollar sign.
Hackett's Superette had red-white-and-blue bunting
draped festively above its door.

Last time Jed looked, it wasn't a national holiday.

While he was watching, Harriet emerged from her
shop lugging a bulky planter filled with pansies. She
set it on the sidewalk just beyond her door, where people would be sure to trip over it as they walked by,
and then dusted off her hands and vanished back into
her store.

Flowers? Flags and flowers? Was the president planning a photo op in town?

No, but the media were here. Word must have gotten
out about those TV people who'd been tramping all
over Erica's lawn that morning.

Of course word had gotten out. There were no se-
crets in Rockwell, other than his grandfather's possible
relationship with Reena Keefer. Rockwell was spruc-
ing up because TV reporters were in town.

Ambling down the street toward his turquoise rental
car, Jed checked out the glistening windows, the flags
and Harriet's pansies. She emerged from her store
again, carrying a watering can, and gave her flowers a

good soaking. She looked a little spiffier than usual, her silver hair tidy, her cardigan tied by its sleeves around her shoulders and hanging down her back like a cape, her sneakers so white she must have used shoe polish on them.

Gee, maybe he should hold a ceremony for his grandfather today so the media could report on it. Surely the death and burial of John Willetz, an authentically crotchety New England Yankee, was at least as worthy of coverage as Erica's box.

His car was parked in front of the Superette, and he ducked inside to pick up some more chewing gum. What he needed was the nicotine gum, but that struck him as the equivalent of methadone; he saw no point in exchanging an addiction to cigarettes for an addiction to nicotine gum. Plain old peppermint ought to be enough for him.

Pop Hackett was hunkered down in front of the checkout counter, tidying the candy racks. "Hey," Jed greeted him.

Pop glanced over his shoulder. "Hey, Jed. You live in New York City—tell me, you think I've got too many rows of M&M's?" He had four rows—brown packages, yellow packages, blue, red. "I'm just thinking you'd be a little more savvy about style and such, that's all."

"M&M's are M&M's," Jed said. "They look the same in New York as they do here."

That seemed to please Pop. He straightened up, dusted the cuffs of his plaid flannel shirt and smiled. Forty years ago, orthodontia would have done him a world of good.

Jed hoped he wasn't destroying the aesthetic balance of the candy display by grabbing a pack of chewing gum. "Where is everybody?" he asked. The store was empty except for Pop.

"Running their own stores and dreaming of fame," Pop told him, sweeping a hand over the sparse strands of hair stuck to his scalp like dried brown seaweed. "Haven't you heard about the TV people?"

"Yeah." He tried to think of any other food items he might need. His stock of peanut butter, milk and bananas was holding up, and while he'd been inventorying the house's contents yesterday he'd stumbled upon a dozen cans of soup, another five of stew and three of canned pears on a shelf in the basement. No canned peaches—and he wouldn't be able to buy any fresh peaches, either, not for another couple of months.

Thinking of peaches made him think of other things. He wandered toward the back of the store, where Pop kept a small and rather pitiful selection of alcoholic beverages. His wines were mostly Château du Jug and Vintage Screw Top, but Jed needed to have a bottle on hand. He searched the shelves in vain for a halfway decent Chianti. That was what Erica had served last night. It had been good; she obviously hadn't bought it at the Superette.

He settled on a Merlot he knew would be mediocre, but mediocre was better than bad. Maybe he'd bring it over to Erica's tonight, and they could split it—once she'd gotten rid of the paparazzi. They could drink some wine, and he could experience something just as delicious as fresh peaches, even though peaches were out of season.

CHAPTER EIGHT

DERRICK TOOK A NIP of scotch, winced because it wasn't Chivas and tucked the bottle under the back seat of Mookie's car. Ordinarily, he didn't indulge before the day's work was done, but he'd been up since five-thirty, so in a sense he'd already put in eight hours. He deserved a pick-me-up.

Actually, other than the unavailability of Chivas in this puny burg, things were looking not too bad. His contact with Erica Leitner that morning had been brief, but he believed he'd connected with her. He always did, sooner or later, especially with women. He could fine-tune the ratio of earnestness to humor in his approach, and he'd been blessed with a rugged and unarguably telegenic handsomeness that had, if anything, been made even more appealing by the plastic surgeon who'd rebuilt his nose. Women like Erica nearly always succumbed.

He'd get his exclusive; he was sure.

But until she was ready to talk to him—and let him film her damn box—he was stuck in Rockwell with time to burn. Sonya had the swell idea of turning the show into a quasidocumentary about small-town New England life. "I'm telling you," she cawed, "the viewers'll eat it up. Crusty Yankees, cute little stores and all those mountains in the background. Mookie, film the mountains, wouldja?"

Mookie obediently swung his camera in the direction of the hills. They weren't mountains. Derrick
ought to know. He'd climbed mountains in his pursuit
of stories. He'd once climbed all the way to the top of
Massachusetts's Mount Everett as part of an interview
with a guy who claimed to have killed his commanding
officer in Vietnam thirty-something years ago. The guy
liked to get away from it all by climbing mountains
whenever the memories of that ugly day in 'Nam
threatened to overtake him. He'd climbed a few mountains out West, in the Cascades and the Rockies, but
fortunately Derrick had caught up with him on Everett
rather than Mount Hood. Derrick had later discovered
that if he mumbled—a skill that didn't come naturally
to him, given his well-honed broadcast elocution—he
could trick people into thinking he'd climbed Mount
Everest rather than Mount Everett.

The guy he'd interviewed during that trek had turned
out to be a dogfaced liar, too. Derrick had located his
sergeant—the officer he'd supposedly killed—running
a Jiffy-Lube in Cincinnati.

The point was, though, Derrick knew mountains.
Those humps on the horizon were *not* mountains.

"You happy with this?" Sonya thrust a clipboard in
front of him. He leaned against the car and skimmed
the text she'd written. He was a journalist, a hard-
hitting reporter who whistled like a missile when he
was going after someone. But to stand on a corner of
Rockwell's picturesque little Main Street and deliver a
monologue about small-town values and the treasures
that might be hidden within the most sleepy, inconse-
quential community, well, that wasn't his strength. For
a task like that, he needed Sonya to put words in his
mouth.

"Yeah, it's fine," he said, handing the clipboard back to her. She'd printed clearly, block letters in black ink on white paper, so he'd be able to read the text from a distance without squinting. Squinting was fine when you wanted to look indignant or determined, but this was a happy story. A fun story. Totally not up his alley.

"I'm thinking, we'll have you stand in front of that crafts store for the first part. I like the flowers. That's such a nice touch. I wish we had some sunlight. Mookie, can you make it look sunnier in the film?"

"Sure." Mookie was too goddamn agreeable. Derrick wouldn't mind—he liked when Mookie was agreeing with him—but Mookie's good-natured acquiescence meant that Derrick always seemed much grouchier by comparison.

"What kind of flowers are those, anyway?" Derrick asked, peering down at the wilting little blossoms. They were yellow and purple—odd colors.

"Pansies," Mookie said.

Derrick straightened up and backed away from the planter. "I don't want to get filmed with any pansies."

"Don't be stupid, Derrick," Sonya scolded. "They're very nice flowers. They make the setting look springlike."

"I don't want to look springlike. Not with pansies." Why couldn't he stand in front of an evergreen somewhere? A sturdy Douglas fir. Or an oak. Were oak trees evergreens? He didn't know much about plant life, but he knew he didn't want to be associated with pansies in front of a TV audience of millions.

"Just stand there." Sonya nudged him back into place next to the planter. Derrick felt a muscle tick in his thigh, a flurry of light spasms, his body's protest against this juxtaposition. A movement to his left caught his peripheral vision, and when he turned toward the crafts shop he saw a couple of women inside, spying on him. They grinned like baboons when he stared at them. Which one of them was responsible for the pansies? Whoever it was, he hoped she'd get stricken by a bolt of fabric.

"Mookie, you set?" Sonya asked.

"Yeah. I got lots of mountains."

Hills, Derrick thought churlishly. Those were *not* mountains.

Mookie switched on a rectangular light attached to his camera. "Is that gonna look like sunshine?" Sonya asked.

"Close enough."

"Okay, then, let's boogie." She smoothed a few strands of Derrick's hair, blotted the surface of his nose with a tissue, then backed up to stand beside Mookie. She held up the clipboard. "Go," she cued him.

"'I'm standing on Main Street in Rockwell, New Hampshire,'" Derrick read from Sonya's script. He heard tension in his voice. The flowers were emitting invisible vibes. He felt them radiating up his spine and tightening his throat. "'When we speak of the heart of New England, we're speaking about places like Rockwell, where the stores are small and the neighbors are friendly.'" Right, like those two friendly apes gawking at him through the shop window. "'No big chain stores here—'" Wal-Mart wouldn't waste its time, he thought "'—but instead a slow, cozy rhythm, the way life ought to be lived.'" What the hell was that supposed to mean, anyway? A cozy rhythm? Was Sonya turning into a freaking poet on him?

She flipped the page and he continued to read her

text. "'Small towns have their histories and their mysteries.'" Great—now she was crafting rhymes. "'The history of Rockwell revolves around some early-Colonial farmers and trappers and a granite quarry. Its most recent mystery revolves around an ancient box that a schoolteacher...'" Sonya had inserted a few words above the line, and he struggled to make them out. "'And her former student...'" Back to the big black print: "Dug up in her backyard."

"Okay, okay." Sonya cut him off. "That was fine, but jeez. Do you mind?"

He realized she was addressing someone behind him. Spinning around, he saw a skinny, bedraggled fellow with bulging eyes and scraggly hair that appeared not to have been shampooed since sometime during the Clinton administration. The clown was mugging and waving, mouthing *Hi, Mom* at the camera.

"We're trying to film something here," Sonya scolded him.

"Yeah, that's why I'm wavin'," he explained. "Tryin' to get in your film."

The man smelled a little ripe. Derrick stepped back from him and banged his leg into the pansy planter. Flinching, he sidled in the opposite direction, toward the store's window. Chivalry might demand that he protect Sonya from this jerk, who was obviously a derelict and quite possibly demented.

Apparently undaunted, she stormed over to the guy and wagged her clipboard in his face. "Look at my notes," she demanded, although she never held the clipboard still enough for him to read them. "Do you see anything in here about having someone standing behind Derrick and waving and saying, 'Hi, Mom'?

Do you see anything even remotely like that in the script?''

''I wasn't *saying* 'Hi, Mom,''' the guy defended himself. ''I was just mouthing it. So's only someone who can read lips would know what I was saying.''

''But you're not in this script, are you?''

The guy tried to follow the fluttering clipboard with his eyes. ''Hey, you wanna film in Rockwell? Well, *I* live in Rockwell, eh? This is *my* town.''

Sonya regarded him. ''What's your name?'' she finally asked.

''Toad Regan. What's yers?''

Toad Regan. Honest to God. If they were about a thousand miles south of here, Derrick would be expecting to hear the ''Dueling Banjos'' theme right about now.

Sonya signaled Mookie to resume taping. ''So, why don't you tell us a little about your town?'' she asked Toad.

Was she actually going to include this rancid morsel of humanity in the show? Derrick scowled, then forced his forehead to relax so he wouldn't deepen his facial creases. He took a steadying breath and watched Sonya go at it, reminding himself that she'd dragged him out of the ratings abyss and that she knew what she was doing.

''My town?'' Toad stood a little straighter and quit mugging. He eyed the funneled lens of Mookie's camera and his smile faded. ''Well, it's just a town, y'know? Not too much happens here. You got yer occasional car wreck, yer occasional death, but other'n that, not much. Sometimes a car'll hit a deer. That's something, I guess.''

''I guess,'' Sonya agreed, straight-faced. ''We're

here in town because of a box someone dug out of her garden. Do you know anything about that?''

"Oh, sure, the box. Everybody knows about the box.''

The door to the crafts shop abruptly swung open, and the two apes emerged. Derrick amended his first impression of them; they looked nothing like a lower orders of primates. Rather, they resembled the sort of women who got orgasms from admiring autumn leaves. One was tall and thin, with silver hair, dressed in exceedingly sensible attire and fringed leather loafers. The other was shorter and rounder, and she carried a quilted bag from which protruded a pair of thick knitting needles.

"I'm sorry but I must interject here,'' the taller one said. "I'm afraid Toad Regan is going to say something about Erica Leitner—''

"You mean, that she's Jewish?'' Toad said helpfully.

Both women rolled their eyes. "Erica Leitner is a lovely young woman,'' the taller one went on. "She's a third-grade teacher—''

"What did I say?'' Toad demanded. "Did I say anything bad about her?''

"You're a drunk old fool,'' the shorter woman declared. "Go home.''

Toad glowered at her. "Yeah? And where might that be?'' Turning back to Sonya, he said, "Did I say anything bad about her?''

"Is the fact that she's Jewish relevant to this story in any way?'' Sonya asked.

"Only that they don't carry any Hebrew National at the Superette, if you get my meaning.''

"We're very proud of our diversity here in Rockwell," the taller woman from the crafts store said.

"She's an excellent teacher," the shorter one said. "My neighbor's little girl had her last year and said she was excellent. She went to Harvard, you know," the woman added, giving Derrick an oddly coy look. "Not my neighbor's daughter, but Erica Leitner did. I'll bet, Mr. Messinger, that being a big TV star you know lots of Harvard folks."

If Derrick wasn't mistaken, the news director who'd fired him for asking unseemly questions of a Supreme Court justice had been a Harvard folk. He couldn't swear to it, but the Supreme Court justice might have been one, too.

"I don't think you should interview Toad," the woman continued. "You'd be much better off interviewing us. Wouldn't he, Harriet?"

The taller one had fixed Toad with a look of diamond-hard disapproval, but at the sound of her name she shifted her attention to Derrick and her face softened. "Yes, I think that would be more appropriate. We've lived in Rockwell longer than Toad has."

"That's on account of you're so much older'n me," Toad pointed out.

Sonya sent Derrick a meaningful look. He interpreted it to mean she wanted him to take over the questioning. Not a problem, except who the hell were these ladies? Where was his research on them?

They smelled better than Toad, at least. "Erica Leitner hasn't lived in town very long, has she?" he asked.

"She's much younger than we are," the short one said.

"So is she an integral member of the community now?"

"There's no temple here, if you get my meaning," Toad commented.

The women from the crafts shop ignored him. "She's very much a part of this community," the short one said. "We've embraced her like one of our own."

"Well, that's not exactly true," the tall one corrected her. "She's certainly a part of this community, and we've embraced her, but you can see she still hasn't lost her big-city ways."

"What do you mean?" the shorter one asked.

"Well, her vocabulary, for one thing."

"Does she swear a lot?" Derrick asked. As far as he knew, the only difference between big-city vocabulary and small-town vocabulary was that living in a big city, a person was exposed to a much wider variety of curse words, in assorted languages.

"Oh, no!" The shorter one shook her head indignantly. "She's a very nice girl. She uses very clean language."

"It's the big words," the taller one explained. "She uses lots of bigger words. And she dresses—"

"In all that L.L. Bean stuff." The shorter one completed the sentence. "It makes her look a little touristy."

"People around here don't wear L.L. Bean stuff?" Derrick asked, surprised. He would have assumed everyone laced on a pair of those trademark Bean hybrid boots in November and didn't pry them off until Easter.

"Well, mostly. Just the summer-home people."

"And the leaf peepers in the fall."

"I don't own anything from L.L. Bean," Toad Regan added vehemently.

A thin, balding man swept out of Hackett's Superette on the opposite corner. "Hey, why don't you do a little filming over here?" he shouted across the street. "I think you've given Harriet's store enough of a plug."

A woman followed him out and continued into the street, brandishing a pen and a pocket-size notepad. "Mr. Messinger? Mr. Messinger, could I have your autograph? Not for me, of course—for my aunt Louise."

"I didn't know you had an aunt named Louise," the tall, silver-haired woman remarked dryly.

"Small world," Toad added. "Your name is Louise, too."

Derrick tried to catch Sonya's eye. The situation was deteriorating. But she was beaming at the proliferation of hicks, and Mookie was capturing it all on tape.

At least the other reporters weren't there. They were a group of local hacks, and he'd made nice with them while they'd been cooling their heels at Erica Leitner's house that morning. But they clearly weren't in his class. The Manchester Fox affiliate? *Please.*

"All right," Sonya announced, her brassy voice slicing through the din. "Let's film a little by the supermarket."

Derrick forced a faint smile as Louise with the co-incidentally named Aunt Louise thrust her pad and pen at him. He preferred to think of himself as a reporter, but in this era of celebrity, what could he do? People recognized him. He had to keep his public happy.

Of course, his scribbling "Best wishes, Louise— Derrick Messinger" onto her pad meant everyone else would start rummaging through pockets and purses in search of paper for him to sign. He braced himself, flexed the fingers on his signing hand and dug into the inner pocket of his blazer for his own pen. To his surprise, no one asked him for his autograph.

Obviously, they respected him more than Louise did. They understood that he was a journalist, not a pop idol.

In front of the Superette, Derrick found himself surrounded by locals, all of them grinning wildly at the camera. The thin balding man who'd requested that they film in front of his store had the temerity to wrap an arm around Derrick's shoulders. There was nothing pansyish about his embrace, but it still gave Derrick the willies.

"Okay, everybody back off," Sonya ordered the crowd. "We'll interview you in a minute. But first, everybody take a giant step away from Derrick and let him do his thing."

Reluctantly, the man disengaged from Derrick and joined the others milling around behind Mookie. Derrick shrugged as if to slough off any residue the man might have left on him. Then he read a couple more pages of Sonya's script.

"Good," Sonya said when he was done. "Now, you." She located the skinny bald man among the crowd, grabbed him by the wrist and hauled him over to stand next to Derrick. "Derrick will interview you. Interview him, Derrick."

Easier said than done. It wasn't as if he were chasing a real story. This wasn't a drive-by shooting. It wasn't a sordid account of drugs and the Mafia. How was he supposed to interview this guy?

"What's your name?" he asked.

"Pop Hackett."

Derrick imagined the twangy lilt of "Dueling Banjos" again. He lifted his mike, gazed soulfully at the camera and said, "I'm standing in front of Hackett's Superette with Pop Hackett. Tell me, Mr. Hackett, have you ever had any experience here in Rockwell with ancient artifacts?"

"Ancient, I can't say. I've got a couple of cans of cream of asparagus soup that've been sitting on the shelf a pretty long time. Don't suppose that'd count."

The onlookers chuckled. Oh, that Pop Hackett. What a card.

"That's *great*," Sonya enthused, her attempt at courting the crowd. Derrick could hear the phoniness in her tone, but they probably couldn't. "That's really funny. Thank you, everybody, for your help. We have to go to another location now."

Mookie lowered his camera and gave everyone a good-natured smile. Sonya slung her arm around Derrick—he didn't mind so much when she did it—and ushered him across the street. "We're going to film over at the school," she murmured. "That's where Erica Leitner teaches. Just to get a sense of who she is and where she's coming from. We want to humanize the story, you know?"

"Sure." Derrick hoped they wouldn't get besieged by another gang of Yankee yokels there.

Mookie drove unerringly to the grade school. Among his many assets, besides his general affability and his skill behind the camera, he seemed incapable of getting lost. Derrick wondered whether he snuck out late at night and cruised whatever town they were in, familiarizing himself with the roads and landmarks, or whether he pored over maps into the wee hours. He was probably the only man in the world who never asked for directions because he didn't need them.

Derrick's mood, not particularly bubbly to begin

with, went seriously flat once they reached the school. The Boston reporter with the Pepto-Bismol-hued suit and the chipmunk cheeks had beaten them to the scene.

"Don't worry," Sonya said, evidently reading his mind. "Let her get her two minutes. Who cares? She hasn't got any more on the box than we do."

"You hope," Derrick muttered.

"Erica Leitner is in that building right now. How could that lady have gotten anything on the box?" She twisted in her seat to face him. "Remember that cartoon *Pinkie and the Brain?* She's Pinkie. You're the Brain."

Derrick didn't remember the cartoon—Sonya was a good ten years younger than him, so she had an entirely different pop culture reference—but he felt better anyway. He considered giving his bottle of scotch a farewell kiss, but thought better of it. Not in a school-yard. It wouldn't be right.

He'd seen sprawling elementary schools before, elaborate structures with angular roofs, banks of windows and awnings along the bus circle. Rockwell Regional Primary School was the antithesis of those schools. A sad box of faded brick, it had undoubtedly been built as a public works project in the Depression, and it was still depressed. The playground was colorful, at least, lots of vivid molded plastic accenting the swing sets and climbers. The playground was empty, though. All the kids must be inside.

Climbing out of the car, he gave Pinkie a polite nod. She sent a grimacing smile his way before resuming her stand-up, chattering calmly into her microphone while her cameraman filmed her. She didn't have a producer with her, he noticed. Probably the cameraman doubled, or else she produced herself. Low-budget. Her station hadn't invested serious resources in this story. She'd be lucky if she got a sixty-second closer after the weather recap at eleven-thirty.

Not like him. He was going to have a whole documentary, with national syndication. *Eat your heart out, Pinkie,* he thought, his spirits lifting.

"My son's in there," a man shouted, loping over to him. "Mr. Messinger? My boy's in there. You've got to talk to him."

Derrick turned from Pinkie to acknowledge the man. He had the longest face Derrick had ever seen, and most of the length seemed to be chin. "Can I help you?" Sonya intervened.

"Glenn Rideout," he said, extending his hand. "I heard from Potter Henley—he's a regular of mine—that you were filming out on Main Street, but by the time I got there you were driving away. So I followed you here."

"How resourceful," Sonya said pleasantly. A hank of hair flopped into her face and she shoved it back behind her ear. "We're trying to set up a shot here. You can watch if you'd like, but please don't—"

"You don't understand. I'm Glenn Rideout. My son, Randy, found the box."

"Your son did?" Sonya leaned closer to him. So did Derrick and Mookie. They didn't want Pinkie to hear this. "According to my research, Erica Leitner was digging in her garden with a former student of hers—"

"Yeah, that's my son."

"And they unearthed the box together."

"That's her story," Glenn Rideout grumbled.

"And your story is?"

"My son found the box. I've got a lawyer says that

box is Randy's as much as the teacher's. If you're going to interview anyone around here, I think you should interview Randy.''

Sonya shot Derrick a look. He shrugged back. Why not?

"Does your son want to be interviewed?" Sonya asked.

"He damn well better. He found the box. You want me to get him out of his classroom?"

"I don't think that's necessary, Mr. Rideout," Sonya said. As if in response to her assertion, a pair of double doors on the side of the school building suddenly swung open and a raging horde of children spilled out, screeching and shoving like wild beasts just sprung from their cages. Pinkie, who'd been standing about twenty yards down along the chain-link fence from where Mookie was setting up, let out a yelp and jumped away from the fence, as if she feared some of the kids might mistake her for a very large piece of bubble gum and leap over the fence to dig their teeth into her.

"He's here," Rideout insisted, scouring the mayhem on the other side of the fence with his gaze. "He's one of the older kids. A fifth-grader."

Derrick searched the group, too, looking for an older boy with a disproportionately long chin. But the kids all blurred into a shouting, running, tumbling mass, and the only people he could distinguish were the adults—teachers and staff. He spotted Erica Leitner hovering on the concrete steps near the double doors, beside her a woman with blunt-cut hair the color of strawberries. Punk, he thought, despite her tailored slacks and sweater set. Anyone who'd color her hair that shade of red had a bit of the rebel in her.

"Look at Erica's friend," he whispered to Sonya.

"What about her?"

"She looks a little out of place, don't you think?"

"Don't be so provincial. They've got Lady Clairol even in Rockwell, New Hampshire."

"Lady Clairol doesn't make that shade of red."

"So...what? You wanna ask her out? What's your point, Derrick?"

"No, I don't want to ask her out. I was just curious about why she was here instead of, say, selling bustiers in some boutique in the East Village."

"What do you know about bustiers?"

"You'd be surprised."

"I already am." Sonya surveyed the raucous scene on the other side of the fence and shouted to Mookie, "You think you'll pick up Derrick's voice over this noise?"

"Huh?" Mookie shouted back, cupping a hand around his ear.

"All right, look, we can't tape here while those banshees are shrieking their heads off. Mr. Rideout, we'll meet with your son after school. How's that? Do you know what time school ends?"

"Around three," Rideout said. "Why don't you come to my neighborhood tavern and meet Randy there. Rideout's Ride, on the corner of Main and Elm. Four blocks down from Hackett's—only, the door's on the Elm Street side."

"Fine. Okay. We'll try to get over there then. Mookie, get some of the chaos on film. We can do a voice-over later."

"Huh?" Mookie leaned toward Sonya and scowled, obviously unable to hear her.

Sighing, she marched over to the fence to confer

with him. Derrick eyed Glenn Rideout skeptically. Did
he want Derrick to interview his fifth-grade son at his
neighborhood tavern, surrounded by smoke and mugs
of beer?

Once again, the "Dueling Banjos" theme rippled
through his mind. The box had better be worth it, he
thought, turning back to watch the mayhem on the opposite side of the fence. The box had better contain
something of great value. Because if Derrick had
trekked all the way here, spent a night in that drafty
little inn and interviewed the offspring of someone who
ran an establishment named Rideout's Ride, and then
the box turned out to be empty...

Well, it had better not be. That was all.

CHAPTER NINE

"YOU DIDN'T RETURN my call yesterday," Erica's mother said.

"I'm sorry." Erica wasn't really sorry, but what else could she say? "I got your message, but by the time I could have called you back, it would have been too late." That wasn't too far from the truth, at least. By the time she'd come home and recovered from Jed's kiss—well, she still wasn't completely recovered, but in any case, phoning her mother at that hour would have given the woman a heart attack. Of course, Erica could have solved the situation by taking her mother's call in the first place, instead of letting the answering machine pick up.

Sometimes dishonesty was the best policy.

"So, you were with friends?"

"Yes." Erica carried her cordless phone down the short hall to her bedroom. The curtains at her front window were crooked, exposing a sliver of window, and as soon as she'd slid her feet out of her loafers, she crossed to the window and straightened the drape. She'd started that day peeking through that sliver of window and discovering the press camped outside her door, as if she were someone famous or important.

"You have friends there?" her mother asked.

"Of course I have friends here." Erica didn't bother to disguise her irritation. She'd been living in Rockwell

for nearly three years. Her mother knew she had
friends. She talked about them sometimes when she
was visiting Brookline. Whenever she did, her mother
would click her tongue and say, ''What kind of people
would live in a town like that?''

People like Erica; that was what kind.

''So you were out partying with your friends on a
school night?'' her mother grilled her.

''Mom.'' Erica laughed to keep from screaming.
''I'm a grown-up. You can't give me a curfew.''

''I don't know how you can stand to live there,''
her mother went on, as if Erica hadn't spoken. ''They
pay you nothing.''

''Nothing goes a long way here,'' Erica pointed out.
She lifted her hair off her neck and shook it loose, then
wandered back toward the dining room, where she'd
dumped her tote and a stack of math quizzes when the
phone had rung. Maybe she should have let the answering machine take her mother's call tonight, as it
had last night. But she'd had only three messages waiting for her when she'd arrived home from school, none
of them obnoxious, so she'd decided to live dangerously and answer the phone.

''And your house. It needs a paint job.''

''My house looks fine.''

''Not on TV, it doesn't.''

Erica paused halfway down the hall to the dining
room. ''How would you know what my house looks
like on TV?'' she asked, bracing for an answer she
wasn't sure she wanted to hear.

''How do you think I'd know? I saw your house on
TV.''

''When?''

''This evening, at the end of the five o'clock news.

Lacy McNair, you know her? The reporter on Channel 4. Of course you know her. You talked to her.''

"I did?'' Lacy McNair must have been one of the reporters who'd invaded her property that morning. "She didn't introduce herself.''

"Why should she? She's Lacy McNair. Everybody knows who she is.''

"Everybody in Boston, maybe. I don't watch Boston news shows.'' Erica cautiously resumed her walk down the hall. She halted in the living room. The curtains on those windows hung wide open, revealing the twilit vista of her front yard, the site of that morning's press siege. Which one had Lacy McNair been? Did it even matter?

"She was talking about some box. It didn't make any sense, but there you were in the spotlight, saying you hadn't opened the box yet. You looked kind of washed out, sweetie. Then they showed your garden, and forgive me, but it's a mess.''

"I haven't finished planting it yet.'' Great. Now all the Channel 4 viewers in the Greater Boston Area had seen her half-completed garden. She would never be able to hold her head up in Brookline again.

"So this box, it was in the garden?''

"If that's what Lacy McNair said, she got it right.''

"And why aren't you opening it?''

"I don't want to break it. It's an antique, I think.''

"So…what? You're never going to open it?''

"I'm going to open it when Avery Gilman gets here. He was a professor of mine at Harvard, and he's—''

"See? This is what I've been telling you. You went to Harvard, you worked with professors like this Avery person, the top people in their fields, and for what? So you could earn nothing in that provincial little town in the middle of nowhere.''

"It's not in the middle of nowhere," Erica argued. *It's off to one side of nowhere,* she added silently. "Mom, I know you don't approve of the choices I made, but we're done having that discussion. Okay? I'm here because I want to be here, because this is where I belong."

"You belong in civilization, honey. Not up there with all those 'Live Free or Die' maniacs."

"They're not maniacs."

"They hunt. They own guns."

"Not all of them." She sighed and continued to the dining room, taking comfort in the stack of work sheets, the red and blue pens lying on her table. She was a teacher, and she belonged in a town where her teaching skills were valued. Brookline was full of teachers with Ivy League degrees. In Rockwell, she could contribute something unique. She could offer a new perspective, and have her own perspectives rearranged. She could learn that people who hunted and ate the game they brought down were not evil, although she still felt a little uneasy about all the antlers decorating walls in town.

A knock on the kitchen door startled her. If she owned a gun, she could hold it while she greeted whoever her visitor was. Probably some pesky reporter again; maybe her good buddy Derrick Messinger, whom she'd spotted skulking around the schoolyard that afternoon.

"Mom," she said, angling her head to peer into the kitchen from the dining-room doorway. "I've got to go. Just tell me, I wasn't on the news yesterday, was I?"

"Shouldn't you have been? You're the one with this fancy box that you won't open."

"The reporters didn't arrive until today. Why did you phone me yesterday?" Peeking through the window, she made out the silhouette of her caller and sighed. It wasn't a pesky reporter. No such luck. It was her next-door neighbor.

She'd resolved to stay away from Jed, hadn't she? Just so he wouldn't kiss her again. Just so she could avoid putting her willpower to such a severe test.

But there he was, standing on her back porch. He must know she was home. Lights were on in the house. Her car was in the shed.

"I'm not allowed to call and say hello?" her mother said with feigned innocence. "I'm not allowed to want to hear your voice?"

"Why did you call?"

"Your cousin Suzanne met this friend of her fiancé's and said he's perfect for you. Robert Goldstein. Yale Law School. You could go to the Harvard-Yale games and bicker."

Erica laughed. "Don't be a matchmaker, Mom."

"You're never going to meet anyone up there."

That's what you think, Erica munbled, her gaze locked onto the shadowy figure on the other side of her kitchen door. Oh, she'd met someone, all right—someone she would have been better off not meeting.

She was probably the only person in Rockwell who locked her doors—old habits died hard—but it seemed downright unneighborly not to let Jed in. She pulled the door open, tried not to react to his smile as she beckoned him inside and then headed down the hall to her bedroom to finish her conversation with her mother in private. "I really can't talk, Mom," she said. "I've got a pile of math quizzes to grade. Just tell me, did that woman on the news—Stacy…?''

"Lacy McNair."

"Right. Did she say anything worthwhile in her report?"

"Just what I told you. And I've got to say, Erica, my phone has been ringing off the hook. All the neighbors saw you. And your ninth-grade English teacher, Ms. Wexler, remember her? She called. She said she was so proud that you had become a teacher. She thinks she inspired you."

Ms. Wexler had been about as inspiring as overcooked pasta. Which reminded Erica of the leftover pasta primavera sitting beneath a sheet of plastic wrap on the bottom shelf of her refrigerator. Had Jed come over in search of food? Just what she needed in her life: a tall, outrageously attractive version of Randy Rideout. Maybe she'd give Jed a handful of chocolate chip cookies and send him on his way.

"Mom, I've got to go."

"Please warn me if you're going to be on TV again, honey. I'd like to set up the VCR so I can get you on tape."

Erica considered that a fine reason for her not to warn her mother if she was going to be on TV again. To be sure, she'd had no idea she was going to be on today. "You seem to know more about my TV appearances than I do," she joked. "I've got to go."

"All those math quizzes," her mother muttered, as if she didn't believe they existed. "All right, Erica. Go take care of the quizzes. Dad sends his love."

"Bye." Erica disconnected the phone and returned to the kitchen. The room was empty. She glimpsed Jed in the dining room, his hands in the pockets of his jeans as he perused the math exam on the top of the pile. "Do you want to grade them?" she asked from the doorway.

He straightened and turned to face her. "God, no. Long division and I have never been on good terms."

Falling silent, he smiled slightly. If he'd come here hoping for her to offer him dinner, he was going to be disappointed—partly because feeding him two dinners in a row would set a bad precedent, but mostly because she'd feel kind of weird entertaining him in her home, offering him the leftovers of a meal that Fern had prepared. If only Erica had mastered a few more recipes; if only she could chop vegetables with Fern's panache; if only she could bake loaves of herb bread, kneading the dough and getting flour on her wrists and knowing what the hell she was doing...

Even then, she wouldn't want to feed Jed. She'd kissed him once; she was too smart to tempt fate by spending more time with him.

He still didn't speak. His gaze wandered over her and she wondered whether he'd dropped by for another kiss, or to transport her to where they'd obviously been heading last night. Finally he cleared his throat and said, "I've got a bottle of merlot at home. I'm not sure how good it is, but I bought it to share with you. I was going to bring it over here, but then I thought that would be kind of presumptuous of me. So I'm inviting you over to my house, instead."

"Your house."

"We could throw together some supper. You fed me so well last night I owe you one." He shrugged. "I'd take you out, but that might not be a good idea. It's so public."

"People would gossip," she agreed.

"Plus the reporters. You're the story they've all come to Rockwell to get. If we went out for dinner they'd find us and drive us nuts."

"Maybe they've all gone home by now."

"As of this afternoon, they were still out in full force downtown."

Erica would hardly refer to Rockwell's sleepy Main Street as "downtown," but Jed's point was well taken. "So," she said slowly, not sure how she felt about it, "you're going to cook me dinner?"

"We could fix it together. I'm not the world's greatest cook."

"Neither am I," she warned. "Maybe we should give Fern a call."

"Fern's got other fish to fry."

Erica felt her eyes widen. How would Jed know more than she did about her best friend?

"I needed to buy a skillet, because my father stole my grandfather's, and while I was driving home I saw Fern hanging out by the Hope Street Inn."

"The Hope Street Inn?" That was the bed-and-breakfast where Erica had reserved a room for Avery Gilman. Why would Fern be there?

"Derrick Messinger and his crew are staying there. I think your buddy was doing the groupie thing."

"What? You think she was going to offer herself to Derrick Messinger?" Erica's laughter sounded hollow. Offering herself to Derrick Messinger was just the sort of thing Fern would do.

Jed held up his hands as if to ward off any criticism. "Hey, it's not my business. All I'm saying is, I don't think you ought to count on her driving out this way to cook a meal for us tonight."

Erica shook her head. She thought Fern had been

hot for Jed. But then, as she recalled, Fern had reacted to Derrick's phone message yesterday with a lot more enthusiasm than Erica had.

"So, you want to take your chances at my place?" Jed asked.

Say no, the voice of wisdom inside her cautioned. She ignored it.

THE KITCHEN of the old farmhouse next door was much larger than hers. The cabinets were polished knotty pine, the floor featured checkerboard tiles of black and white, instead of a quease-producing foamy green pattern, and the ceiling fixture infused the room with sunshine brightness. A large four-burner gas range stood in one corner, a double-basin stainless-steel sink occupied a space beneath the window and the refrigerator was a relatively new model, with side-by-side doors and a built-in ice dispenser. Erica gazed around, wondering if her awe was visible. This was the kitchen she should have had. It was a kitchen an earth mother could bake bread in—assuming the earth mother knew how to bake bread.

Jed lifted a bottle of wine from the table at the center of the room. "We'll probably need this," he said, carrying it to a counter and pulling a corkscrew from a drawer, "given that neither of us can cook."

"I can cook," Erica argued, crossing to the stove and lifting a large Teflon-coated skillet from one of the burners. The bottom of the skillet was a pristine shining silver. This must be the new pan Jed had bought. "I'm not as good a cook as Fern, but I'm learning. Why did your father steal your grandfather's pan?"

"Because it was there?" Jed guessed with a shrug. He levered out the cork, which made a happy little pop as it came free of the bottle. "He was just helping himself to whatever caught his eye. You'd have to ask him why he chose the pan."

"It's just that pans are not that valuable." She lowered the new pan to the burner.

"He's a junk dealer. What does he know about the value of things?" He filled two goblets with wine and handed one to her. "I picked up some chopped beef, but burgers don't go with merlot. You think we could come up with something more interesting to do with the meat?"

"Sure," she said, once again aware that it was an answer destined to lead her into trouble. If she were Fern, she could take chopped meat and assorted other ingredients and whip up a marvelous meal. She wasn't Fern, though.

She'd have to fake it. She could brown the meat and season it, and throw in some vegetables if he had any, and turn the mixture into a stew. With enough wine to wash it down, the dish might not taste too bad. "Do you have any spices?" she asked.

He swung open a cabinet to reveal an array of small jars. "I have no idea how old some of this stuff is," he said. "For all I know, my grandmother might have bought these, and she's been dead more than ten years."

Erica pulled some of the jars down from the shelf and stared at them as if she knew what to look for. Spices didn't spoil, she was pretty sure. They might lose some tang, but they didn't rot or turn moldy.

Jed removed the meat, a loaf of bread, a carrot, a bell pepper, a tomato, an onion and a couple of potatoes from the refrigerator. "Let's fire up the stove and see what happens," he said.

He seemed awfully cheerful, as if this potentially doomed project was a great, joyous adventure. Erica decided to cheer up, too. As long as they were cooking, they'd be too busy to kiss. In fact, she didn't sense much sexual heat coming from him, not like last night, when they'd sat too close together on the porch swing. This spacious kitchen gave them plenty of room to evade each other.

"So, did you do any interviews today?" he asked as he set to work cutting the pepper.

She sipped her wine, then dumped the meat into the new pan and turned the heat low under it. "Just this morning's little press conference outside my house. My mother saw it on TV."

"What?" He stared at her.

"That was who I was talking to when you showed up at my house. My mother. She said one of the reporters broadcast a report about the box on the local news out of Boston."

"What kind of report? What the hell could they have said?"

"That I dug up a mystery box and its contents haven't been revealed. You know what TV newscasts are like. They report on the weather, the sports scores, a burning building, a controversial new diet, a celebrity divorce and a cat that walked a thousand miles to get home from a campsite in Montana where it had been abandoned by accident. What better way to end the broadcast than with a story about a mysterious box found in a schoolteacher's garden?"

The beef began to sizzle. Erica stirred it, feeling Jed's gaze on her and wishing she looked more adept with a spatula. "Isn't that a little cynical for you?" he finally said.

She shot him a glance. He was regarding her with a blend of curiosity and amusement. "I'm not cynical," she defended herself.

"I didn't think you were, but…"

"But what?"

He smiled. "You've got your edges."

What edges? What was he talking about? She'd had plenty of edges while growing up outside Boston and matching wits with Ivy League intellectuals, but now she was a wholesome, holistic country girl, learning to garden, learning—not nearly fast enough—to cook, learning to center herself in Rockwell's cozy environment.

If she still had edges, it was only because she hadn't yet succeeded in becoming the person she wanted to be: an unedged woman.

She stirred the meat as it browned. With what she hoped resembled flair, she reached for a jar of garlic powder, opened it, sniffed and detected the faintest whiff of garlic, and shook some onto the meat. If she'd been at home and alone, she would have searched for a recipe, dug out her measuring spoons and practiced precision. But with Jed as her witness, she wanted to appear as if she knew what she was doing.

"So, should we stick this pepper in with the meat?" he asked, displaying the chunks of green on his cutting board.

"Why not?" she said bravely. It would all cook together, like her mother's stuffed-pepper recipe. She recalled that her mother used tomato sauce with that. "You have any tomato sauce?"

"Maybe." Sipping his wine, he perused the contents of a cabinet. "Tomato paste," he said, producing a narrow can.

Erica had seen tomato paste on the supermarket shelves, but she'd never had any idea what to do with it. "Okay," she said. "Let's put some of that in."

They fumbled along, adding onion, ginger powder and dense globs of tomato paste that gradually thinned in the heat of the pan. Jed peeled and sliced the potatoes and she tossed them in. Everything simmered together into a disgusting-looking hash. It didn't smell too bad, though, and the wine added a pleasant shimmer to the proceedings. Jed cut the tomato into wedges and the carrot into sticks. He set the table with two plates, silverware and squares of paper towel in place of napkins. "I can't find where my grandfather kept napkins," he explained. "I don't know, maybe he never used them."

"The paper towels will work. Fold them so they look like napkins," she suggested. Jed dutifully folded them in half and centered the forks on them. "I guess this is done. Pasta primavera it's not."

"Who wants pasta primavera? We just had that last night," Jed remarked, making her feel better.

She ladled the slop onto their plates. Jed added the bread and a tub of butter to the table, then carried the half-consumed bottle of wine over and gestured for her to sit. She dipped the tines of her fork into the meat and licked them off. Not too wretched. She'd be able to eat it without gagging. "I'm not a very good cook," she told him again.

He shrugged. "Neither am I," he assured her once more. "This looks fine." He scooped up a manly forkful, ate it, swallowed and nodded. "It's fine."

"Thank you."

"I thought you were a good cook. Last night you knew what you were doing."

She smiled. "I was cutting the bread. That I can handle. Fern did everything else." She took another delicate nibble of the concoction on her plate. It went down her throat without any problem. "I'm learning to be a better cook, though. I've done some baking—cookies, mostly. Randy Rideout thinks the store-bought are better, but he doesn't have much taste."

"His tastelessness is a genetic thing. He's Glenn Rideout's son." Jed dug into his food with more enthusiasm than Erica could muster. "You've probably already figured this out about Rockwell," he went on, "but there are no decent restaurants. Bars, yeah. But if you want some Chinese, or Mexican, or even just a perfectly cooked steak, you're not going to find it here."

"Granted, Rockwell isn't New York City. But it has its compensations."

He chuckled. She liked the way his eyes crinkled in the corners when he smiled—and she wished she didn't notice things like that about him. "What compensations might those be?" he asked, his tone holding a clear challenge.

"The peace and quiet. The clean air. The way the snow stays white all winter long. In Boston—and I'm sure in New York—the snow is usually gray within a day of hitting the ground. Not here."

"In New York, the snow usually doesn't stick around more than a day. They've got municipal employees who plow the streets and sidewalks."

"Yes, and the pollution probably helps the snow to melt faster, too," Erica pointed out. "Particulate matter in the air contributes to global warming, you know." Dangerously pedantic, she thought, silencing herself with a sip of wine. "In Rockwell, you can plant a garden out your back door and eat the very vegetables you've grown."

"Gardening's a lot of work," Jed said mildly. "Some people enjoy it. I sure as hell don't."

"Did you garden when you lived here?"

He gestured toward the window. "That whole field behind the house used to be corn and potatoes. I spent a lot of summer days working for my grandfather. Not fun." He ate a little of the stew, then helped himself to a slice of bread. "Tell me, Erica, someone with your schooling, you could have gotten a teaching job anywhere. Why Rockwell?"

"I liked the name," she admitted, then smiled. "I liked the size and location, too. I wanted to live and work in a small town, one where my students might not have access to the cultural benefits of a more cosmopolitan community. Rockwell fit the bill on all those counts. And then the name. *Rockwell.* I pictured Norman Rockwell."

Jed laughed so hard he started to cough. "Norman Rockwell? Hell, you associate Norman Rockwell with a town that has one bar for every three citizens?"

"With antlers on the walls," Erica conceded, joining his laughter. "All right. Rockwell has less in common with Norman Rockwell than I thought it would. With the quarry nearly mined out, there's too much unemployment. And all the bars with the antlers..." She sighed, experiencing a genuine sympathy for her adopted home and its economic woes. "But there's something pure here."

"What?" Jed was still smiling, but his eyes held a challenge. "What's pure about this place?"

She searched her mind for an answer. The air, the white snow, but what else? Kids here used bad language and bullied one another. Adults had affairs and got pregnant. Her best friend dyed her hair bright red and set her sights on Derrick Messinger. Glenn Rideout hired a lawyer to protect his presumed interests in the ownership of a box. Rockwell even had its homeless: that strange, mumbling guy named Toad. Whenever she saw him shambling along the street, smelling like hot tar and morning breath, he'd issue incoherent comments about God and religion that Erica preferred not to listen to.

"I don't want to be a city person," she finally said, even though that didn't really answer Jed's question. "I want to be in touch with nature, connected to the earth. I don't want to walk on concrete all the time. I want to walk on grass and dirt."

"Mud," Jed muttered, then chuckled. "We've got grass and dirt in New York. It's called Central Park. You've got it in Boston, too. Boston Common, right? And that other place, where they have the Pops concert on the Fourth of July."

"The Esplanade," she informed him. "But those are contained parks surrounded by city. It's not like that here. Here you've got grass and dirt and trees and mountains for miles around."

"And long, winding two-lane roads, and there's always some truck loaded with logs right in front of you, doing twenty miles an hour and you can't pass him. In New York, you don't even need a car. You can walk everywhere, or grab a bus or the subway. And we don't get any of those twenty-mile-an-hour logging trucks jamming up our streets."

"Well, I'm glad you're happy in New York," she said, realizing with a pang that she wasn't glad at all. Eating with him, cooking with him, sipping wine with

him, even arguing with him—it was all too lovely, too
natural, too—dare she think it?—romantic. If only he'd
stay in Rockwell… But he never would. He wouldn't
linger a moment longer than necessary in this unpaved,
muddy village.

"I'm just trying to figure out how you could be
happy here. I mean it, Erica. The nearest movie theater
is, what, thirty miles away?"

"Hackett's Superette has a nice selection of video
rentals."

Jed shook his head. "Pop Hackett refuses to stock
NR-17 movies. Some Rs, too. He's got a damn good
selection of Disney flicks, if that's what you like."

"Why are you so eager to put Rockwell down?"
Erica challenged him. "Okay, so you like New York
City. That doesn't mean you have to bad-mouth Rock-
well."

"I grew up here. I know what I'm talking about.
This place is the end of the road—and it's a narrow,
potholed road. Anyone with half a chance tries to get
out of here."

"I don't know about that," she argued. "Fern
stayed."

"Maybe she didn't have half a chance."

"It's more than just Rockwell that drove you
away," Erica said, her mind digesting his words more
easily than her stomach digested the stew. "Everything
you say is true, Jed—no first-run movies, too many
bars. But that's not why you left."

"Sure it is."

"What happened? Did someone break your heart?"
The question was brazen, but she had nothing to lose
by asking it. Jed already thought she was crazy to want
to live in Rockwell, and he wasn't going to stay in

town once his grandfather's ashes were buried. So what if she offended him with her nosiness?

He swallowed the last of his bread, then settled back in his chair and drank some wine. "Not a lover, if that's what you're asking."

He didn't seem annoyed, so she dug deeper, as if she might unearth a mysterious treasure beneath his hard Yankee exterior. "Who, then?"

"You've met Jack."

His father. She nodded slightly. "We haven't actually gotten acquainted."

"Count your blessings. He's a real son of a bitch. Leaving town was the best way to get him out of my life."

"What about your mother?"

"They split when I was maybe three or four. She married someone else when I was twelve—a huge improvement over my dad—and my senior year of high school, my stepdad got a job near Albany, so I moved in with my grandfather to finish out the year. I see my mother when I can. She's a good woman."

Erica experienced a sudden urge to meet Jed's mother. She wouldn't mind getting acquainted with his father, either, if only so she could learn just how much of a son of a bitch the man was, how strong his influence on Jed might have been, how difficult their relationship was. She wished she'd been friendlier with Jed's grandfather, old John Willetz, but he'd been a private person, taciturn and crusty.

And damn, she shouldn't care about getting to know any of them. The main reason she wanted to was that it would be a way to get closer to Jed, and that was a doomed exercise. He hated Rockwell. He wasn't going to stick around, no matter how close she got to him or his family.

But his eyes were searing; his gaze, seductive. And he hadn't insulted her cooking. He was a native of the town she longed to be a part of, a product of its soil, molded by its schools and its close-knit society, its bars and its brisk, clean air. So what if he'd left? Perhaps if she'd been born in Rockwell she would want to leave, too. But in a way, he was what she was hoping to become: self-sufficient, capable, as solid and strong as the slabs of granite that formed the town's foundation.

Noticing her empty glass, he lifted the bottle to pour a refill. She waved him away. "No, I've had enough," she said. She felt relaxed and warm inside, but not drunk. Not drunk enough to want to risk drinking any more wine when she was feeling the way she felt about Jed right now.

He lowered the bottle and lifted her hand, instead, folding his long, strong fingers around it. "Erica," he said quietly.

His eyes continued to burn into her, but his mouth curved in a smile, as if to remind her that none of this was serious or significant.

It felt way too serious and significant to her. She rose to her feet, scrambling for a polite way to go when saying goodbye was the last thing she wanted to do.

He stood, as well, his hand still surrounding hers, warm and hard. "Don't tell me you're leaving."

"I'm leaving." He didn't tighten his grip on her hand, yet she seemed unable to slide it free. "Jed, what happened last night—"

"Was fantastic," he said completing the sentence.

"Come here." He pulled her toward him and wrapped his other arm around her.

"Jed."

He brushed his lips against her forehead. Unwanted heat spiraled down through her.

"Jed, really. Let's not get started."

"We already got started. We're just continuing," he said, as calmly as if they were debating semantics.

"Let's not continue then. You're going to leave Rockwell, Jed. I'm going to stay."

"So?"

"So, what's the point of continuing?"

He touched his mouth to her forehead again, a simple, devastating kiss. "The point is," he murmured, his body as warm and hard against her as his hand had been, "we're two adults, and we're attracted to each other, so why not take advantage of the situation?" He lifted her hand to his mouth and grazed her knuckles.

Oh, God, he was good. Way too good. Erica might have degrees from Harvard and Brown, but she was pretty ignorant when it came to men this good. This *bad*. All her book learning, all the seminars and lectures and symposia she'd attended within the ivy-covered walls of her esteemed schools, had failed to teach her how to distinguish bad from good at a time like this.

"I'll feel awful afterward," she said, sounding like a skittish teenager.

"No, you won't. I'll make sure of it." He slid his free hand down her back to her waist and then back up again. She imagined his hand directly on her skin, rather than stroking her through layers of clothing, and the notion made her shudder. As long as he was touching her, she wouldn't feel awful.

"I meant after you're gone."

"Why? We're not talking marriage, Erica. We're not talking commitment and forever. Just something nice and sweet and in the present." He kissed her forehead again, then the tip of her nose and at last her mouth, her waiting, eager mouth.

She tasted wine on his lips. She tasted heat and sex. Why not? she thought. Why not just this nice, sweet, present thing? Afterward could take care of itself.

She reached up to cup her hands over his shoulders. He deepened the kiss and she clung to him so she wouldn't do something awkward, like lose her balance and collapse—or start arguing about the propriety of what they were doing, what they would likely be doing in just a few minutes if this kiss didn't cool down fast. She held on tight and let him kiss her, and kissed him back.

He sighed, obviously sensing only her acquiescence, not her ambivalence. His tongue slid deep into her mouth and he pulled her even tighter, tangling his fingers into her hair, pressing his thighs against hers.

She heard music, soft and tinkly, a few bars of what sounded like an old Pearl Jam song performed on a glockenspiel. She'd never heard bells from a kiss before, but she thought that if they signaled her being swept away by passion, they might play something a bit more romantic than Pearl Jam.

Jed leaned back. She heard the same few bars of the song again. "Damn," he said, breaking from her and moving to the refrigerator. He leaned against the counter there, breathing deeply for a moment, apparently struggling for control. On the counter next to his hands sat a cell phone. It emitted another Pearl Jam riff in gentle bell tones. "I should have ignored it," he muttered before hitting the button and lifting it to his ear. "Jed Willetz," he snapped into the phone. She tried to read his expression as he listened to his caller: first irritation, then bewilderment, then anger. "Derrick Messinger?" he growled. "How the hell did you get this number?"

CHAPTER TEN

ADD TO ALL THE THINGS Jed already didn't like about Derrick Messinger—his phony-looking hair, his phony-sounding voice, his ego-driven, sensationalistic reports on totally stupid topics, his sweeping into town like a whirlwind of attitude—the fact that he had somehow gotten hold of Jed's cell phone number and phoned just in time to interrupt one of the most luscious kisses Jed had ever experienced. Right now, Messinger held the number-one spot on Jed's deserves-to-die-a-painful-death list.

His heart was still beating a bit too hard. His groin was still feeling a bit too primed for action. Across the room, Erica watched him, her lips glistening from the kiss, her eyes slightly unfocused, her chest heaving with each uneven breath. He ought to disconnect the damn phone and carry her upstairs to bed.

But Messinger was talking, babbling in his trademark baritone, smooth but with an edge of excitement, the sort of delivery that could make the opening of a gas station sound as though it was part of a horrible plot to destroy the world's population of sperm whales. Messinger's words spilled out of the phone so fast Jed couldn't make much sense of them. Then again, his mind was miles away—or, more accurately, about ten feet away, across the room where Erica stood.

"How did you get this number?" he asked again when Messinger paused to catch his breath.

Messinger chuckled. "I'm an investigative reporter, Mr. Willetz. I know how to find things out."

The steam in Jed's brain slowly dissipated. "My father," he grunted. He'd given his cell phone number to his father last year, when advancing age had begun to stake its claim on Jed's grandfather, so his father could contact him if the old man started to fail. John had died three months ago, and Jed had assumed his father would have forgotten the phone number by now, or at least forgotten where he'd placed the scrap of paper on which he'd jotted it. Apparently Jack wasn't quite as stupid as Jed had counted on him to be. "How much did you pay him?"

Messinger only chuckled again.

Jed didn't join the laughter. "It better have been a lot," he muttered. "If he sold my number cheap—"

Messinger shut down the chuckles with an abruptness that proved how fake they'd been. "I know there are other reporters nosing around town," he said, "but let's face it, I'm the marquee name. I'm the one with the resources to put together a class story about Rockwell."

Given how little class Rockwell had, Jed doubted that. "If you want to do a story, be my guest. Just don't expect me to help you."

"Mr. Willetz." Messinger paused for dramatic effect, then said, in a creamy, let's-get-friendly voice, "Jed. You're the story's lynchpin. You're the son of one of the town fathers."

If Jack Willetz was a town father, Jed was the secretary of state. "Give me a break," he snapped. "You want to kiss butt? You're wasting all those smooches, buddy. I'm not going to be a part of your class story."

He pulled the phone away from his ear, searching with his thumb for the off button, but Messinger's voice drilled through the air and he lifted the phone back to his ear. "You live right next door to her. If you don't want to contribute to what's going to be a fair, balanced report—"

About what? Jed wondered. How fair and balanced the citizens of Rockwell were? How fair and balanced that dirt-crusted old box Erica had dug up was?

"You're in a position to facilitate a meeting with my people and Erica Leitner. All we want is to talk to her, to expand our coverage of the phenomenon she unearthed in her backyard garden."

"It's not a phenomenon. It's a box."

"The thing is, Erica Leitner is the person I need to reach, to get the unvarnished story from the source, as it were. But she's not home right now."

Jed gazed at Erica. She'd regained some control over herself. Her cheeks were no longer flushed; her breathing, no longer ragged. She got busy carrying the dirty dishes to the sink, but he could tell she was listening to his end of the conversation. "Am I supposed to know where she is?" he asked Messinger.

"That's not what I'm saying. The thing is, we want to narrow in on her and the box, to create a layered, textured report. Who she is. Where she lives. What the box represents."

"It's a box," Jed reminded him again. "It doesn't represent anything."

"That's where you're wrong, Jed. It represents *everything*." Messinger said this with such authority Jed almost believed him. Then he caught himself. To say the box represented *everything* was bullcrap, the inflated words of a man who inflated stories so he could satisfy his inflated ego.

"I've got to go," Jed announced into the phone. Erica had turned on the water and added a squirt of dishwashing soap to the sink.

"Fine. I'm sure we'll be speaking again. Meanwhile, if you happen to see your neighbor, please tell her I'm going to get her." With a smug, silky laugh, Messinger hung up.

At last Jed did what he should have done five minutes ago—pressed the off button. "Derrick Messinger said to tell you he's going to get you," he informed her.

She sighed and stared into the mound of suds in the sink. "That sounds like a threat."

"You want me to run interference?" he asked, approaching her.

"How can anyone run interference? I'm not going to hide in my house. I can't. I've got my job, I've got to finish planting my garden, and Dr. Gilman is arriving in town tomorrow. Poor Dr. Gilman. Derrick Messinger is going to pounce on him."

"He's a hotshot Harvard man. He can defend himself," Jed predicted. Soapsuds skittered over Erica's narrow wrists, leaving streaks of shine on her skin. He imagined she would look spectacular in a bubble bath. She'd probably look even better in a clear bath, without bubbles obscuring any part of her anatomy. He wondered how he could delete Messinger and Gilman from the discussion and get back to where he and Erica had been before the phone had rung.

As if she could read his mind, she said, "No."

"No, what?"

She rubbed a sponge diligently over a plate. "No, I'm not going to sleep with you."

He resisted the impulse to argue. Arguing wouldn't get him where he wanted to go. "Okay," he said, doing his best to sound agreeable. "We can just stick with kissing for now." He slid his hand under her hair and caressed her nape.

She tossed down the sponge and turned to face him, backing up until his hand fell away. "Don't, Jed. And don't give me another line about how we're two adults in the present. You may not like to think beyond the present, but I do."

She reached for the sponge again, but he blocked her before she could lift it. "I don't need you doing my dishes."

"You helped with the dishes last night."

"Yeah, well, that was the past. I'm thinking in the present." Instead of returning to her neck, he cupped his hand under her chin, letting his fingers stretch along her cheek. Her skin was cool and smooth. "So maybe nothing more is going to happen between us. We're still neighbors, right?"

"Temporarily," she said in a taut voice.

"In the present. And I just protected you from *I'm Just the Messinger,* so you ought to be bursting with gratitude instead of acting like a fussy little virgin."

"Bursting with gratitude?" She cracked a tepid smile. "What did he want, anyway?"

"He wanted to know everything about you—your blood type, your taste in music, whether you wear thong underwear."

"Yeah, right." Her smile grew fuller.

"He wants me to—what were his words? 'Facilitate a meeting' between his people and your people."

"For heaven's sake. If he wants to view the box, he can view it along with everyone else when Avery Gilman opens it. It's not such a big thing."

"He thinks it is." He stroked his fingertips along her cheekbone, then traced a line down to her chin. "Just like you think our having a little fun together is such a big thing."

"It is," she said, her smile gone and a glint of anger flashing in her eyes. "One thing is about a box. The other is about…" She faltered.

"Sex?" he suggested helpfully.

"Intimacy. Emotions."

"Fun."

"That, too," she conceded. "If I'm not going to help you clean the dishes, Jed, I should go home. I've got math quizzes to correct."

"And I've got a bottle with some wine still in it."

"Perhaps you can polish it off after I'm gone."

"Drown my sorrows, you think?" He grinned. She was so flipping earnest, taking everything so seriously. "Should I go on a bender after you walk out the door?" He swooped down and dropped a light kiss on her mouth. She didn't kiss him back, but she didn't flinch and gasp and act like a fussy little virgin, either. "I think I'll save the wine. We'll share it the next time we're together," he said.

She looked as if she thought that might also be a threat. If it was, he hoped she preferred it to Derrick Messinger's threat to "get her." Jed wanted to get her, too, but in a way that would leave them both sweaty and smiling.

Her box wasn't a phenomenon. But sex with her would probably be just that. She believed he was unable to think beyond the present, but as he released

her, as he walked with her out of the kitchen and down
the hall to the front door, he was thinking plenty about
the future. Tomorrow, or the day after, or the day after
that, if luck was with him, he and Erica were going to
experience something pretty damn phenomenal.

"So, YOU STRUCK OUT with Derrick Messinger?"
Erica asked Fern.

Lunchtime, and the nurse's office was quiet. No
emergencies, bleeding or vomiting, no kids whining
about headaches or stomach cramps minutes before
their geography tests. Erica spooned cold, smooth
yogurt into her mouth and acknowledged that it was
tastier than the slop she and Jed had thrown together
last night.

But of course the slop had only been a pretext for
them to be with each other. It had only been a prelude
to what had followed—and what *could* have followed
if Erica had been a little more daring. Good God, Fern
and every other woman of a certain age in Rockwell
were allegedly willing to drop their panties for Jed
Willetz, and he'd chosen *her* for that honor. Yet her
panties had remained firmly in place.

Just barely.

"What makes you think I struck out with him?"
Fern asked before taking a bite of her Muenster-
tomato-and-lettuce sandwich. "In fact, what makes
you think I was trying to hit a home run with him?"

Erica couldn't reveal her source without revealing
that she'd been with Jed. "It's a small town," she said
vaguely. "Nothing remains a secret for long." She
wondered how long it would take before the whole
town knew she and Jed had had dinner together last
night.

Fern shrugged, apparently accepting this explanation as legitimate. She took another bite of her sandwich, then a sip from her box of apple juice, and shrugged. "I just thought it would be fun to mosey over to the Hope Street Inn and introduce myself. And I baked a banana bread as a kind of 'Welcome to Rockwell' present. On behalf of the town, you know? If we treat him and his crew nicely, he'll be more likely to do a nice show about us. And banana bread is so easy to make."

Not for Erica, it wasn't. If she ever finished planting her garden, though, she'd be too busy learning how to bake tomato bread and zucchini bread to have time to bake banana bread.

"So I got to the inn," Fern said, "and the man himself was sitting in that wingback chair by the bay window, you know which one? It's got that awful chintz fabric covering it that looks like wallpaper from a little girl's bathroom. Anyway, he had his cell phone in one hand and a glass of scotch in the other, and he kept making eyes at me, even as he was phoning just about every living person in town. Then this officious woman with short hair and a voice like a foghorn cornered me and started grilling me. She was his producer, apparently. Sonya, or Sofia, something like that. She wanted to know all the gossip in town."

"Did you share it with her?"

"Of course not!" Fern pressed her hand to her chest, as if the mere idea made her apoplectic. "I only mentioned a few tidbits. The stash of girlie magazines in the basement of the library—for research purposes, they always say. And Elaine Hackett's obsession with James Mason movies. That kind of thing. But I realized this Sofia person wasn't going to let me get close to Derrick, so I finally just left the bread and took off.''

"But he was making eyes at you?" Erica pressed her.

"I think so." Fern took another sip of juice, then sighed. "Up close he doesn't look as good as he does on TV. His hair—I don't know. It doesn't look quite real. I think it is, but it doesn't look it.''

Erica almost blurted out that Jed had wanted to bet her that Derrick Messinger was wearing a toupee, but she caught herself in time. She didn't want Fern to think she was spending time discussing things like Derrick Messinger's hair with Jed.

"He's the first new guy to venture into town in a while, you know? Getting acquainted with him might be more fun than trekking all the way to Manchester in search of a willing gentleman. If he offered to run away with me, I might be tempted. I'd finish out the school year first, of course.''

"Of course." Erica scraped the bottom of her yogurt cup and swore to herself that if Jed offered to run away with her she wouldn't be tempted. "So are you going to bring more home-baked goodies to the Hope Street Inn again today?"

"No." Fern looked indignant. "One banana bread is all he gets for now. I don't want him thinking I'm easy." She munched on a bit of crust. "I'll probably go back to the inn, though. This time I'll offer only myself. He can get his bread elsewhere.''

"I'll go with you," Erica said.

Fern looked aghast. "No! If you come, he won't even notice me!"

"He will so notice you," Erica argued, surprised by Fern's outburst. They had never been competitive that way. When they'd traveled together to Manchester in search of a nightlife, they'd never vied for the attention of men. They'd never compared themselves with each other, fretting over which one was prettier or more attractive. Their friendship was too important to them to jeopardize it with jealousy.

"I didn't mean it *that* way," Fern reassured her. "It's just that he wants to do his show about you. You walk into the inn and you're the only person he's going to see, the only person who'll matter to him."

True enough. "How about if you position yourself as my best friend—which you are—and the only person in Rockwell who might be able to get him access to me?" She recalled what Jed had said last night, about how Derrick wanted Jed to put his people in touch with Erica's people, as if she had any people. If anyone was going to facilitate anything, it ought to be Fern. "He'll be so indebted to you love won't be far behind."

"You think?" Fern toyed with the straw from her juice box as she considered the plan. "Maybe I could win a few points with him that way." She stuffed the straw back into the box and drained the juice from it with a loud, gurgling slurp. "It might work even better if you don't come with me. I can tell him I'm his only chance for access to you. Without my cooperation, he doesn't see you."

"That would work, except I've got to go there this afternoon. Avery Gilman is arriving today, and I reserved a room for him there."

"The Hope Street Inn?"

"It's the nicest bed-and-breakfast in town. I thought he'd like it. He'll think it's rustic and New Englandy. And the building is a hundred years old, which will push his buttons. You know all that antique stuff in the front parlor, the firedogs and the stereopticon? Dr. Gilman will be drooling.''

"You're sure he's able to defend himself? Him and Derrick Messinger under one roof... The Hope Street Inn isn't that big."

"Maybe Messinger will decide to do his show about Dr. Gilman instead of me,'' Erica said hopefully.

"Then how am I going to win points playing go-between?'' Fern pouted. "Well, whatever. I'll figure something out. You can busy yourself getting your professor settled in while I ply my wiles with Derrick.''

They agreed to meet after school and travel to the Hope Street Inn together. School ended later than usual, thanks to a staff meeting that began ten minutes after the kids vacated the building. During the meeting, more than a few faculty members hovered near Erica, making her uncomfortable. She'd thought the excitement generated by her front-page appearance in the *Rockwell Gazette* would have died down by now, but apparently some of her colleagues had heard about the story's being mentioned on a news show out of Boston, and the gawking and ribbing had resumed. Wendy Williams, the reading specialist, made a crack about Erica being the darling of the ancient-box world. Dorothy Hines, the music teacher, hummed a few bars of the *Entertainment Tonight* theme song. When the agenda reached "New Business," Burt Johnson, the principal, noted that several people had observed Derrick Messinger skulking around the schoolyard and he reminded everyone how important it was for them all to maintain decorum so the school would look good on television. He also mentioned that he was establishing a committee, comprising Fern, Roger Basmegian, the gym teacher, and Hazel Nagy as a representative of the community, to discuss the current sex education curriculum.

Fern was fuming when they left the meeting. "We don't need a committee. Especially one with Hazel Nagy on it. Her idea of sex education is, men can pee standing up and women can't. The end. And Roger? His idea is probably, men can write in the snow with their pee. Women can't."

"Forget about it," Erica murmured. She didn't want Fern's upcoming meeting with Derrick Messinger spoiled by her anger over sex education. Right now, Fern's cheeks were splotchy with color; her eyes, burning; her hands, curled into fists. Erica was no seductress, but she knew enough to suspect that no man would want to get romantic with a woman that close to the boiling point.

"How can I forget about it? Basmegian is such a Neanderthal. You know what he calls his wife? The little lady."

"She *is* little."

"That's not the point. The point is, he has no idea what the current pedagogy is when it comes to sex education. The last literature he read on the subject was probably *Penthouse Forum*."

"Then he'll balance Hazel Nagy and her prude brigade. Really, Fern, forget it. We're on our way to see Derrick Messinger."

Fern nodded, but the color didn't fade from her cheeks. "Maybe I'll suggest that he do a show on sex ed in the New Hampshire sticks."

"Don't. Burt'll fire you for making the school look bad on TV."

"Let him fire me," Fern huffed. "I'll run off with Derrick."

They climbed into their respective cars. Erica followed Fern to Main Street and then down it to Hope Street. The first block of Hope Street east of Main featured a Laundromat, the Eat-zeria and a bar, but the second block was prettier, lined with modest but stalwart houses and stout oak trees, the branches of which bore tiny green buds, harbingers of spring. On the corner of the block stood the Hope Street Inn, a rambling Victorian with a broad porch, a smattering of gingerbread trim and a sign dangling from an overhang. Erica steered up the driveway to the small parking area behind the building. A car with Massachusetts plates occupied one of the spots. Dr. Gilman's car, she concluded, then reminded herself that he wanted her to call him Avery.

The drive seemed to have given Fern a chance to control her temper. After getting out of her car, she hunkered down to inspect her reflection in the side mirror and stabbed her hair several times with her fingers to fluff it out. She quickly added a smear of plum-hued lipstick to her lips and straightened up. "How do I look?"

"Gorgeous," Erica said, meaning it.

Fern scowled. "I feel empty-handed. Maybe I should've baked another banana bread."

"If all he wants you for is your banana bread, he's not worth your time," Erica advised.

"Right." Fern didn't sound convinced. But she gave her snug-fitting sweater a tug, squared her shoulders and preceded Erica around the building to the porch steps and inside. A cute little bell tinkled above the door as they swung it shut.

The parlor was empty—and Fern was right, the fabric on that wingback chair *did* look like bathroom wallpaper—but lively chatter floated through the arched doorway of the dining room. Nellie Shoemaker hurried into the parlor, a short, stocky woman in her fifties who had taken over the inn from her parents when they'd retired to Florida a few years ago. Her hair was the same color as the granite poking out of the topsoil throughout the region, and her eyeglasses were so large they gave her a bug-eyed appearance.

Her smile zinged with energy. She must be feeling quite proud of herself, housing not just a TV celebrity but also a Harvard professor in her bed-and-breakfast.

"Hi. I'm wondering if Dr. Avery Gilman has checked in yet," she said.

"Well, yes, he has. He just got here a short while ago, and he's having some tea and banana bread now. I'm not sure where the banana bread came from. I didn't bake it. I always put pecans in mine. This one has walnuts in it."

"Walnuts taste the same as pecans when you bake them," Fern muttered, obviously not pleased that the bread she'd baked wasn't being consumed by the person it had been intended for. "Derrick Messinger isn't around by any chance, is he?"

"Well, yes, he's having some tea, too. It's amazing to have this many guests when it's not even ski season."

Erica couldn't imagine Derrick Messinger indulging in an afternoon cup of tea. This was the intrepid journalist who'd set off in search of Jimmy Hoffa's corpse, armed with nothing but a camera and great quantities of attitude. Hadn't Fern said he'd been drinking scotch yesterday?

Then it dawned on her that Derrick might be using teatime to interrogate Dr. Gilman. Jed might think Avery was a hotshot professor, but he was much more the tweedy, absentminded type, with his scruffy beard, his scruffier hair, his gangly body clad in baggy khakis and old sweaters stretched out at the elbows. Avery Gilman could hold his own against any other Colonial-era historian-archaeologist, but against a shark like Messinger? Erica wasn't so sure.

She strode toward the dining room, Fern right behind her. Her entrance into the room, bright with late-afternoon sunlight, brought the conversation at the long, linen-covered table to a halt. Derrick, with his too-perfect blond hair, leaped out of his chair. So did Dr. Gilman. Erica recognized the other two people at the table: one was Derrick's beefy cameraman, and the other a woman she was pretty sure she'd seen at her house that morning, too. She must be Sofia or Sonya.

Erica saved her smile for Dr. Gilman, who looked exactly as she'd remembered him from her undergraduate days, all elbows and knees, steel-wool hair bushing out from his scalp and chin. He wore a ribbed V-neck sweater of indeterminate brown, baggy twill trousers and scuffed shoes. He extended his right hand. "Erica Leitner! So good to see you!"

"Dr. Gilman." She shook his hand, then grinned. "I'd like you to meet my friend, Fern Bernard. Fern, this is Dr. Gilman."

"Avery," he corrected her as he released her hand and turned to Fern.

Erica turned to her, too. She stood transfixed, just inside the dining-room doorway, staring at Dr. Gilman as if he were a creature from another planet.

He didn't look that strange. With her spiky, persimmon-red hair, Fern arguably looked stranger. As though someone had nudged her from behind, she stepped into the room, her hand outstretched. Dr. Gilman clasped it in his own. She sighed, then said, "It's a pleasure," although forcing out the words seemed to be a serious challenge.

What was wrong with her? She was a college graduate; she'd met professors before. Even if she hadn't, she was never cowed by anyone. She was brassy and sassy, possibly the most sophisticated resident of Rockwell.

She lowered her gaze slightly and sighed again. If Erica didn't know better—if she didn't know that Fern had designs on Derrick Messinger—she might think Fern was smitten with Dr. Gilman.

Absolutely absurd. Avery Gilman represented the antithesis of everything Fern yearned for: excitement, electricity, cutting-edge style. He was a slightly moldy, slightly musty pedant. Why did Fern seem on the verge of swooning?

Erica wasn't the only person to notice Fern's odd reaction. Derrick Messinger cleared his throat loudly, as if to remind everyone that he was, after all, the most important person in the room. While Fern hovered near Dr. Gilman, her hand still clasped within his, Derrick clamped his own strong hand on Erica's shoulder. "Erica! This is perfect! Why don't we do a sit-down right here? Sonya, get your notes. Mookie, fire up the camera—"

"We're not doing a sit-down," Erica cut him off, not exactly sure what a sit-down was. "I'm here only to welcome my former professor and make sure he's all settled in." She glanced back at Dr. Gilman and found him gazing down at Fern with that same goo-goo look in his eyes.

Good God. What had happened to their plan? Erica was supposed to resist Derrick's attempt to interview her, and Fern was supposed to be the liaison, the hero-ine who persuaded Erica to contribute to Derrick's show, and then Derrick was supposed to reward Fern for her assistance by falling for her. But right now, Fern seemed unaware Derrick was even in the room.

"I baked that banana bread," she purred. "I hope you like it."

"It's great!" the cameraman said.

"It was quite tasty, as was Ms. Shoemaker's tea. A welcome tonic after my long drive." He gave Fern's hand a slight squeeze before releasing it.

"Okay, look," the other woman interjected. Yes, her voice did sound like a foghorn, one with a New York accent. "Enough with the banana bread. We're all here, so let's figure this out. Av, you're gonna open the box tomorrow night, agreed? Eight-thirty, so we can get the live feed out of Manchester."

"I don't know," Avery said, arching an eyebrow just enough to inform Erica he didn't like being called Av. "As I've said all along, I have to examine the specimen first. I don't work according to some net-work's broadcast schedule."

"Maybe you don't, but schedules are schedules," the foghorn lectured. "We've got a lock on eight to nine tomorrow night. A half hour of 'Welcome to Rockwell'—which I'll be editing tomorrow morning at the studio in Manchester—followed by the live feed at eight-thirty, during which you open the box, followed by reaction to whatever happens to be inside it."

"What if the box is empty?" Erica asked. "Are you

going to broadcast a half hour of stunned silence?''
Avery laughed. Fern managed a dazed smile.

"There's always a reaction. Don't worry. I'm a
pro.''

"So am I,'' Derrick interjected, just in case anyone
had forgotten about him.

"And I've busted my tail to get us this live feed,''
the foghorn said. "We get to be front and center when
you do open it. *I'm Just the Messinger* gets the exclusive. Right?'' Before anyone could respond, she addressed Erica. "We were thinking of having Av open
the box here, in this room. For one thing, the decor is
great, very antique in style. For another, the lighting is
excellent.''

"No,'' Erica said. "We're not going to open the box
here. We're not moving the box from my house until
we have a clearer idea of its age and value.'' She shot
Avery a glance and was gratified to see his nod. "I
don't care about the lighting.''

"When you're taping a TV show, the lighting is
important.''

"But the box was found behind my house. That's
where it should be opened. As far as I know,'' Erica
added pointedly, "journalists don't stage events.''

Derrick's smile vanished. The foghorn hadn't been
smiling in the first place. If the cameraman was
wounded by Erica's insinuation, he salved his hurt
feelings by slicing himself another piece of Fern's banana bread.

"Let's have a look at this box, then, shall we?''
Avery suggested, apparently oblivious to the tension in
the room. His gaze lingered for a moment on Fern, and

then he addressed Erica. "At your house. Perhaps your friend would like to join us?"

Erica glanced at Fern, who peered up at Avery with dewy eyes. "I'm sure she would," Erica said.

CHAPTER ELEVEN

WHERE HAD ALL THESE CARS come from? Derrick wondered irritably as he guided the rental car behind the line of vehicles parked in front of Erica Leitner's house and turned off the engine. He recognized a disgusting old gray pickup in the spot nearest her driveway—it belonged to Jack Willetz, that little worm. The guy had squeezed ten bucks out of Derrick in exchange for his son's cell phone number, and a lot of good that had done. These small-town hicks had gall. Some of the locals went out of their way to make Derrick feel special, but others—for instance, everyone he'd met with the last name of Willetz—wrung him out.

God knew what was in the damn box. At this point, Derrick was having trouble pretending he cared. Well, they'd get it open tonight, broadcast the big event and be done with it.

Last night, Gilman had looked the box over and said he was sure he'd be able to open it tonight. That morning, after a breakfast of coffee, orange juice and gooey blueberry muffins—Ms. Shoemaker had laughed so hard she'd suffered an asthma attack when Derrick had inquired whether she had any low-fat muffins, a question he failed to see the humor in—he'd sat Avery down in the inn's front room and interviewed him on tape for an hour. It had been excruciating. He'd asked Avery what he thought might be inside the box, and

Avery had pontificated for a full ten minutes on some no-name nobody who'd apparently been a confidant of Ethan Allen's and had helped to recruit soldiers for the Revolutionary War. It had taken Derrick a while to remember that Ethan Allen was a Colonial-era war hero and not just the name of a furniture-store chain.

Fortunately, Sonya was a genius when it came to editing. She and Mookie had left the inn at ten and driven to the studio of a network affiliate in Manchester to edit everything they'd taped in and around Rockwell, including the fawning merchants, that long-faced bartender and his equally long-faced son, and the town drunk. Derrick had spent the day dozing, watching a *Dirty Harry* flick on TV in the rear parlor—no cable in the rooms, let alone pay-per-view adult fare—and sipping scotch out of a delicate porcelain coffee cup with flowers painted around the edge. They looked suspiciously like pansies, but he wasn't going to guzzle straight from the bottle when Ms. Shoemaker was around, acting as though she believed she was running a high-class establishment.

He hoped tonight would go smoothly. At this point, all he wanted was to do his *I'm Just the Messinger* gig, jump on the next plane to LaGuardia and sleep in his own bed.

Maybe he'd have wanted to stay longer if he could have slept in the funky red-haired chick's bed. He thought he'd played Erica's friend Fern very nicely two days ago, simultaneously ignoring her and sending her vibes. He happened to emanate extremely potent vibes; they'd carried him to a pinnacle of stardom once and would again. The redhead had seemed receptive, too. But as of yesterday afternoon, she had eyes only for Herr Professor.

All right, so maybe Derrick wasn't destined to score with a local while covering the biggest story in Rockwell's boring little history. Maybe the Man from Harvard would open the damn box, it would be empty and Derrick would escape from this hellhole, whereupon he'd return to the world of doormen, gorgeous twenty-something secretaries in miniskirts and free delivery from every Chinese restaurant within a ten-block radius. Freedom was only hours away. He could hardly wait.

He got out of the rental car, locked it and reached inside his pocket to make sure he had his lucky rubber band with him. Then he strolled along the row of cars toward Erica's front door. He didn't recognize the professor's car among the vehicles lining the road. Avery Gilman had to be here, though. He'd probably gotten a ride with Fern. Derrick didn't know what kind of car she owned. If this were a halfway believable town, she'd be driving something sharp—a Corvette or a Miata, maybe—but in Rockwell, the mountains were hills, the scotch was low-test Johnny Walker and the cool girl probably drove a minivan.

Actually, the only minivan parked outside Erica Leitner's house was the one Mookie and Sonya had driven back from Manchester, with the satellite dish on its roof and the local affiliate's logo painted, blinding red against a yellow background, on its sides. Most of the vehicles were pickup trucks, none quite as seedy looking as Jack Willetz's, and SUVs.

Sonya must have been watching for him, because she barreled out the front door as he started across the straw-brown lawn. "That Barbie doll from the Boston local news is back," she announced in her braying Bronx accent.

"She's not filming the opening, though," Derrick half asked. "We've got exclusive rights to that, don't we?"

"Erica Leitner didn't sign anything with us, but I'm pretty sure the Boston reporter doesn't know that. There are people from the *Globe* and the *Herald* and from papers in Portland and Nashua, but they can't do anything with the story until tomorrow, so who cares?" Sonya babbled as she trooped back into the house with Derrick, painfully hip in her black stretch pants and black turtleneck. He followed her inside and grimaced at the hubbub of chattering voices that greeted him as he crossed the threshold, a sound he associated with cocktail parties. Did they have cocktail parties in Rockwell? It was Friday night, after all. And Erica was Harvard educated. Perhaps she'd have some quality thirst-quenchers available for the guests.

Right. And where would she obtain quality thirst-quenchers around here? He should have asked Mookie to pick up a bottle of Chivas while he'd been in Manchester earlier today.

Erica's cocktail party to celebrate the grand opening of her box comprised maybe twenty people. They milled about her living room, which was furnished with less money but more taste than the parlors at the Hope Street Inn. No chintz, no frills, no upholstery or curtains or knickknacks featuring a pattern of pansies. The walls were that cheap off-white shade of paint that landlords always used to conceal dirt and stains before they showed a unit to a new tenant. The brownish-gray carpet wore indentations and ruts from the previous residents' furniture.

Derrick surveyed the room. Sonya had buttonholed the perky reporter from Boston. A few guys carried still cameras; they must be print-media people. In one corner stood the long-faced bar owner and his kid, who wore a cap featuring a logo for Triple-X Beer, whatever the hell that was.

He spotted one of the ladies from the crafts store engrossed in a conversation with a moon-faced woman holding a large spiral notepad. She looked more apt to hit someone over the head with the pad than to write in it, but she did have a pen in one hand, so who knew? The fellow who owned that minigrocery store in town meandered around the room, setting out paper plates filled with Ritz crackers garnished with canned cheese and chunks of what appeared to be beef jerky. Rockwell's version of hors d'oeuvres, Derrick thought with a grimace. Jack Willetz and the town drunk—what was his name? Some amphibian. Newt, maybe?—were stuffing their mouths with cheese-smeared crackers, as if they hadn't eaten in days. Resisting the urge to curl his lip, Derrick moved toward a doorway filled with glaring light.

The doorway opened onto the dining room, and when Derrick peeked inside he saw Mookie busy setting up bright lights to illuminate the table. It was covered with a clean white cloth, and at the center of the table sat the box. With all the light and the white linens, the room looked sterile enough to serve as a hospital's OR.

And why not? Gilman would be performing surgery in there soon enough.

Derrick moved on to the kitchen, a gloomy room in dire need of renovation. Erica and Gilman were there, spying on Mookie's preparations through the dining-room doorway and sipping from tall glasses of water—although it could be vodka or gin, Derrick thought op-

timistically. Hovering beside them were Fern, her hair
the color of a cherry jelly bean, and the youngest Willetz, tall and thick shouldered, clad in a plaid wool shirt
over a navy-blue T-shirt and faded jeans. He looked
like some sort of laborer, a lumberjack down from the
mountain in search of sex.

Derrick wasn't sure why that image had jumped into
his brain, other than the fact that sex was never far
from his thoughts. But there was something…not quite
predatory but definitely hungry in Jed Willetz's pale-
gray eyes. Hungry and possessive. He held a brown
bottle in his hand, some brand of beer. Better than
water, Derrick thought.

"Hello there, Erica," Derrick said in his smoothest,
most reassuring voice. "Dr. Gilman. Are you all set to
become a TV star?"

"Why are you doing this live?" Jed Willetz asked.
"It could be a disaster. What if the lock is stuck?"

"That's part of the excitement," Derrick explained,
not caring if he sounded condescending. "No one
knows what will happen. The network's been promot-
ing this story since yesterday. They bumped two sit-
com repeats off the hour just to accommodate my
show. People want to see it live. They want to be surprised."

"What people?" Jed shook his head. "This is like
one of those stupid reality shows, where people make
asses of themselves because they want to be famous."

"No one is going to make an ass of himself," Derrick said, not adding that the reason most people tuned
in to live broadcasts like this was that they hoped
someone *would* make an ass of himself. That was the
big draw: the possibility that someone would do some-

thing foolish or dangerous or downright ridiculous on the air.

He checked his watch. Eight-ten. The show was already being broadcast, not the live part but the prologue, Sonya's minidocumentary about cute little Rockwell.

"Why don't we go into the dining room and get ourselves organized," he suggested.

Erica sighed and spun around to face Fern. "How do I look?"

"Gorgeous," Fern assured her. Behind her, Jed Willetz nodded.

Erica's frown expressed disbelief. "My mother thought I looked washed out on TV the other night."

"Who are you going to listen to, your mother or me? You look fine." Fern reached up and brushed a long, wavy strand of hair behind Erica's ear. "Break a leg, honey. You, too," she added, giving Gilman's hand a squeeze.

He smiled faintly and followed Erica into the dining room. Derrick dismissed Jed Willetz and Fern—the tasteless bitch, choosing a Harvard professor over him—with a nod and joined the others in the dining room.

The doorway into the living room began filling with onlookers, some of them chewing crackers and canned cheese, a few wielding disposable cameras. What a circus. But after all, circuses were the oxygen *I'm Just the Messinger* breathed.

Fortunately, Sonya was able to organize the clowns so they'd make good background scenery without imposing on the central drama. "Remember," she hollered above the din, "you can watch, but you've gotta keep quiet. We can't have a lot of distracting noise. If you folks don't remain quiet I'm gonna have to clear you out of the room.'' She carried a clipboard, which lent her a certain authority.

''My kid has to be in the front row,'' the bartender shouted, shoving his son forward through the small crowd. ''My kid, Randy Rideout. He found the box. He gets to stand in front!'' The kid looked sheepishly at his father, who continued nudging him forward.

''He can stand near the front if you want,'' Sonya conceded. ''But he can't say a word.''

''How about he just says he was the one who found the box?''

''Not a word,'' Sonya said so fiercely Rideout Senior fell back a step. Rideout Junior remained where he was, however, just inside the doorway, his stupid hat in full view of the camera.

''Can he take the hat off?'' Derrick suggested to Sonya. ''We don't want brand advertising in our broadcast.''

Sonya nodded. ''The hat goes.'' She tugged it off the kid's head and tossed it through the doorway in the general direction of his father.

Gilman settled himself at the dining-room table, a small, leather carrying case of tools open in front of him and his face scrunched into a squint from the bright lights. Erica batted her eyes a few times as she dropped into a seat next to the professor. Mookie clipped microphones to the necklines of Gilman's crew-neck sweater and Erica's denim jumper. ''Talk a little so we can get a sound check,'' he said.

''Hello,'' Erica said awkwardly.

Gilman rose to the occasion by bursting into a lecture. ''The box appears to be early nineteenth century,

although I'll be better able to date it once it's opened.
It appears to be a gentleman's caddy—''

"Yeah, yeah, save it for when we're live," Derrick
cut him off, then glanced at Mookie, who nodded that
the sound levels were good. Then they all stood
around, silent and bored, waiting for the live feed to
begin. Derrick didn't wear a clip-on mike; he preferred
to have his mike in his hand. It was like a weapon,
long and hard, with that rounded tip, kind of—no, it
wasn't phallic. Absolutely not. He just liked holding a
mike; that was all.

The town drunk's jaw pumped as he munched on
crackers in the living-room doorway. Jed Willetz
loomed in the kitchen doorway like something carved
out of native granite. The dining room, Derrick realized, was way too small. They should have set this up
somewhere else.

Sonya pressed her earphone tight against her temple,
nodded, then silently counted Derrick down. The light
on Mookie's camera blinked on and Derrick shaped
his trademark smile—conspiratorial, not cheery. "Hi,"
he addressed the camera, reading the text that scrolled
through the prompter. "*I'm Just the Messenger* is now
coming to you live from Erica Leitner's house, where
Dr. Avery Gilman is prepared to open the box. Earlier
in our broadcast, Dr. Gilman, a Harvard University
professor specializing in Colonial artifacts, described
some of the strategies historians like him use to narrow
down the date of an artifact. He offered some theories
as to how the box might have wound up buried in Erica
Leitner's vegetable garden.''

"My son dug it up," Rideout's voice drifted in
through the living-room doorway, but Sonya gave him

such a lethal glare he wound up covering his words with a cough.

"We've got some interested parties here at Erica's house, looking on," Derrick ad-libbed smoothly. "Some folks from Rockwell, including many you've met during the first portion of this show. We've asked them to be very quiet so Dr. Gilman can concentrate. Dr. Gilman, what exactly are you going to do?"

The camera swiveled slightly to Derrick's left, zeroing in on the professor, who held up a tool that appeared to be a brush with a rubber bulb attached to it. "I'm going to use this to clean the dirt from the lock. The device has both a brush and a blowing mechanism." He squeezed the bulb a couple of times. "See? It blows."

Just so long as this show didn't blow. Derrick smiled encouragingly while Gilman began blowing and brushing at the lock, and then the hinges. "This box may have been buried only recently, but my guess is that it's lain unmolested in the ground for well over a century," Gilman lectured. Derrick nodded; *unmolested* was a terrific word for this kind of show. "My reason for assuming that," Gilman explained as he gingerly dusted the hinges, "is that the wood appears deeply and evenly stained from the soil. With the right kind of wood soap, we could scrub off some of that stain and get to the original maple. I'd need some equipment I don't have with me to test the finish on the wood, but it seems to be authentic. No evidence of polyurethane or some other modern finish. Now I'm going to use this tool—" he lifted a narrow silver tool from his case "—to gently clean out whatever dirt might be lodged inside the keyhole of the lock."

"You'll forgive me, Dr. Gilman, if I say that looks like the sort of thing a thief would use to pick a lock."

"Well, that's what I'm going to do, isn't it? Pick the lock."

"I certainly hope so. So does Erica—" he gestured toward Mookie, who pivoted the camera to encompass Erica seated beside Gilman "—and so do the millions of people in our TV audience tonight." *Please, God, let that TV audience number in the millions,* he added silently.

"Old locks are a bit simpler to break into," Gilman noted. "They don't have the complicated barrel system modern locks have." He dug bits of dirt out of the keyhole, and they fell like crumbs of chocolate cake onto the pristine white tablecloth. "Of course, you have to be very gentle. We don't want to break this. The more intact we can keep an artifact, the more it can tell us."

"What is this artifact telling you, Dr. Gilman?" Derrick asked.

"It's telling me it sat in the dirt for a long time." Gilman poked a little more dirt out of the lock.

Derrick had to admit the guy was doing better than expected. A little stuffy, a little pompous, but not deadly dull. The silence of the crowd peering in through the doorways lent a nice taut mood of anticipation to the scene. The network broadcasting *I'm Just the Messinger* was one of the small ones, but maybe this stupid box, this ridiculous story he'd hated from the get-go, was going to catapult him back into the land of the major networks.

"Erica," he said, deciding to get her more involved in the moment, "what are you thinking right now?"

Erica had been watching Gilman fuss with his delicate little tools, and she jerked upright and stared glassy-eyed at the camera for a moment. Then she let out a breath. "I'm just—curious about what's inside the box."

"Tell us now, before Dr. Gilman gets it open. What do you predict will be inside?"

"Oh, I don't know." Her cheeks colored slightly, and she gave a nervous laugh. "Dirt, maybe?"

The crowd chuckled. A quick, chastening frown from Sonya silenced them all.

"Okay," Derrick pressed her, "let me put it this way. In your *dreams,* what would you like the box to contain?"

"Well, I'm not—I mean, vast wealth is unimportant to me, so I'm not dreaming that it's full of diamonds or anything like that." She moistened her lips and glanced at Gilman's meticulous motions as he worked on the lock. "It would be nice if there was something historically important inside, like old letters. Love letters, maybe."

The Rideout kid curled his lip and rolled his eyes. Over by the kitchen, Jed Willetz smiled mysteriously. A faint murmur in the far reaches of the living room might have indicated that someone approved of her idea.

"Love letters," Derrick said, turning to face the camera. "Imagine it. Some ancient love affair—a Revolutionary War hero's heartfelt epistles to the woman he left behind, perhaps a farmer's daughter, a beautiful young thing knitting sweaters and waiting for her soldier to come home. And why, we have to wonder, would the letters have been kept locked inside a box? Perhaps it was an illicit love. Perhaps she was a farmer's wife, not a daughter. Perhaps the soldier was a Redcoat, and their love was treasonous!'' He was on a roll now. ''Perhaps there was an out-of-wedlock child. Perhaps she wrote to the soldier that she was pregnant and he was married, so he had to hide her letter from his wife.''

''I believe he would have been inclined to burn such a letter,'' the professor interjected.

''Well, it's more romantic my way. How are you coming along?'' he asked when Sonya pointed at her watch.

''Getting there, getting there. The lock is clean now. I'm going to anoint the hinges with a bit of lubricant so they'll be less likely to break once we lift the top.'' He used a cotton swab to dab what appeared to be mineral oil on the hinges, and then on the lock. ''And now I'm going to pick the lock.''

''Just like a common street thug,'' Derrick said.

Gilman eyed him dubiously. ''Not exactly, no.'' Then he inserted another narrow tool into the lock and carefully jiggled it around. ''This feels pretty easy,'' he said. ''It's a simple lock, nothing elaborate, nothing customized. Yes...I can feel some movement in there...''

Erica leaned toward the box. So did Derrick. So, he noticed, did everyone else except Mookie, who was too stolid and responsible to risk shifting the camera's aim during a live feed.

''There.'' With a nearly inaudible click, the lock gave way. Gilman eased his tool out of the hole and wiggled the lock free of the box's latch.

''He's going to open it now,'' Derrick murmured to the camera, deliberately lowering his voice to a suspenseful hush, as if he were announcing at a golf tournament. ''The moment of truth is here, ladies and gentlemen. We are now going to see what this mysterious box holds.''

Mookie zoomed the lens in toward the box as Gilman painstakingly lifted the latch and then the box's lid. Slowly the light slid over the rim, slowly it filled the box, slowly Gilman pulled the lid as far back as the hinges would allow.

Derrick gasped so loudly, he drowned out anyone else who might have gasped. And who wouldn't gasp at the sight of the box's contents: a pile of glittering gold coins.

PANDEMONIUM, Erica recalled from her years of rigorous education, was derived from the Greek words *pan,* meaning all, and *daemon* meaning demon. The instant everyone saw the gold coins inside the box, demons reigned all over.

"Ladies and gentlemen," Derrick Messinger was babbling into his microphone, "this is amazing! It's incredible! There must be millions of dollars in gold coins inside that box!"

"No, no!" Avery outshouted Messinger, hastily lowering the lid. "It's not millions of dollars! Don't be silly!" He bowed over the box, protecting it from the descending hordes.

They spilled in through both doorways, all of them shrieking and demanding and hooting. "Lemme see!" "I gotta see this!" "A buried treasure!" "The school-teacher's filthy freakin' rich!"

"My boy found it!" Glenn Rideout bellowed. "Don't forget, my boy's got a claim on it!"

"Maybe there's more where that came from!" someone shouted. "Let's go dig up her garden!"

"It's my dad's garden," Jack Willetz bellowed. "If anyone digs it up, it's *me*."

"We need to see these coins up close," Messinger informed Avery. "You have to open the box again."

"They may not even be genuine," Avery said unconvincingly. "They need to be examined by an expert numismatist."

Erica's head started to pound. The lights were so bright, the noise level so high…and a pile of gold coins sat inside a box on her table. Heaven help her. People wanted to get at the box—and they wanted to tear apart her garden, which she hadn't even finished planting yet. How would she ever learn to bake zucchini bread if her wonderful Rockwell neighbors ravaged her backyard?

She felt a hand on her shoulder, strong and firm and comforting. "No one's going to dig up your garden," Jed whispered. "Especially not my father." He released her and moved away, probably to stand guard over the property, she thought vaguely.

Another hand gripped her shoulder, this one smaller and lighter. "Can I peek?" Fern asked, brushing against Avery. "Just one little peek?"

"We all need a peek," Derrick said, his composure and his hair remaining firmly in place even as the cramped dining room filled with people. "The charming residents of Rockwell," he recited at the camera, "are understandably excited about this amazing turn of events. Few people have ever seen such an abundance of gold in one place."

"It's not an abundance," Avery warned. "It's a few coins."

"Gold coins. Are they old? Are they priceless? Ladies and gentlemen, this is live. You are witnessing the discovery of the century, here in a sleepy little village in central New Hampshire.''

"This is not the discovery of the century," Avery argued. "The discovery of Norse settlements in what is now the Maritimes, eastern Canada, thus proving that the Vikings sailed to North America long before Columbus made his voyage—now, *that* was the discovery of the century.''

"That was the discovery of the last century," Derrick retorted. "And this is gold. Open the box.''

"He's not going to open the box until everyone takes a giant step backward," Erica declared. A third-grade-teacher tactic, but it worked. Everyone—even Messinger—fell back a step. She gazed around her at the avid faces of her neighbors. They still seemed too close. "Another step back," she ordered them. Reluctantly, everyone complied.

Avery sent her a nod of approval, then inched the box open. The room grew eerily still, as if a collective breath was being held.

The box did not contain millions of dollars in gold coins. Erica wasn't an expert when it came to precious metals, but she didn't think the box contained more than twenty coins, and they couldn't each be worth upward of a hundred thousand dollars. Some shone more than others, but they didn't look dirty or eroded. Didn't pirates bite gold coins to see if they were real? She couldn't see any tooth marks in the coins.

The crowd started to lean in again. A sharp stare from the woman with the foghorn voice sent them backward.

"Professor," Messinger said, his voice dangerously obsequious, "do you think it would be possible to hold up one coin for the television audience to see?''

Avery glanced toward the living room, then the kitchen. Pursing his lips, he lifted one coin from the box. "It's dated 1802," he said, holding it up in front of the camera. "I can't attest to its authenticity or provenance. We'll need to have someone better versed in numismatics examine it." He hastily placed it back in the box and lowered the lid.

"Eighteen-oh-two," Messinger said breathlessly. "Can you believe that, folks? Eighteen-oh-two. That's before Jefferson was president."

"Actually, no," Avery corrected him. "Jefferson took office in 1801."

"Well, whatever. Folks, that is a true antique. A *gold* antique. This buried treasure is worth a small fortune."

"A large fortune," Glenn Rideout yelled.

"Most likely a small one," Avery corrected him.

"Is there chocolate inside those coins?" Toad Regan asked. "Ever see those chocolate coins? They look just like that."

People started drifting back into the dining room, and Avery tucked the box securely under his arm. Messinger began interviewing various people—"You've met so many of these wonderful Rockwell people during the first half hour of our show. Let's finish up by hearing what they think of this astonishing discovery"—and Avery seemed to be thinking the same thing Erica was thinking: that the box and its valuable contents needed to be protected. Erica admired her fellow Rockwellians, she truly did, but she wouldn't be surprised if any one of them discreetly pocketed a coin, given the chance.

Almost unnoticed as the crowd gathered around Messinger, vying for a minute or two of nationally tele-

vised fame, Erica and Avery escaped to the kitchen
with the box. Fern stood near the sink, wide-eyed and
edgy, and Jed had positioned himself by the back door.
"No one's assaulted your garden yet," he assured her.

Erica didn't want to acknowledge how good it felt
to have him there, tall and strong and prepared to defend her territory. She imagined his presence would be
more effective than any of her assorted kitchen knives.
She hated feeling dependent on him, just as she hated
fearing what her neighbors might do to her property.
But he was so...so tall and strong. So male.

They'd seen each other again last night. After Avery
had examined the box, he and Erica had driven over
to Fern's house, where, in her well-lit, relatively modern kitchen, Fern had whipped up a feast of herbed
chicken, steamed asparagus and wild rice, and Erica
had wound up feeling like a fifth wheel. Whatever bug
had bitten Fern and Avery had bitten hard; her sarcas-
tic, funky friend and her erudite former professor had
chattered on and on about their favorite episodes of
The Brady Bunch until Erica had finally taken her
leave. Less than a minute after she'd driven her car
into the shed behind her house, Jed had appeared, carrying last night's leftover wine.

"Just sit on the porch with me," he'd invited her.
"I promise I won't touch you."

To her regret, he didn't touch her. They'd sipped the
last of the wine and talked about the arrangements he
was making for his grandfather's ashes and his uncer-
tainty about whether to sell his grandfather's house or
hang on to it for a while. "Until I figure out what to
do, I won't do anything," he'd said.

"Obviously." She'd been flattered that he'd wanted

to bounce ideas off her, to discuss his day with her, his concerns. As if they were friends. Close friends.

And he hadn't touched her. Which made her think he was trustworthy. Which was ridiculous, because it didn't matter how much she trusted him—he was going to leave Rockwell, leave her and return to New York.

She shouldn't be as glad as she was that he was in her house now, close by, watching out for her. "Everybody's too busy being a TV star to dig up my garden," she told him.

"Yeah. But wait until Messinger and his techies disappear. They'll be out there with picks and shovels like the forty-niners."

"They'd be trespassing," Erica pointed out. "I could have them arrested."

"Now, *there's* a neighborly attitude." He gazed through the window in the back door, thoughtful. "What are you going to do with the box?"

"I don't know." She glanced at Avery. "I assumed you would take it back to Harvard for further analysis."

"When I go back to Cambridge, yes." Avery's gaze traveled from Erica to Fern and he smiled wistfully. He clearly wasn't ready to go back to Cambridge yet.

Erica turned to Jed. "I'm sure it'll be safe here."

"Are you?" He spun away from the window and observed the frenzied scene in the dining room for a minute. "I'd tell you to give it to the police for safekeeping, but I don't know how trustworthy the local cops are. Maybe you ought to lock it in a safe-deposit box at the bank."

"We need to inventory the contents first," Avery said, obviously in agreement with Jed. "I wouldn't want a coin to disappear unnoticed. We can inventory it, then sign a notarized statement of its contents, and then lock it in the bank.''

''The bank won't be open now,'' Erica observed.

''For this, they'll open it. We can phone Peter Goss. Is he still the head honcho over at Rockwell Community Bank?''

''Rockwell Community Bank no longer exists,'' Fern informed him. ''It became a branch of Fleet Bank a couple of years ago. But Peter's still the manager.''

''Let's call him.'' Jed started toward the phone.

''Wait!'' Erica felt overwhelmed, dizzy, as if the mass of people in her house, the cameras, the reporters, the noise, the box itself were sucking all the oxygen out of the air. She gulped in several breaths and waited for her mind to clear.

When it did, she saw Jed, Avery and Fern watching her. Fern looked devoted; Avery, avuncular; and Jed...unbearably sexy. Why hadn't he touched her last night? If he had, she might just have been foolish enough not to stop him.

She had to get her life back under control. No lustful yearnings for her transient next-door neighbor. No letting the crazed people in her dining room stampede her or her property. No panic about what was going to happen to her life now that she was apparently the owner of an artifact of potentially enormous value.

She might wish she were a sweet, mellow, accommodating earth mother, but as of this moment, she would have to be what she was: a smart, sophisticated warrior with an Ivy League pedigree and the fortitude to manage her own fate.

''*I,*'' she announced, striding across the kitchen to the phone, ''will call Peter Goss.''

CHAPTER TWELVE

SHE'D BARELY DRIFTED OFF to sleep, when a noise woke her. Actually, an assortment of noises: rattling, stumbling, thumping.

Someone was in her house.

Her heart stuttered a beat, but she willed herself not to panic. This was Rockwell, after all, a safe, cozy, small town where everyone knew everyone. Of course, some weirdo might have hitched into town from somewhere else, a psychopath with a big hunting knife who hid out in the Moose Mountains and descended into Rockwell whenever the urge to rape and pillage overtook him. Erica had locked her doors, but the maniac had gotten past her locks and was inside her house. The rattling, she realized, was her silverware drawer. The thump had been one of the kitchen chairs colliding with the table.

Oh, God—oh, God—oh, God. She'd moved to Rockwell to make a life for herself far from the crime of the city, and here she was, trapped in her own house with a bloodthirsty killer. And dialing 911 would do her no good in Rockwell.

She took a few deep breaths and waited for her eyes to adjust to the dark. Whoever was in her house sounded as though he was still in her kitchen. Maybe the invader was just a raccoon foraging for food. An incredibly smart raccoon who knew how to open locked doors.

She heard the clap of a cabinet door shutting and decided it wasn't a raccoon. What was the phone number of the police station? She had it programmed into the telephone in the kitchen, not the bedroom phone.

She could dial Jed's cell phone number... No, she couldn't. She'd been far too grateful for his presence that evening during the opening of the box and the hysteria that had ensued. Having him close by had made her feel too safe, too secure. Too dependent. She couldn't depend on him. He'd be gone any day.

But she'd depended on him just hours ago, when happy hell had broken loose in her dining room, in full view of a live camera broadcasting the discovery nationally. Who would have thought the box would contain what had turned out to be twenty-two gold coins, their movement cushioned and their jingling muffled by the thick burgundy velvet lining the box's interior? Suddenly, unexpectedly, Erica was in possession of wealth—possibly significant wealth—and everyone, not just in town but across the country, knew about her bounty, thanks to Derrick Messinger and all the other media vultures.

Amid the havoc, Jed had quietly taken over. He'd wrapped the box in a paper bag, taped the bag and made her and Avery Gilman sign the tape. He'd answered her incessantly ringing phone for her and told every caller she was unable to come to the phone. He'd removed the paper plates of cheese and crackers from the living room so mooches would have an incentive to leave. And once she'd finally cleared everyone out of her house, he had accompanied her and Avery to the bank to have her treasure locked in a safe-deposit box. She'd thought they ought to bring it to the police station, but Jed had said the police weren't necessarily the most trustworthy folks in Rockwell, and she'd deferred to his wisdom.

So the box was locked inside the bank for the night. But Erica wasn't. Whoever had been banging around in her kitchen seemed to have moved into another room—the living room or dining room, she wasn't sure which. In either case, he had moved closer to the hall, closer to her bedroom. Closer to her.

She briefly contemplated climbing out a window, but she still had the storm panes up, so exiting through a window would entail breaking through the double layer of glass. She might cut herself, to say nothing of the expense and hassle of replacing the Thermopane.

She stood, tiptoed to her closet and pulled out an empty hanger. It was wood, with a hard metal hook. If she could fight her way to the kitchen, she could phone the police—and grab a knife. She'd feel a lot better if she had a knife in her hand.

The hanger alone might not be enough weaponry. She lifted one of her thick-soled L.L. Bean work boots from the closet floor. It weighed a good two or three pounds. If need be, she could throw it at the creep, then whack him with the hanger.

Drawing in another steadying breath, she tucked the hanger under her arm and eased the door open. She heard the invader's heavy footsteps and the thud of her own heart, now beating in a dirge tempo. Appropriate, if death was imminent.

No, Erica wasn't going to die. She had her hanger and her boot. She could make it to the kitchen, grab the phone—or bolt through the back door. And flee to Jed's—not because he was Jed, not because he was so damn tall and strong looking, but because he was her only neighbor.

She peered down the hall. The living room was dark, but light from the kitchen spilled a glowing rectangle through the doorway and onto the carpet. She crept down the hall, wishing she'd paused to throw on a bathrobe over the baggy cotton T-shirt she slept in, then froze when she heard another cabinet door slam, followed by the incoherent growl of a male voice. Edging closer, she was able to decipher a couple of the words. They were uniformly foul.

She sidled a little closer to the doorway, tightened her grip on her weapons and charged through the door, screaming, "Get out! Get out!" while waving the hanger and the boot above her head.

"Jesus Effin' Cripes!" Toad Regan screamed back, flattening himself against her refrigerator, looking terrified.

"What are you doing in here? Get out!" Erica shrieked, hoping volume would frighten him off. He smelled like cheap booze and old dust, and cracker crumbs were caught in his scraggly beard, probably left over from the snacks he'd wolfed down earlier that evening.

"I'm not doin' anything! Stop waving that stick at me." He seemed to regain his courage, unfortunately. Pushing away from the refrigerator, he approached her.

If she fell back, she'd appear weak. She held her ground and continued to brandish the hanger. "How did you get in here?"

"Walked," he said. "I'm not askin' for any trouble—"

"You broke into my house!"

"Oh, come on. You know who I am. It ain't no big thing."

"And you're banging around in my cabinets—" He took another step toward her and she extended the hanger as if it were a sword. "Breaking and entering. That's a crime, Toad."

"I didn't break nothin'."

"Get out of my house."

"Come on. Just show me the box and then I'll go."

She sighed. Of course. Her first burglar, hoping to steal the box. "It isn't here."

"Yeah, right." He snorted, then lunged for the hanger. For a disheveled, malodorous town drunk, he was pretty quick, and his eyes glinted with malice. He gripped her wrist with surprising strength, but she refused to let go of the hanger. "Just show me the box and I'm outta here," he promised. "And don't give me none of this stuff about it's not here. School-teachers ain't supposed to lie."

It occurred to her that now would be a good time to start being frightened. Toad Regan tightened his hold on her. He stood nose to nose with her, his breath beery, his gaze nasty, his fingers meeting in a bruising circle around her wrist. He could hurt her.

She swung her left arm up and smacked the side of his head with her boot. Her left hand wasn't her dominant one, but even if the impact didn't stun him, it startled him.

"Hey, you bitch! What're kickin' me for?"

"I didn't—" She hesitated, realizing that in a way she *had* kicked him—and realizing further that this wasn't a good time to argue with him. He was still holding her wrist, squeezing it so tightly her fingers began to go numb as they clung to the hanger. "Let go of me!"

"I'll let go when you show me the box."

"It's not here," she snapped.

"Let go of her," a voice came from the kitchen doorway. A man's voice. A hushed, threatening voice.

Toad released her and spun around. Jed stood on the threshold, tall and hulking and powerful. His hair was mussed; his eyes, squinting; one hand was fisted and the other held a candy cane.

And she'd thought she might have looked silly carrying a hanger and a boot.

Even wielding a candy cane, Jed cast a menacing shadow across the room. Toad seemed to lose an inch in height. "Hey, Willetz," he muttered. It occurred to Erica that, Toad's thinning hair, hollow cheeks and sunken eyes notwithstanding, he might be not much older than Jed.

"What are you doing here?"

"Just looking for a place to sleep. You know me." Toad laughed nervously.

"I don't think Ms. Leitner wants you sleeping with her," Jed said, his tone laced with such deep condemnation that Erica couldn't take issue with his phrasing. "Were you planning to bed down in her kitchen?"

"Well, I was just…you know, looking around before I settled down."

"Looking for what?"

"The box," Erica said.

"Okay, so…so…" Toad shifted from one foot to another, refusing to meet either Jed's or Erica's gaze. "So, okay, so what's one coin, right? To you it's nothing. You got plenty more. You wouldn't 'a even noticed."

"Get out," Jed snapped.

"How'm I gonna get back to town?" Toad whined.

"Same way you got here. Go away, Toad. And don't you ever come back here uninvited. You understand?" Jed stepped farther into the kitchen, leaving Toad a clear path to the door.

Toad took it, casting Erica a final, doleful look as if he actually expected her to ask him to stay. She glowered at him and he slunk out of the house. Jed slammed the door behind him, then wedged a chair under the knob.

"That door was locked," she said. An unwanted tremor tugged at her voice, and her knees suddenly felt wobbly.

"Are you all right?" Jed strode toward her, clasped her arm and led her to one of the other chairs. She sank into it and understood from his worried expression that she must have appeared on the verge of fainting. He moved to the sink and filled a glass with water for her.

"I'm fine," she said shakily. Damn. She didn't want to faint. Not in front of Jed. Not while all she was wearing was an oversize baby-blue T-shirt and panties.

"Drink this," he ordered, pressing the glass into her hand. Noticing the bruise Toad had left on her wrist, he cursed. "Son of a bitch. I can't believe he did this to you."

"I don't understand." She took a sip of water. It felt cold and soothing, so she took another sip. "The door was locked—"

"I could break that lock with a credit card," Jed told her. "People don't take locks seriously in Rockwell, because no one except you bothers to use them. Maybe we should ice your wrist."

"Oh, it's nothing." She studied it belatedly. More red than blue. It would probably fade in a few minutes.

"I should have punched his lights out," Jed muttered, hunkering in front of Erica, gently probing her hand and wrist as if he thought the bone might be fractured.

She flexed her fingers to show him her limb was operational. His touch irked her, made her want to touch him back, to weave her fingers through his and feel his palm against hers. Heaven help her, she was sitting just inches from Jed, dressed in next to nothing. She definitely should have put on her robe before she'd ventured out of her bedroom.

"Stop being so macho," she chided, wishing she could put some distance, both physical and emotional, between Jed and herself. "I had the situation under control."

"With a boot and coat hanger?"

"A dress hanger," she said. "It's better than a candy cane. What are you doing here, anyway, Jed? How did you know to come over?"

He leaned back on his haunches and grinned sheepishly. "Okay," he said, as though about to embark on a long, involved story. "I quit smoking a few months ago. I still have cravings. I was having a real bad one tonight. I'm sick of sourballs and chewing gum, and I've gone through most of my grandfather's supply of toothpicks, so I was poking around in his cabinets, hoping to find something to take the edge off. And I found this candy cane." He eyed it as if seeing it for the first time, and laid it on the table. "I don't know how long the stuff has been sitting in that cabinet. I'm assuming it's from this past Christmas and not some Christmas ten years ago."

He paused, apparently waiting for acknowledgment. Erica nodded dutifully.

"So I took the candy cane and went out on the porch. Because I wanted the whole experience, you know? I always used to go outside to have a smoke, so tonight I went outside to have a candy cane. And I saw your back door standing open, and I heard voices. And…" His smile faded as he searched her face. "Are you upset that I'm here?"

"No." She would have liked to have handled Toad by herself, but she hadn't been able to get rid of the jerk on her own. Her hanger and her boot hadn't been anywhere near as effective as a few pointed words from Jed Willetz.

She wanted to be self-sufficient. She wanted to be connected to her town, her neighbors and most of all to herself and her own inner resources. If Jed hadn't come along, though… She was pretty sure Toad was harmless, but she just didn't know.

Another tremor fluttered through her. Jed must have noticed, because his eyes narrowed slightly, his face tightening with concern. "Are you okay?"

Yes. No. He was still hunkered down in front of her, his face close to hers. His hair glinted with blond highlights in the overhead light, and his expression was so worried, more worried than a neighbor might have been, much more worried than any guy just passing through town ought to be. He was way too close, and she knew what kissing him was like, and she didn't want to be alone right now. She'd just survived a traumatic incident, and she didn't want Jed to leave her.

HE RECOGNIZED THE LOOK in her eyes. It spoke more eloquently than her "let's not get started" and "what's the point?'' and everything else she'd ever said to turn him away. She'd had a scare—*he'd* had a scare—and now they both needed some comfort. That was what her eyes told him.

He straightened up, lifting her to her feet as he stood, and then covered her mouth with his. She tasted like spearmint, and her cheeks were still warm and soft from bed. Her shirt did little to conceal the curves of her body, and the fabric was so thin he could practically feel the texture of her skin as he flattened his hands against her back.

She could have gotten hurt. That idiot Toad Regan could have injured her just so he could steal a gold coin.

Jed was a modern man, with great respect for feminism. Most of the women he knew could defend themselves, and wanted to. Erica had defended herself with a boot and a hanger. Christ. If something had happened to her, it would have just about killed him.

She kissed him with more passion than he'd known her slender body could contain. She held on to him more tightly than she'd been holding on to her hanger. He felt the roundness of her breasts through her shirt, the swollen tips of her nipples, the heat down below, where her hips met his. If they hadn't been standing in the middle of her kitchen, he'd have torn off her shirt. And his own.

They were going to have to get the hell out of this kitchen, because he needed them both naked, and soon. His body ached with a craving much deeper and more harrowing than his craving for a cigarette just a few minutes ago.

He broke from her, and she made a desperate little moan. He had to close his eyes and take a breath to keep that sound from triggering something crazy inside him. He liked women, he loved them, but he'd never wanted one as much as he wanted Erica right now. This brave, crazy woman with her boot and her hanger, her dark, dark eyes and all that hair, and her ability to turn a pound of ground beef into the most tasteless slop he'd ever eaten—but he'd eaten it because she'd made it, because she was Erica and he wanted her.

She gazed up at him, and her expression made him want her even more. He bowed to kiss her again, just a quick, light kiss to tide him over until they reached her bed. Gathering her hand in his, he ushered her out of the kitchen and down the hall. Halfway there he had to stop for another kiss. She pulled him to her, sliding her hands under his flannel shirt and across his T-shirt, following the contours of his chest. He pressed her up against the wall and leaned into her, making himself even crazier. He couldn't seem to help himself, though. Her hair rained over the backs of his hands and her tongue tangled with his and her hips met his, and he wanted to break out of his skin, to burst wide open, to give himself, body and soul, to her.

He shoved up her nightshirt, bunching it up around her waist and sliding his hands underneath. She jumped, then sighed as his hands moved over her, tracing her waist, the lower edge of her rib cage and upward. She moaned again when he cupped her breasts. He moaned, too.

''Jed,'' she whispered.

Don't stop us, he prayed silently, brushing his thumbs over her nipples and feeling her jump again. *Whatever you do, Erica, don't shut me down.*

She arched slightly, her fingers fisting against his sides. ''I have...'' Her voice faded into a sigh.

"What?" he asked.

"Condoms."

Thank you, God, he mouthed. He hadn't brought anything with him. He hadn't expected this.

"They're in the bathroom."

That was an odd place to keep them, unless she was in the habit of having sex in the tub. But then, if Pop Hackett had been telling the truth about her social life, she wasn't in the habit of having sex at all. Maybe she kept the things there because that was where she stored items she never used.

He slid his hands out from under her shirt and backed up, giving her room to pass. He was so aroused it hurt to walk. She led the way into the bathroom off the hall. Opening the mirrored medicine cabinet above the sink, she stared at the bottle of ibuprofen, the tube of first-aid cream and the small white box of dental floss, then abandoned that for the vanity under the sink. There, amid stacks of toilet paper, bottles of shampoo and a plunger, she located an unopened package of rubbers. Bless her. Bless the world. Jed wasn't a religious man, but he was definitely experiencing the more miraculous side of life right now.

He took the package from her, then clasped her hand and drew her out of the bathroom, this time heading straight to her bedroom. No more detours, no more delays. He needed her now.

Without fanfare, he shrugged out of his flannel shirt and dropped it on the floor. His T-shirt followed, and when she ran her hands over his bare shoulders, her fingers cool and graceful, it felt so good he fumbled with his fly. If he couldn't even handle a belt buckle and a zipper, how was he going to handle her? He felt like a kid again, that first time—with JoAnn Meese, in

the back of Stuart Farnham's flatbed. He'd been six-
teen years old, awkward and way too eager. Fortunately, she'd been kind of tanked, so she hadn't noticed
what a lousy job he'd done of it.

Erica would notice, and there was no way in hell he
was going to do a lousy job with her, if he could only
slow down a little, get a grip, catch his breath. But
how was he supposed to do that when she nudged his
hands away and undid his fly for him, when she
skimmed her hands under the slack waistband of his
jeans and pushed them down? His briefs got caught on
his erection, and when she freed him from the fabric
he gasped at her touch.

Erica.

He hauled her nightshirt over her head, then hesitated at the sight of her panties. They were cream-
colored lace, fancy and sexy without being obvious.
Feminine. Ladylike—no, *woman*-like. He stroked her
bottom through the lace, then brought his hand forward
and down between her legs. She sank onto the bed,
and with some small regret, since they were so allur-
ing, he pulled the panties off her.

Where was the package of condoms? He'd tossed it
onto the bed, but the blanket was rumpled and…damn,
he had to slow down. Had to touch her all over, first.
Had to kiss her all over, had to taste the skin of her
throat and take her breasts with his mouth. They were
plumper than he'd expected, not large but big enough.
Oh, and her belly button, a narrow slit centered on her
flat, smooth abdomen. He slid his tongue down into
the dark curls between her legs and she let out a cry.
He nearly came just from that sound.

Where the hell were the condoms? He rose onto his
knees and groped the bed linens in search of them,

distracted by the dance of her hands on his back, on his thighs, grazing his balls. He located the box behind a lump in the blanket, tore frantically at the plastic wrap and finally broke it open. Square foil packets spilled out, and as he grabbed one she made his life difficult by rising up and kissing his chest. Did she know how insane she was making him? Did she have any idea?

Of course she did. She was intelligent, a teacher, a Harvard grad. She knew exactly what she was doing, brushing her tongue over his nipple, reaching down again to caress him. When he pulled back to look at her, he wasn't surprised to see a shy smile curving her lips.

Shy. Yeah, right. Any shier and she'd be giving him a heart attack.

He barely got the sheath on before she lay back, bringing him down with her, guiding him home. Oh, it was good. She was so hot, so tight and wet. So sweet, her hips rising to welcome him, her legs wound around his, her hands on his back, one at his waist and one sliding up into his hair. Her whole body moved with every thrust, every part of her responding, every bit of flesh, bone and blood sharing in the pleasure of it. She breathed in rhythm with him.

His muscles ached from holding back. His soul ached from wanting something so much, wanting *someone* so much. He'd never realized making love could be so wonderfully painful.

Making love. This wasn't just sex. This was Erica, smart and stubborn, the worst cook he'd ever met, not much better at gardening, but so optimistic, so eager to find beauty in a place as crummy as Rockwell. So willing to give. He'd wanted to give himself to her, but she was doing all the giving, opening to him, drawing him deep, holding nothing back.

Her hand fisted at the small of his back. Her other hand tugged at his hair. Her body tensed like a bowstring and he stopped moving. ''No,'' she whispered, ''Don't stop, Jed, I need...''

He started moving again, harder and faster, and she let go, shaking, pulsing, clinging to him as a quiet sob tore from her throat. She seemed to surround him, wrapped as tight as a second skin around him, and it was all he could do to keep pumping, trying to give her just a little more, take her just a little further. He felt the second wave sweep through her, heard her cry and gave up, gave in, gave her everything he had.

For a long time afterward he remained where he was, on top of her, buried inside her. The sweat on his back began to dry, cooling him. Her hands roamed slowly along his spine, his sides, the back of his neck, and her breath danced across his shoulder. He tried to think but his mind seemed to have short-circuited. Every half-glimpsed thought sizzled and fried and dissolved into nothing. He ought to get off her, but he wasn't sure he had the energy to move, and anyway, he didn't want to. Lying right where he was, still hard inside her, felt way too good.

''Jed?'' Her voice came out low and scratchy.

He hoped she wasn't going to start a conversation. He lacked the brainpower to sustain his half of one.

''What?'' he asked warily, finding the strength to lift himself enough to see her face.

She smiled hesitantly. ''Don't leave,'' she said.

Perfect. No demands for commitments. Just two words, two perfect words. ''I won't leave,'' he promised, then lowered his lips to hers.

CHAPTER THIRTEEN

SOMEONE WAS POUNDING on the back door.

Erica opened one eye and squinted at the clock-radio. Ten-thirty. She heard the pounding again.

The heavy arm slung around her waist shifted, and she began to piece together where she was, what she'd done and whom she'd done it with. That sinewy arm offered a pretty strong hint. So did the solid warmth of the man lying behind her, his chest against her back and his legs paralleling hers, his knees bent behind hers, his insteps offering a convenient perch for her feet.

Jed. Having him in her bed made her feel deliciously lazy, suspiciously achy and in no hurry to find out who was knocking on her door. "Ignore it," he whispered into her hair.

"It could be reporters."

He hoisted himself high enough to peer over her at the clock. Then, probably because, like Everest, it was there, he kissed her shoulder.

Heat flooded her. She had figured Jed would be good in bed—he had such a rugged aura, such certainty in his movements, such confidence in his attitude—but she hadn't expected the tenderness, those little kisses and caresses that had nothing to do with pleasing him and everything to do with making her feel special and beloved.

"If reporters were going to come to your house," he said, pushing her hair out of his way so he could drop another kiss behind her ear, "they'd have shown up hours ago."

She remembered the morning a few days ago when reporters had indeed shown up before sunrise. They'd remained in her front yard, too. This morning's visitor was at her back door. It must be someone local, someone she knew. Fern, maybe? Fern and Avery Gilman, armed with a bottle of champagne to celebrate their engagement?

Where in Rockwell would they get a bottle of champagne?

"I'd better go see who it is," she said, reluctantly pushing herself up to sit. Jed groaned, but he didn't restrain her.

She found her panties on the floor and her T-shirt dangling over the edge of the dresser. After donning those items, she pulled her bathrobe from its hanger and tied it around her waist. She'd learned her lesson last night. A lot could happen if you wandered out of the bedroom without a bathrobe on.

Turning, she gazed at Jed for a minute. The blanket covered certain sensitive parts of his body, but enough was exposed—the muscular hump of his shoulder, one lean leg, a sleek stretch of chest—to ignite another rush of warmth inside her. His jaw sported a stubble one shade darker than the tousled hair on his head, and his eyes were closed. He looked exhausted.

As if that was surprising. What they'd done last night—all through the night, one heavenly time after another—had required a greater output of energy from him than from her.

"You can go back to sleep," she offered.

He rolled onto his side and burrowed into her pillow. The motion sent a square foil packet flying from the folds of the blanket. They'd used a fair number of condoms last night, but not her entire supply, the remains of which lay scattered about the bed. "If it's Toad," he mumbled, "scream loud."

It wouldn't be Toad. Jed had scared the spit out of him last night. He wouldn't dare to come back, unless it was to apologize.

Still, she tied the sash of her robe a bit more securely around her waist before shuffling down the hall and into the kitchen. Through the window in the back door she spotted a baseball cap with the inscription Triple X, the Sexy Beer.

Sighing, she moved the chair Jed had used to bar the door, and opened it. "Hi," Randy Rideout greeted her in his shrill, prepubescent voice. "Check this out!" He unzipped his jacket to reveal a T-shirt reading Rockwell—the Town of Hidden Treasures. Below the words was a rendering of a treasure chest, its lid open and gold coins mounded above the rim, with a few stray coins outside the box.

"Where did you get that?" Erica asked, stepping aside and waving him in.

"They're for sale in town. Pop Hackett's got 'em at the Superette, and my dad got some to sell in his bar."

"How did they get them printed up so fast?"

"There's this silkscreen place..." Randy gazed around the kitchen. Looking for food, Erica guessed as she pulled a bag of store-bought chocolate chip cookies from a cabinet. Not a healthy snack, especially not at that morning hour, but she wasn't about to whip up a batch of whole-grain pancakes for the boy. Her legs were sore; her breasts, tender from all the attention Jed had lavished on them last night. The skin under her chin felt tingly from whisker burn. She wasn't in the mood to cook something nutritious.

Even if she hadn't spent the night making love with Jed, she wouldn't be inclined to make whole-grain pancakes. She'd tried making them once and they'd come out flavorless and gritty.

Randy gave her a grateful smile before digging into the bag of cookies. "Anyway," he continued, "Pop Hackett called up this silkscreen place and ordered some T-shirts. They said it would take a week, but Derrick Messinger—you know that TV star—well, he was at my dad's bar and he said he could pull some strings and get the shirts printed up overnight."

"Really." Erica pursed her lips. Messinger struck her as just the sort of man who could pull strings.

"Hey, is that a candy cane?" Randy scampered to the table, lifted the candy cane and laughed uproariously. "It's April! Who has a candy cane in April?"

Someone who's just quit smoking, Erica almost answered, wondering if Randy had noticed the hanger and the hiking boot lying on the floor in the table's shadow. She discreetly picked up those items and carried them into the dining room.

Randy tossed the candy cane back onto the table, opting for the more substantial satisfactions of chocolate chip cookies. "I think that Derrick Messinger guy charged my dad to get the shirts printed faster," he said as Erica returned to the kitchen. "My dad and Pop Hackett were talking about paying him."

She nodded and beelined to the coffeepot. After placing a filter in the basket, she measured the coffee, adding a few extra scoops even though she hoped Jed would remain out of sight.

"And Mrs. Ettman said she ordered these little souvenir boxes shaped like the actual box, and she was gonna sell them. She said the boxes already existed, but she was gonna put stickers on them that say Rockwell—the Town of Hidden Treasures just like the shirts. She says this is going to put us on the map."

"Wonderful." Erica couldn't quite bring herself to share Randy's enthusiasm. Was her backyard find going to turn Rockwell into a tourist destination? Were legions of treasure seekers going to descend upon the town armed with picks and shovels? Was this quiet little village in the shadow of the Moose Mountains going to become the site of the next American gold rush?

If she'd wanted to live in a community overrun with money-hungry treasure seekers, she could have settled in Boston.

The coffeemaker gurgled and the air grew heavy with the aroma of fresh coffee. "Would you like some milk with those cookies?" Erica asked as Randy bit into a second cookie.

He opened his mouth to answer, then froze, staring past her. She spun around to discover Jed looming in the doorway. He was clothed, thank goodness, but disheveled, his eyes squinty and his jaw in need of a shave.

"I smelled coffee," he said.

Randy might be somewhat naive, but he wasn't an idiot. Would he figure out why Jed Willetz, sleepy, rumpled and barefoot, was standing in her kitchen at ten-thirty in the morning? When she was wearing a bathrobe? Not that she'd done anything to be ashamed of, not that she had to justify her private life to anyone, let alone an eleven-year-old kid. But this wasn't Boston, or New York, or even Brookline. It was Rockwell, where folks made everyone else's business their own and where she was a third-grade teacher to whom Rockwellians entrusted their children for six hours every weekday.

"You're that guy," Randy said, evidently recognizing Jed. He wagged a finger. "That guy from the picture in the *Gazette,* with Ms. Leitner and the box. And you came into my dad's bar, too."

"That's me," Jed said amiably. He opened cabinets until he found the one containing coffee mugs and pulled out two. "I just need a little coffee to start my engine, and then I'll be on my way," he told Erica.

"Oh, you don't have to..." Well, yes, he did have to be on his way. He had things to do. So did she. She had to go to the bank with Avery, retrieve the box and send it and him back to Cambridge, where he and his expert colleagues could figure out the box's age and significance and what it was worth. She had to return at least some of the calls she'd gotten last night—a list Jed had neatly jotted on a pad beside the phone. Her mother, her college roommate and her cousin Diana all merited calls from her. She wouldn't bother returning the calls from three old and nearly forgotten boy-friends, who probably assumed she was now rich and therefore worthy of their renewed passion.

She had no passion for them. She had passion for only one man, an amazingly virile, tender man who, in a matter of days, would be gone from her life.

Why on earth had she slept with him last night, knowing he was only passing through?

She'd been needy, frightened, overwhelmed. No, that wasn't why. Once Toad had been banished, she hadn't been frightened anymore. Or overwhelmed. A stiff drink would have calmed her nerves. She hadn't turned to Jed for therapy.

She'd turned to him because she'd wanted him, because she was no better than any of the other women in town eager to drop their panties for him. She'd turned to him because he was a friend and a sounding board, and because on the excitement scale, kissing him had surpassed receiving her *magna cum laude* diploma from Harvard University, and if kissing him could be that fabulous, making love with him would be even better.

She'd turned to him because last night she'd gotten tired of running away from her own desires, because she could no longer pretend he meant nothing to her. He meant a lot. Too much. And as soon as he drank some coffee, he would be on his way.

Okay, she assured herself. *You did this, it was worth it, and you'll have plenty of time to recuperate once he's gone.* What better place than Rockwell for such a recuperation? Nothing ever happened here. She lived alone—and she'd be even more alone as soon as Jed vacated his grandfather's house. Her life comprised simple routines and nothing unexpected: teach, come home, master wholesome recipes, grade papers, read, garden. Surely she could schedule in some time for nursing a broken heart.

"So, I was wondering," Randy said as he polished off his third cookie, "can we finish planting your garden?"

"You're not just saying that because you're hoping to dig up more treasures, are you?" Erica asked him. She was grateful for the opportunity to focus on her garden—and on her young friend. It spared her from having to think about Jed standing just a few feet away, his strong, deft hands lifting the decanter and filling a mug with coffee, his lips pressed to the rim of the mug, his tongue bathed in the hot, fragrant brew. She'd rather look at Randy, with his tacky shirt and tackier cap, than at Jed, with his luminous eyes and his irresistible smile. She'd rather think about her silly garden, which would wind up overrun either by zucchini or by crazed treasure seekers armed with rakes and spades, than about the intimacies she and Jed had shared throughout a long, astonishingly X-rated night.

"Oh, I don't think there's anything else buried in your garden," Randy said. "I mean, like, it wouldn't make sense. Someone wants to hide his gold, if he had more than one box, he wouldn't hide it all in one place. Right? He'd spread it around. I mean, if he was going to hide it all in one place, he'd put the whole amount in a bigger box, right?"

"That makes sense." Erica glanced over at Jed to see if it made sense to him. He was watching her above the curved rim of his mug, his gaze pensive. "Doesn't that make sense to you?" she asked brightly. *See?* she hoped to convey. *We can forget about last night and spend the morning theorizing about the box. We can act as if nothing more important than that stupid, gold-filled artifact exists between us.*

His expression unchanging, he shrugged.

All right. Maybe he couldn't forget about last night. *She* could, damn it. *She* could pretend last night was ancient history and this morning she and Jed were nothing more than friends and neighbors, which was probably all they were, anyway. "I'll tell you what, Randy. Let me change into some appropriate gardening clothes, and then we'll plant the rest of those seedlings.

But then I've got to go into town and take care of business.''

"Yeah, and maybe buy a shirt." He pulled at his loose-fitting cotton T-shirt. "Buy it from my dad, okay?"

"We'll see." She wasn't sure she wanted to own such an ugly shirt, and if she did decide to buy one, she wasn't sure she wanted to purchase it from a man who'd hired an attorney and was making legal claims against her. She didn't hold Glenn Rideout's behavior against his son, but she was no fan of Glenn's, especially when he might wind up becoming her adversary in court, fighting over the fate of the box.

God, these small-minded small-town people. If someone had dug up a box of antique gold coins in Cambridge, the commemorative shirts would have featured more appealing designs—some interesting colors, teal and mauve, maybe, and better lettering, and an illustration that resembled the actual box. But if it had happened in Cambridge, she wouldn't have spent the next day working on her garden. In Cambridge, only multimillionaires could afford enough land to plant a garden, and even if all the coins in the box turned out to be genuine gold, she was no multimillionaire. Only in a town like Rockwell could an untenured third-grade teacher inching into her late twenties afford enough property to plant a garden.

Rockwell was fine. She was fine. And when Jed Willetz left town… She'd still be fine. She'd garden and cook and continue to fix up her house, and she'd join some committees. She'd find a way to weave her life more thoroughly into the town's fabric. She had a good situation in Rockwell, a town so warm and friendly that when someone broke into her house she knew the trespasser by name.

Even when Jed was long gone, she'd be all right.

FLAGS AND BANNERS were out along Main Street. So were reporters, lurking on street corners, interrogating pedestrians and doing stand-ups in front of Hackett's Superette, which sported a big placard reading We've Got Official Treasure T-shirts! right above the sign advertising fifty cents off on all varieties of Cap'n Crunch. The sight of those reporters and the hoopla made Jed want to climb back into his turquoise rental car and floor the gas.

How far would he drive? Back to his grandfather's house or back to New York City? He had to leave; he knew he had to. But...

Erica.

After phenomenal sex, wasn't he supposed to want a cigarette? All he'd wanted after making love with her—all he *still* wanted—was her. It hadn't just been sex last night. They'd talked, too, about her students, about some of his more profitable junk purchases, about what Avery would do with the box, about what she found so appealing about this hideous little town, and what he found so hideous about it.

How could Erica stand it here?

It didn't matter. She had a dream, and she'd made a choice. So they'd had some good healthy sex, and now he would bury his grandfather's ashes and go back where he belonged.

Too bad Erica thought she belonged in this dive.

He'd already stopped in at the Congregational church to talk to the Reverend Pith about having a graveside ceremony for his grandfather. Last night, around 2:00 a.m., after he and Erica had made love for the third time and they'd been lying facing each other, her hands resting against his chest while he toyed with her hair, winding it around his fingers and then releasing it so it slid against his palms, he'd asked her what she thought about skipping a church service and just saying a few words at the burial site. "My grandfather wasn't exactly a religious guy, you know," he'd said. "He probably wouldn't have been thrilled about the church service we did back in January. Two church services would really piss him off."

"Then just do the graveside ceremony."

"I think Reena Keefer would be okay with that, if she'd even bother to show up."

"Reena Keefer?"

"The syrup lady. She and my grandfather had a thing going."

Erica had leaned back and stared at him, obviously surprised. "I didn't know that."

If she'd truly belonged in Rockwell, she would have known it. But Jed hadn't lingered on that thought. "I need to work it all out with Reverend Pith and Sewell McCormick."

"The podiatrist? What does he have to do with it?"

"He manages the cemetery."

"You're kidding. And he's the town manager, too."

"A regular Renaissance man, ol' Sewell."

Erica had laughed, allowing Jed the tiny hope that maybe she understood what a joke Rockwell was. But that hope had flickered out like an extinguished flame when she'd opted to work on her garden with the Rideout kid today. A woman planning to pull up roots didn't plant zucchini in her backyard.

So he'd gone to the church himself, awakened the

minister from an early siesta at his desk and secured his agreement to say a few appropriate words next Tuesday over John Willetz's ashes before they were buried next to his wife's remains on the hill overlooking the moribund granite quarry. "Don't make the words appropriate," Jed had cautioned Pith. "Make them nice."

He'd found Sewell McCormick outside his podiatry office, doing an interview with a reporter from the *Burlington Free Press.* Sewell was cheerleading about Rockwell with such spirit Jed wished he had some pom-poms to give the guy. Not wanting to hang around while Sewell did his town-booster routine, Jed decided he'd work out the cemetery arrangements later and headed back down Main Street to where he'd parked his car. Along the way he passed Harriet Ettman's crafts shop, its window filled with brown wooden boxes adorned with cheap decals reading Rockwell—the Town of Hidden Treasures on the lids. Why would anyone buy such an ugly box? What would you put in it? Cigarettes, if you smoked. And cigarettes were nobody's treasure. As he walked past, the shop's door swung open and two vaguely familiar-looking women bounded out carrying paper bags, each of which contained a bulge the shape of the boxes.

All right. People were making money from Erica's find. She'd make money, too. Derrick Messinger, with his idiotic TV special, would make money. Why not? If Jed could earn a living out of junk, why shouldn't the residents of his hometown do the same thing?

He was nearing Rideout's Ride, when Derrick Messinger's two colleagues—the woman with the Noo-Yawk accent and the burly cameraman—emerged. The cameraman had on a Town of Hidden Treasures

T-shirt, but the woman maintained her urban chic, dressed in formfitting black. "Hey, there, you!" she called to Jed.

Jed could have pretended not to hear her, but Sewell McCormick at the other end of Main Street had probably heard her, and Jed wasn't that good an actor. He approached the concrete steps leading up to the bar's entry. "Yeah?"

"I hear you're living in Manhattan," she said.

Great. The Rockwell grapevine had sprouted runners beyond town limits. "That's right."

"What I was thinking, since you've got connections here, maybe you could be our liaison. You know what a liaison is?"

Jed scowled. "We may be Yankee rustics up here, but we're not morons."

"Well…" She glanced behind her at the bar. "The majority of the people in there did not know what a liaison was."

"The majority of the people in there probably started drinking hours ago," Jed pointed out, although he wouldn't be surprised if even a completely sober Matty Blancher wouldn't know the word. "And no, I'm not interested in being your liaison."

"You wouldn't have to do anything," the woman explained, determined in spite of his rebuff. "Just let us know if there are any new developments. This being our story, after all, the story Derrick Messinger broke on national TV."

"He did a hell of a lot better with this story than with his search for Jimmy Hoffa, didn't he."

The woman's expression hardened to stone, but the cameraman let out a guffaw. "Hey, sometimes you've

gotta shoot a lot of arrows if you want to hit a target,"
he said.

"If you've got bad aim," Jed countered.

The cameraman laughed again. He struck Jed as
someone it would take a lot of effort to insult. "Sonya
still hasn't gotten her sense of humor back after that
fiasco."

"I have, too," said the woman as she dug through
the black canvas purse hanging from a shoulder strap.
"As a matter of fact, the numbers from yesterday's
broadcast did wonders for my sense of humor.
Here—" she presented Jed with a business card
"—just in case. I thought about giving your dad my
card, but I got the feeling he'd charge an arm and a
leg for any information."

"That's him," Jed said with a nod. He pocketed the
woman's card and hoped he'd remember to remove it
before he tossed his jeans into the laundry.

"How about you give me your phone number, just
in case?" she persevered.

"Just in case what?"

She sighed. "You're the only person in town who
knows what a liaison is. Come on, be a sport." She
pulled out a notepad.

He considered, then recited the phone number of his
showroom. "City Resale," he told her. "That's my
store."

"Great. You be my liaison, and maybe I'll buy
something."

"Whatever." He turned to the cameraman. "So how
much is Rideout asking for the shirt?"

"I don't know. I bought this down at the grocery
store. We came in here looking for liaisons, and the

bartender got steamed that I didn't buy my shirt from him. It's pretty awful, isn't it.''

"The shirt or the bartender's reaction?"

The cameraman laughed again. "Both."

"Come on," the woman said, starting down the steps. "We've got to go rescue Derrick before he makes a fool of himself with that redhead. Thanks again," she said to Jed. "Jack, right?"

"Jack's my father," he corrected her.

"Oh. John, then, is it?"

Before he could correct her again, she was strutting down the sidewalk, checking her watch and adjusting her chichi sunglasses. The cameraman nodded his farewell and lumbered down the street after her.

Since Jed was already on the porch, he decided to enter Rideout's Ride. If his father was there, he could discuss his plans for the graveside ceremony. It seemed that the only reason he ever entered Rideout's Ride was to see if his father was inside.

Once Jed adjusted to the dim, smoky light, he realized Jack Willetz wasn't among the bar's patrons. The place was a bit more hopping than usual—maybe a dozen guys in late middle age occupied the tables, interspersing friendly conversation with shots of booze. Glenn Rideout looked atypically happy, his smile emphasizing the length of his chin. Right across the bar from him, Jed's father's accountant perched on a stool.

"Jed!" the man bellowed. "Remember me? Potter Henley." He shoved his beefy right hand toward Jed, who gave it a polite shake.

"I was just searching for my father," he told Rideout before the guy could pressure him into ordering a drink.

"He's not here," Rideout said. "You want to buy

a T-shirt?'' He lifted one from behind the counter, shook out the folds and displayed it in all its tasteless glory.

"No, thanks. I've got more T-shirts than I know what to do with.''

"But this one's a collector's item.''

"I'll pass.''

Rideout scowled, crumpled the shirt into a ball and tossed it onto a shelf behind the bar. "Don't know why I care. By the time my lawyer is done with Erica Leitner, I'll be so rich a few T-shirt sales won't make a difference.''

An alarm bell sounded inside Jed's skull. "What do you mean, by the time your lawyer is *done* with Erica?'' he asked.

Potter Henley broke in, yelling, "I bet you're going to have to sell old John Willetz's place to cover the taxes.''

The interruption annoyed Jed. "Why?'' he asked impatiently.

"It's always that way. Someone inherits a nice piece of real estate and then has to sell it to raise money to cover the taxes. I'm betting your grandfather's place has a huge tax assessment attached to it. And you're not even going to be using the house. 'Course, it's possible you could do away with that tax bill altogether by handing title to the house over to someone else.''

"Who would I hand it over to?''

"Your dad,'' Potter shouted. "You sell him the house for a token amount—say, a dollar—and then he has to pay the taxes on it.''

Jed laughed sourly. "You're my dad's accountant. You know what he'd do if I sold him the place for a buck. He'd turn around and sell it for a couple hundred thousand and pocket the profit.''

"You'd save yourself a nice little tax bill," Potter noted.

"Big deal." Jed turned back to Rideout, who was grinning smugly. "So, Glenn, what exactly is your lawyer going to do to Erica?" he asked, struggling to keep his voice low, under control.

"He's just talking big," Potter Henley explained, not making any effort to keep his voice low. "He thinks that old box is actually worth something."

"The box, I don't know," Rideout said. "But what's inside the box, all those pretty gold coins? You bet they're worth something. And my boy found them. My lawyer's gonna make sure everyone, starting with the schoolteacher and ending with *everyone,* knows who dug 'em up. It wasn't the schoolteacher. It was my son. Finders, keepers.''

Jed doubted a lawyer could successfully argue that the box belonged to Rideout—or his son. If the kid had gone into Erica's house and found a diamond necklace in a drawer, would he have a claim on it? This was pretty much the same thing: the kid had been on Erica's property and found a box. That didn't make it his.

But Jed didn't like Rideout's implication. He knew what lawyers were like. They could badger and intimidate a person until she gave in out of fear or weariness. Erica seemed tough, but she was trying so hard to be a part of the community here, she might not be willing to fight someone as established in Rockwell as Glenn Rideout.

Even if she was willing, she shouldn't have to fight him. The guy was a jerk, and he'd probably gone and hired himself a bottom-feeder who'd make Erica feel like a traitor to Rockwell if she didn't share her bounty with the Rideouts.

"Actually," Jed said, straightening his shoulders and staring directly into Glenn's marble-hard eyes, "the box was on my land. If anyone has a claim on it, it's me."

"What are you talking about?"

"It was technically on my grandfather's land—which is now mine."

Rideout appeared agitated. He hissed a breath into his lungs. "My son told me the garden was being planted squarely on Miss Leitner's side of the fence."

"Have you seen that fence? It got knocked over years ago. It doesn't mark the property line. I went to town hall to check the survey on the land, and wouldn't you know? The box was on my property. So if you think you've got a claim on it, your lawyer is going to have to get through me before he even talks to Erica."

Rideout hissed again. "My lawyer's damn good."

Jed smiled. "My lawyer's in New York."

That shut Rideout up. Even he had the sense to realize a New York lawyer would be much sharper than whoever he'd hired from around here. "So you're gonna snatch the box away from Miss Leitner? Is that what you're saying?"

"What I'm saying is, if something is mine, it's mine."

"That's a good point," Henley said helpfully.

"The hell it's your land," Rideout argued. "And even if it was, my son found the box. If you'd found it, it would be yours. If your dad found it, it would be his. Finders, keepers, like I said."

Jed didn't give a damn what Glenn Rideout said. He

was sick of him—and sick of Potter Henley, and his father, and the pictures of dogs staring down at him from the walls, and the antlers aimed at him, and the smell of cigarettes hovering in the air. He didn't want a cigarette. He didn't even want a candy cane. He didn't want to think about selling his grandfather's place for a dollar, about the many ways his father would rip him off given the opportunity, about the property lines, about the stupid T-shirts Glenn was marketing, about the box, about all the reasons he hated Rockwell.

He wanted to go back to Erica's place, carry her off to her bedroom and pretend nothing existed on the other side of her door. Especially not Rockwell, the place she yearned to make her home.

But Rockwell did exist on the other side of her door. And if he had half a lick of sense, he'd pack his bags and hit the road.

"Tell your lawyer he'd better not make a move against Erica," Jed said, pointing a threatening finger at Rideout. "The box is mine. If you think you've got a snowball's chance in hell of claiming ownership of it, you're going to have to deal with me."

Before Rideout could respond, Jed stormed out the door.

CHAPTER FOURTEEN

IT TOOK LESS TIME to plant the rest of the garden than it had taken to plant the row and a half she and Randy had completed last weekend. She no longer cared about spacing the seedlings six inches apart and setting them three inches deep. Nor did she care if the zucchini choked out the broccoli, if the peas shriveled and died, if she wound up with too many tomatoes.

She ought to care. She wanted to care. But she didn't.

Randy yakked nonstop as they dug holes, nestled the seedlings into them and patted the soil snugly around them. Some new video game had just been released, he told Erica, and all the kids were saying it was the coolest game, but Randy had played it at Nick Hunkel's house after school yesterday and it wasn't so great. The cars didn't skid enough and the blood looked completely bogus.

Once the seedlings were in, Erica realized she needed to water them. She hadn't hooked up her hose yet, so to irrigate her newly planted garden, she and Randy traipsed in and out of the kitchen lugging a blown-glass pitcher and a plastic milk jug filled with water from the sink. If Erica had planned this whole earth-mother thing better, she would have bought a watering can when she'd purchased the seedlings and the trowel.

Randy emptied the milk jug onto the pea plants and prattled about how computer games were really the way to go and any kid who was still relying on video games for amusement was stuck in the wrong century, while Erica stood swaying, trying not to collapse as she stared at her soggy garden and realized she was never going to make peace with those budding tomato vines, those innocent-looking zucchini plants that might someday consume the entire yard. She was never going to learn to bake zucchini bread. She'd probably never learn to bake anything edible at all. She wanted so badly to fulfill her dream of becoming integrated into this clean, wholesome environment, with its crystalline blue sky, the Moose Mountains shaping proud purple humps on the horizon, the harmony of a rural town awakening to spring. And it just wasn't going to happen.

She was always going to be Erica Leitner, the Harvard graduate from Brookline, Massachusetts, and she was not going to become one with the world of Rockwell. The only thing she might become one with around here was Jed Willetz—in a strictly physical sense.

Her dizziness left her. Of course she was going to become one with Rockwell, with her garden, with the muddy soil beneath her shoes and the open sky arching above her. Sleeping with Jed, who rejected everything she chose to embrace, didn't change her goals and plans. She'd made her commitment to Rockwell, and one night of fabulous sex wasn't going to change anything.

"Stick with the computer games," she urged Randy as she gathered their tools. "You're better off sitting in front of a computer than sitting in front of a TV, even if all you're doing is playing.''

By one-thirty, the garden work was done and the tools put away. After letting Randy scrub his hands and face at the kitchen sink and devour a few more cookies, she sent him on his way and scanned the phone messages that had accumulated while she'd been toiling outside. A few distant relatives, the boy who'd taken her to the senior prom in high school, an investment adviser—''calling you on a Saturday, Ms. Leitner! Surely that proves how dedicated I am!''—Burt Johnson asking her if she intended to renew her contract for next year now that she was rich, and her mother again, reminding her that with her newfound wealth, she could probably afford a nice little pied-à-terre in Back Bay. No messages from Avery, which meant he was probably still at the Hope Street Inn. He wouldn't leave Rockwell without the box, and he couldn't retrieve the box from the bank without her.

She changed from her gardening clothes into a pair of soft black jeans and a rose-hued sweater and brushed her hair. The mirror above the dresser reflected her unmade bed, the rumpled sheets and indented pillows and the stray condom packets caught in the blanket's folds. A broken sigh escaped her.

He's gone, she reminded herself. Even if he hadn't actually departed from Rockwell yet, he was gone in every way that counted. He'd magnificently ravished her, and now he would return to the big, crowded, noisy city. Last night had never been about love. It couldn't be, because she and Jed were walking different roads. Hers was a two-lane blacktop weaving over hills and through pine forests, and his was the interstate that led south to Manhattan.

If only he'd stay. He could live at his grandfather's house—*his* house now. He could collect junk up here, although that would probably entail doing business with his father, the town's official junk collector, and he wouldn't like that—but he could do it. He could rehab the junk in Rockwell and transport it to his store in New York every few weeks. And then he could come back. He could help her keep the garden flourishing, and they could learn to bake bread together. And every night while he was in town, every long, loving night...

No. It wasn't going to happen. She couldn't keep him where he didn't want to stay.

Aware that she'd gone too long without consuming anything but coffee, she detoured to the kitchen, searched for inspiration on the shelves of the refrigerator, then opted for a couple of the store-bought cookies she kept on hand for Randy. They weren't bad, actually. Much tastier than her last attempt at homemade cookies. Next time, she promised herself as she headed out the back door and locked it, she'd eat something healthy and earth-mothery. For the moment, she needed sugar, fat, refined flour and preservatives.

She got into her car, backed it out of the shed and headed in the direction of the Hope Street Inn, promising herself she would think only about Avery and the box. No more mooning over Jed Willetz.

She mooned over him all the way into town. Main Street looked as spruced up as it did on the Fourth of July when Rockwell staged its grand parade, which invariably featured two fire engines, a phalanx of children on bicycles with red-white-and-blue crepe-paper streamers fluttering from the handlebars, a few 4-H kids accompanied by pigs and cows and some convertibles with World War II veterans enthroned in the back seat. Erica spotted almost as many flags hanging from storefront brackets today as she saw on the Fourth. On this slightly overcast spring day, however, instead of the sidewalks being lined with folks in lawn chairs drinking iced tea and beer and waving at the parade marchers, the sidewalks were lined with outsiders armed with cameras and notepads, latching on to passersby.

Erica avoided eye contact with townspeople and reporters alike as she cruised down Main to Hope Street. She'd had her moment in the spotlight last night. She didn't want to be the star of anyone's story today.

Fortunately, no reporters were visible in the vicinity of the Hope Street Inn. She parked behind the building, climbed the steps to the wraparound porch and went inside.

Nellie Shoemaker hustled into the entry hall wearing an apron marked by multicolored stains that implied that she was engaged in real cooking. "Oh, hi!" she said, obviously recognizing Erica. "Thank goodness you're not someone looking for a room. We're booked solid—all these reporters from out of town! I've got to tell you, your little box is the best thing that ever happened to my business!"

Erica smiled faintly. Just as she didn't want to be viewed as Rockwell's media darling, she also didn't want to be viewed as its economic savior. "I'd like to see Dr. Gilman," she said. "Is he here?"

Nellie shook her head. "He checked out last night. I was annoyed about that because his reservation was until Sunday, but then a reporter all the way from Syracuse showed up around 11:00 p.m., desperate for a place to stay, and I was able to give him Dr. Gilman's room—at twice the price! So it all worked out just fine.''

Pain played a drum solo inside Erica's head. Maybe thinking about Avery and the box wasn't such an improvement over mooning over Jed. ''What do you mean, he checked out? Where did he go?''

''He didn't tell me,'' Nellie said with a sly grin.

''He ran off with the redhead,'' Derrick Messinger's mellifluous voice emerged from the parlor.

Erica managed another smile for Nellie, then turned and followed the voice to its source. Derrick was ensconced in one of the chintz wingback chairs in the parlor, a porcelain cup in one hand and a bottle of scotch in the other. His hair, as always, was impeccable. His outfit—crisp khakis and a starched oxford shirt—was equally impeccable. Beside him stood a wheeled suitcase. He looked miserable.

''Avery Gilman ran off with Fern?'' Erica asked, afraid to consider all the possible connotations of ''ran off.''

Derrick took a delicate sip from his cup, then refilled it from the bottle of scotch. ''They left here together last night, with his suitcase. You tell me, Erica. You're the VIP today. You tell me.''

Tell him what? ''I'm not a VIP,'' she argued, pulling over an ottoman and sitting on it. ''I spent the morning planting my garden. No one's interviewing me—which I like,'' she hastened to add, on the chance that Derrick might whip a camera from his suitcase and start taping this exchange. ''And Dr. Gilman's a man with a lot of responsibilities, not the least of which is that he's supposed to take the box back to Harvard for analysis. And Fern has a job here in town. She's the school nurse. She can't just run off.''

"Why not?"

"Because..." Erica had to think. "Because when a student loses her tooth in school, Fern's got these little treasure chest-shaped plastic containers for storing the tooth so it won't get lost. And she cleans up after kids with stomach bugs."

"If I were her, I'd run off," Derrick said before sipping from his cup.

Erica conceded privately that she would, too. If Fern had fallen in love with Avery, why stick around in Rockwell to mop vomit? Even if she *hadn't* fallen in love with him, why stick around?

"I would have taken her to New York with me," Derrick muttered. "What does that musty professor have that I haven't got?"

"A job at Harvard?" Erica suggested. Some people might be impressed by that. Fern had never been impressed by Erica's Harvard degree, so she probably wouldn't have been influenced by Avery's prestigious faculty position. But to list for Derrick everything else Avery had going for him—modesty, intellectual breadth and hair that didn't appear glued into place— would be tactless.

"He was good on the show, at least," Derrick admitted. "We did great in the overnight ratings. I guess I should thank you, too."

"You're welcome."

"I'll return to New York a conquering hero. Fern could have ridden that wave with me if she'd wanted." He sighed, then focused on Erica. "I don't suppose you'd...?"

"No."

"Didn't think so. You weren't sending out vibes. Fern was. Unless I misread her. That's the scary thing,

Erica. I'm good at reading people. I've got to be. It's essential for an investigative reporter to be able to read people, and I thought I'd read her perfectly, from the title page to the appendix. Oh, well.'' He sipped again, sighed again. ''There are plenty of women in New York. Plenty of women with vibes. Countless vibrating women.''

And most of them would undoubtedly be happy to vibrate right out of their panties for Jed Willetz, Erica thought glumly.

Damn—she wasn't going to think about him. ''I've got to go,'' she told Derrick. ''I've got to find Dr. Gilman.''

Avery couldn't have run off with Fern, she knew. Fern was impulsive, but not *that* impulsive. Avery wasn't impulsive at all. She recalled his patient, methodical approach to opening the box last night. If he'd been impulsive, he would have just broken the lock.

Donning her sunglasses as insurance that none of the reporters would recognize her, she drove down Main Street and then east to Fern's house, a few blocks from the primary school. She parked alongside the dead grass of Fern's tiny front lawn and raced around to the back door. No one used front doors in Rockwell.

Fern's back door was unlocked, and Erica opened it to discover Fern and Avery seated at the kitchen table eating apple pie. The room was warm and tangy with the perfume of hot apples and cinnamon. In fact, Fern's kitchen looked exactly like the sort of place in which a person would bake apple pies. Copper pots hung on a wall rack. The white walls and pale tiles on the floor enhanced the room's lighting. The counters were polished granite, which Fern had pointed out was relatively cheap in these parts, since granite was mined locally. Relatively cheap wasn't cheap enough for Erica, who was still reeling from the expenses she'd incurred by purchasing her house and signing a mortgage, but perhaps one day, if she ever got a raise and saved a little money, she might install granite counters in her kitchen, too.

Granite counters would not endow her with the ability to make such a gorgeous, fluted piecrust from scratch, however.

"Erica!" Avery leaped to his feet, smiling so broadly his teeth seemed to be biting through his beard.

Fern smiled, too, a subtler, sneakier smile. "Hey, TV star! How about a slice of pie?"

"Did you just make it?" Erica asked, slumping into a chair.

"Avery helped." Fern stood and fetched a plate and fork for Erica. "He did all the peeling." She winked at Avery, who blushed. Erica couldn't believe her fusty professor was blushing. "Have you bought one of the souvenir T-shirts yet?"

"No," Erica replied. "And I don't intend to."

"Oh, but you should! They're so Rockwell." Chuckling, Fern cut a slice of pie for Erica.

"The development of a market for T-shirts is really rather interesting, actually," Avery observed. "The box itself contained coins that are no doubt of substantial value, but the wealth it's bringing to the town is only indirectly related to that value."

"All that kitschy merchandise is going to disappear in a few weeks," Erica predicted. "Derrick Messinger will do some new show about a lottery winner in Idaho and everyone will forget all about Rockwell."

"I won't," Avery said, sending Fern a dewy-eyed

gaze. "It's only two hours from Cambridge. Less, if I can compel myself to exceed the speed limit."

"I bet you can," Fern purred.

Erica dug into her pie so she wouldn't have to witness the goo-fest in progress between Fern and Avery. The apples were tart and spicy, with a hint of crunch. The crust was light and crisp, still warm from the oven. How did Fern do it? Was her skill at baking innate? Was Erica doomed because she'd grown up in a semiurban home where her mother never baked because, "Let's face it, there are a dozen gourmet bakeries in this town that make better pastries than me, so why should I knock myself out?"

She continued to eat while Avery and Fern murmured to each other on the subject of speed limits. The pie filled her as the cookies she'd snacked on before leaving her house hadn't. When she was done, she pushed her plate away and said, "Avery, I don't know how long you're planning to stay in town, but if you want to get access to the box, we have to arrange it with Peter Goss. The bank is closed on weekends, so we'd have to contact him and see if he could meet us there."

"I was thinking I'd stay until tomorrow," Avery said, addressing Fern more than Erica.

"I can get Peter to open the bank," Fern assured him. "He's scared of me."

Before Erica could ask why, Avery said, "I'm not surprised." Erica decided to let it lie.

"Well. Okay, then," she said, forcing enthusiasm into her voice. "We're all on the same page. I just wanted to make sure."

"I think you should hire an attorney, Erica," Avery said abruptly.

Erica flinched. "Why?"

"We talked about it," Fern chimed in, surprising Erica even more. Surely they had better things to do than talk about Erica. "Now that everyone in the world knows what's in that box, Glenn Rideout's going to be making all kinds of claims. He's got a lawyer. You should get one, too."

"Is there more than one lawyer in Rockwell?"

"I'd recommend someone from Cambridge," Avery suggested. "We might even be able to hire someone through the university—although if you did that, the attorney would be representing Harvard's interests more than yours."

"I can't afford a lawyer," Erica said. She couldn't even afford granite counters in her kitchen.

"If the box and its contents are worth as much as I'm starting to think they are," Avery pointed out, "you can afford an attorney."

"I don't even want the box! What would I do with it? It's an antique artifact. It belongs in a museum."

"If it's yours," Avery explained, "you can donate it to a museum. But first you've got to ascertain that it's yours."

"And not Glenn Rideout's—the greedy creep," said Fern.

"All right." Erica rested her head in her hands. It still thrummed with pain. "My cousin Naomi's husband is a lawyer down in Cos Cob, Connecticut. Maybe I'll call her." Naomi's husband, Sheldon, charged top dollar—he was quite the hotshot, according to Erica's mother. Naomi had met him at Cornell. Why couldn't Erica have met a hotshot at Harvard? If she had, she could have been living in a four-bedroom Colonial with central air in Cos Cob, too.

She'd call Naomi tonight. She'd call her mother. She'd do everything everyone thought she should do. Her life had been slipping out of her control ever since the box had been found. She hadn't wanted anyone to see it, yet that very first evening Meryl Hummer had managed to finagle a photo for a front-page story about it, and Erica had never regained her footing.

That very first evening, Jed had entered her house and her world. She'd armed herself with a knife, but unlike Fern, she inspired no fear.

God, she was a failure. At everything. Her garden was a muddy mess, the plants unevenly spaced and poorly chosen. Her culinary skills were zilch. Her family didn't approve of her career. She had an Ivy League degree with high honors and she felt like an idiot.

And the man she wanted, the man allegedly every woman in town except for Fern wanted, the man who had loved her all night long, so sweetly, so wildly that merely remembering caused a wave of heat to surge through her, was going to bury his grandfather's ashes and disappear.

A stupid box had changed her fortunes, and instead of making her feel grounded and rich she felt lost and impoverished.

SEEING HERSELF as a fifth wheel, she refused Fern's offer of a second slice of pie. Avery promised to phone her tomorrow, once Fern had worked out a time with Peter Goss to meet them at the bank. "Buy a T-shirt," Fern urged her as she headed out the back door. "I mean it, Erica. You don't ever have to wear it, but you should own one, just in case."

Erica didn't want to contemplate just in case *what*. She drove back toward town, wondering whether buying a T-shirt would make her feel better or worse. She decided to buy one. If it turned out to make her feel worse, she'd send it to her mother.

An impressive crowd swarmed outside Hackett's Superette, watching a TV reporter ply his trade on the sidewalk. Erica kept driving, heading down to Rideout's Ride. For Randy's sake, she'd buy her shirt from his father.

The bar was not as lively as the sidewalk outside the Superette, but its clientele seemed relatively spirited. At least a dozen people, mostly male, occupied the tables at the rear of the tavern. They conversed, they smoked cigarettes and they shuttled glasses of booze between their cocktail napkins and their mouths. They seemed well suited to the place, their faded plaid shirts and burly demeanors making her think of hunters, just as the antlers hanging on the wall made her think of the hunted.

Randy's father stood behind the bar, energetically polishing its surface with a rag. A rotund, balding fellow in twill trousers and a V-neck sweater—clearly not a hunter—sat on a stool across from him, nursing a highball glass containing a brown, and no doubt potent, liquid. "Well, well," Glenn Rideout greeted her. "If it isn't our very own celebrity! What can I get you, Miss Leitner?"

Erica wasn't sure how to interpret his congeniality. She'd been in his bar twice a couple of years ago, both times to discuss Randy's schoolwork when he'd been a student in her class. Glenn had not been so warm and affable those times, so she couldn't rationalize his cheerful mood as standard bartender behavior. Maybe he'd made a lot of money selling T-shirts today. Glenn

Rideout struck her as the kind of guy whose mood could be buoyed by large influxes of cash.

Perhaps he was treating her with particular conviviality because he was planning to claim the box was half his. She didn't want to hire a lawyer, but Avery and Fern were probably correct. The happier Glenn Rideout seemed, the more strongly Erica felt she needed legal representation.

"I was thinking of buying a shirt," she told him, ignoring the insistent throbbing in her skull. "How much do they cost?"

"Nineteen-ninety-nine. A steal, if you ask me."

Right, Erica thought, *you're stealing nineteen-ninety-nine from me.* Did she really have to buy a damn shirt? She didn't want to. "What sizes do they come in?"

"Small, medium, large, extra large."

"And extra-extra," a chubby man on a bar stool hollered, as if he wanted people in the next county to know. "That's my size."

Erica smiled politely at him, then turned to look at the shirt Glenn Rideout was displaying for her. She suppressed a grimace. It truly was ugly. "I don't know," she hedged. As aggravating as her mother could be, Erica loved her too much to unload such a hideous shirt on her.

"You better buy it," the man on the stool shouted. "It could be as close as you ever get to that box."

Erica frowned. She'd assumed everyone in town knew who she was by now, but evidently this fellow didn't. "Actually," she told him, "I'm pretty close to the box."

"Don't expect that to last," the man said.

Erica shot Glenn an accusing look. Was he boasting

publicly that he was going to claim ownership of the box? Let him try to claim it. She'd line up a lawyer. Sheldon Mandel of Cos Cob would shut Glenn down.

"What are you looking at me for?" Glenn asked, radiating spurious innocence.

She ordered herself to remain polite. "I know you're planning to argue that the box might belong in part to your son, Randy—"

"The hell with what I argue," Glenn said, folding the shirt neatly and nudging it toward her as if she'd already purchased it. "Your neighbor, Jed Willetz, says the box is his."

"Jed? Why would he say that?" Her body had been his. Her heart might be his. But the ancient, coin-filled box from her garden?

"He was just in here a while ago," Glenn informed her. "Said the box was on his property and it belongs to him. What do you think of that?"

She didn't know what she thought. She couldn't imagine why Jed would say such a thing. He'd checked and double-checked the property lines. He'd granted that her garden was on her own property. The question had been asked and answered long ago, before she and Jed had spent the night together. "I think you must have misunderstood him," she said as calmly as she could.

"Glenn misunderstands a lot, but he didn't misunderstand this," the chubby man declaimed. "I was sitting right here, Miss Leitner. I heard every word. I'm a certified public accountant, so when the discussion turns to money and ownership, I'm pretty much on top of things." He nodded for emphasis.

"But Jed—no," she insisted. "He would have told

me if he thought the box came from his property. We talked about it.''

''Before or after he saw what was inside?'' the chubby man asked.

Before. Before he'd known the box was full of potentially valuable gold coins.

''He's got a lawyer in New York City,'' Glenn told her. ''A sharp one, he says. What I'm thinking, Miss Leitner, is you and me oughtta join forces and fight him. What gives him the right to lay claim to the box when everybody knows you and my son dug it up? Derrick Messinger broadcast that bit of news all over the country, so it must be true, right? Jed Willetz is the son of a scumbag. I'd say he's inherited a few of his dad's scummy genes. But you and me together, with a good lawyer we could chip in on… We could beat him.''

The notion of joining forces with Glenn Rideout in opposition to Jed made the apple pie she'd just eaten churn unpleasantly in her stomach. As queasy as she felt, though, her headache vanished. Jed—the bastard—was going to contest her for claim on the box? Let him try. Sheldon might not be a shark, but he'd fight for her—if she could afford him, which she could if ownership of the box and its contents was decisively assigned to her and the coins proved valuable. Maybe he'd take the job on contingency. Or he'd take it because Erica had hung out with Naomi at dozens of family bar mitzvahs over the years, sharing lipstick, giggling over Aunt Marion's blue-rinsed hair and sneaking glasses of wine when the bartenders weren't looking. Family was family. Sheldon would get the job done, without any help from Glenn Rideout.

But who cared about the box? Jed—that bastard!

He'd kept an eye on her, guarded the box for her, raced to her house to protect her from Toad Regan and then spent the night making love to her, and now he was going to hire a lawyer to argue that the box was his?

She didn't care what the box was worth. She never had. But she'd cared about Jed, and about what last night was worth. It had been worth so much to her, much more than all the two-hundred-year-old gold coins in the world.

Now she knew what it had been worth to Jed, too.

The only positive aspect of this entire disaster, she thought as she stormed out of Rideout's Ride, was that she was so angry she forgot to buy the damn T-shirt.

CHAPTER FIFTEEN

JED WAS NOT A HAPPY MAN when he steered the turquoise Saturn up the driveway to his grandfather's house. He'd just spent an hour arguing with his father, who claimed that the memorial service for Jed's grandfather should be held in church, not graveside. As best Jed could tell, the only reason the man was agitating for a second church service was to give him something to barter with. He'd probably hoped Jed would say, "Okay, you can take whatever other junk you want from the house. Just let me do the service my way."

Jed hadn't given him that satisfaction. Most of his grandfather's possessions weren't worth much, but money wasn't the point. Jed was still royally ticked that his father had stolen his grandfather's favorite cast-iron skillet. There were principles involved.

He'd stopped at the Superette on his way home and picked up a chilled six-pack of Michelob. He would have preferred a dark lager to match his dark mood, but Pop Hackett's inventory of beer was pretty limited. Jed had also picked up a pack of red licorice whips to chew on if the urge for a cigarette overcame him.

But he hadn't wanted a cigarette since last night. Since Erica. He wondered if sex with her tapped into the same pleasure center as nicotine, although he'd bet sex with her wouldn't cause cancer. High blood pressure, perhaps.

Driving back to his grandfather's place only increased his gloom, because she was next door. Of all the women in this godforsaken town he could have fallen for, why did it have to be the only one who lacked the sense to see Rockwell for what it was?

Okay, maybe *he* was the one who lacked sense. Maybe there was something to be said for clean, pine-scented air. A person could re-create that fragrance in Manhattan with a can of air deodorizer, but it wasn't the same thing. Maybe living surrounded by open space, having the freedom to plant a garden right outside your back door, being able to greet everyone you ran into by name, knowing that the most dangerous human threat in town was a bonehead like Toad Regan—so all right, maybe Rockwell wasn't synonymous with hell.

It came close, though.

He was so busy fuming about how close Rockwell came to his definition of hell that he didn't notice her on his front porch until he was already out of the car. She rose from the swing and watched him as he strode toward the porch steps. In the long shadows of dusk, he couldn't quite make out her face. He knew it was Erica, however—not just because of her resplendent hair, her posture, the specifics of a body he'd grown intimately acquainted with overnight, but because whenever he was near her his nervous system and at least one other part of his anatomy sprang to high alert.

He'd spent the day trying to avoid her, reminding himself that last night had been a one-time deal. But to discover that she was waiting for him on his own front porch—it was too gratifying. He was too damn glad to see her.

His joy ebbed a bit when he got close enough to

read her expression. She was not the least bit glad to
see him.

"Hey," he said cautiously.

She glowered.

He climbed the steps and balanced the six-pack on
the porch railing. "I'm not in a real great mood," he
warned her. "I've just finished fighting World War III
with my father. You want a beer?" He removed a bottle from the cardboard tote and extended it toward her.

"No, thank you."

Shrugging to cover his apprehension, he twisted the
cap off the bottle and took a swig.

She gestured toward the five remaining bottles. "Are
you planning to get drunk?"

"No."

"Then why did you buy six beers?"

"It was cost-effective." This conversation wasn't
going well. He was standing less than two feet away
from a woman he had become obsessed with, consuming beer when he only wanted to consume her, to taste
her instead of cold, sour bubbles on his tongue, to feel
her instead of the chilled round glass of the bottle. He
wanted to scoop her into his arms like a Neanderthal,
and carry her off to bed, and make her come so many
times she'd take a week to recover.

A week. He'd be gone before that week was up.

No sense indulging in X-rated fantasies. That she
hadn't shown up at his house with the intention of
deepening their friendship was clear from the dark glint
in her eyes and the fierce set of her chin.

"So," he said even more cautiously, "how was your
day?"

"My day was swell," she snapped. "Glenn Rideout

invited me to pool resources with him so we could fight you in court.''

''Oh.'' He took another swig of beer and rested his hips against the railing. He wanted to sit, but as long as she was standing he'd remain standing, too. Not out of chivalry but because being taller than her gave him a tactical advantage. ''Let me offer you some advice. You don't want to join forces with Glenn Rideout. Ever.''

''Thank you.'' The words dropped out of her mouth like two small chips of ice.

''So, you want to fight me in court?''

''Glenn told me you've got a New York lawyer lined up and you're going to claim legal ownership of the box. Your contention is that it was found on your property. I thought we'd already straightened that out, Jed. I thought—''

''Okay, okay.'' He held his hand up to silence her. She clamped her mouth shut, but he felt waves of rage rolling off her. ''I only told Rideout that to get him off your back.''

''Is that so?''

''He's like a termite, Erica. He gnaws on things, nibbles away at them, and you think he's just a bug. But he can bring your whole house down if you don't watch out. He's got this dumb idea that he can claim half the box because Randy found it.''

''Randy *did* find it.''

''But it wasn't on his property. In my work, I can't go into people's houses, say, 'Gee, I really like this table—I could refinish it and sell it for a nice profit,' and help myself to the table. It's in their house. Just because I see it doesn't make it mine.''

"But nobody saw the box. It was buried. Randy dug it up."

"On your property."

"Or maybe on yours," Erica said with a sniff. "You want a cut of the action, Jed? Just say the word."

The action he wanted had nothing to do with her damn box. He sighed. "Who are you going to believe, Glenn Rideout or me? I thought I was doing you a favor by threatening to bring a New York lawyer into it. If you'd rather I back away and leave you to take on Rideout all by yourself, just say the word."

She eyed him dubiously, her teeth playing over her lower lip in an unintentionally sexy way. He cooled himself off with a quick gulp of beer.

"Fine," he said, hoping to goad a response out of her. "Believe Rideout. Go be his partner. Sue me."

"I don't believe him," she admitted, lowering her eyes, suddenly deflated. "I don't know who to believe, but he's certainly not at the top of my list."

"Come to New York with me," Jed said. The invitation slipped out, startling him as much as it seemed to startle her, but he didn't regret it. In fact, saying it made him feel better than he'd felt since he'd climbed out of her bed that morning. He set his beer bottle on the ground, took her hand and drew her down onto the swing with him. "How about it?"

She shook her head, as if unfamiliar with the language he was speaking. "What are you talking about?"

"I'm talking about New York. Where I live. Tall buildings, lots of people, rude drivers and a hundred brands of beer available in every liquor store. How about it?"

"You're asking me to go to New York with you?"

He thought hard about what he'd suggested and decided it sounded all right to him. "Yeah."

"To visit?"

"I don't know. To visit, to stay, whatever." He wasn't prepared to get specific. He hadn't even been prepared to invite her in the first place. Not that he regretted the invitation, but he didn't want to get tangled up in details or overanalyze his motives.

"I live here," she reminded him.

"I used to live here. Big deal."

"Jed." She sounded shaky, and her hand fluttered like a frightened moth against his. "It *is* a big deal. I own a house here."

"So do I." He gestured at the farmhouse extending back from the porch.

"And I have a job."

"They need teachers in New York."

She lifted her gaze to his. Her eyes swarmed with emotion—panic, doubt, yearning and a bunch of other possibilities. He tried not to see love in them. This discussion wasn't about love. He had already jumped way ahead of himself. He wasn't going to put himself in deeper peril by making bold declarations and commitments. All he wanted was Erica—somewhere that wasn't Rockwell.

"What are you suggesting, Jed? I should go to New York with you and get a job there?"

He shrugged. She was looking for a bold declaration and a commitment. He hoped she'd be willing to settle for honesty. "I don't know. We could see how it worked out."

"Why?"

Maybe she wasn't trying to wrangle a promise out of him. She seemed to be aiming for something else:

logic. A handle around which to wrap her Harvard-honed brain. "We like each other," he noted. "We're good together. Last night…" He retrieved his beer bottle and drank some beer, buying time. *Go for honesty.* "Last night was incredible. I don't know about you, but I haven't ever experienced anything like that before. It was just really good."

She smiled, not the sexy, kittenish smiles she'd given him last night but something deeper, acceptance mixed with bemusement. "It was really good," she agreed.

"Not just the sex," he added. "The part where you took on Toad Regan with a boot and coat hanger. A *dress* hanger," he corrected himself before she could set him straight. "I admire your courage, Erica."

Her smile widening, she turned away. He nudged the floorboards to set the swing in motion, and they rocked together gently. "I live here," she said again. "I settled in Rockwell for a reason."

"Yeah, and I'm having one hell of a time buying it."

"All my life I've pictured myself living in a small town like this," she said. "Tossing aside the razzle-dazzle of urban life and surrounding myself with tranquillity. When I was in college, my world was filled with all these brilliant people, every single one of them ambitious and brimming with entitlement, ready to take over the planet. I don't want to take over the planet, Jed. I want to become a part of it. I want to find my way back to old-fashioned values, to live a simple life."

"What's so simple about Rockwell?" he argued. "This is a very complicated town."

"What's complicated about it?"

"Half the people here are crazy. The other half are close-minded. Old-fashioned values around here mean, 'I'm your best friend unless you happen to find a box full of gold coins. Then I'm going to sue you or break into your house.'"

"All right. Maybe simple isn't what I mean," she conceded, poking at the floorboards with her toes as he pushed with his heel, so they could both propel the swing. "Maybe *natural* is a better word. Like my garden. And my attempts to learn how to cook with the food I grow. I want to get back to nature, immerse myself in nature—be a part of nature."

"What's so great about nature? Nature sucks." He waved his hand toward his scraggly front yard. "Take mud season, okay? Nature is mud season."

She laughed. "Mud eventually dries."

"Mud is not even an issue in New York City." He tried to figure out why he was fighting so hard for this. He had female friends in New York, no one as intriguing as Erica, but it wasn't as if he couldn't get a date. He didn't *need* her to come to New York with him.

But it irked him no end that she'd choose Rockwell over New York—over *him.* How could she want to stay in this stifling town that he'd been so thrilled to escape from? How could she make that choice when the possibilities between him and her were so enticing?

"Well, it was just a thought," he said, then forced a grin to prove he didn't care that she preferred Rockwell to him. "You want to stay here, suit yourself. I think you're crazy, but maybe that's why you fit in so well here."

"I don't fit in so well," she argued, getting serious just as he was trying to lighten things up. "I wish I did. It's been my dream to fit into a town like this.

And in time, I think that dream will come true. It's not easy, but I haven't given up yet."

No surprise that she was stubborn. That was one of the things he liked about her. But he was still infuriated by the thought that she'd turn her back on what they'd shared last night for *this*—this dead quarry town full of busybodies and scammers, people who'd ignore you until they thought you might be rich or famous or, God help you, both, and then they'd target you for friendship or legal action or burglary.

She'd chosen Rockwell over him, and it hurt.

ERICA UNFOLDED HERSELF from Fern's car and met Fern at the rear bumper. They'd driven over together from the school in time for John Willetz's graveside service Tuesday afternoon. Fern had suggested they travel together because it would be easier to find one parking space than two.

Erica hadn't imagined that anything—even John Willetz's burial—could cause a parking problem in Rockwell. Obviously, her imagination was much too limited. The sides of the road near the gate that led into the cemetery were packed with cars, most of them protruding halfway into the roadway and narrowing the space for traffic like an artery narrowed by cholesterol deposits. Why anyone would have created a cemetery without a parking lot was beyond her.

She wished she could have thought of a good excuse to miss the service. But the only excuse she'd come up with was the truth, and the truth—that she'd slept with Jed and then he'd asked her to go to New York with him, without any promises or plans, and that for reasons she still couldn't fathom, she'd said no—was better kept to herself. If Fern found out Erica had been the most recent Rockwell female to drop her panties for Jed... Well, it was just better if no one knew.

As it happened, Fern had other things on her mind. "Avery invited me down to Cambridge this weekend," she'd told Erica on the drive over to the cemetery.

"He did? When?"

"He called last night. Well, he called Sunday night, too."

He hadn't called Erica. She hadn't expected a call from him, other than to report on his continuing examination of the box and its contents, but still, the box was what his trip to Rockwell had been about.

No, it wasn't. It had started out that way, but then he'd met Fern. "Are you going?" Erica asked, keeping her tone casual.

"Do you have to ask?" Fern's eyes shimmered. "Cambridge, Massachusetts! Avery told me it's full of boutiques and little cafés and movie theaters that show films with subtitles. He said Boston is right across the river, and it's got even more boutiques and theaters and restaurants with food from all around the world. Hungarian, Greek, Thai, Ethiopian—I don't even know what they eat in Ethiopia. Camels?"

"It's kind of similar to Middle Eastern food," Erica told her.

"He said Harvard's got all these old buildings— *really* old. Older than the box. Three hundred years old."

"I know. I was a student there, remember?" Impatience had colored Erica's voice, and when Fern had looked wounded, she'd suffered a twinge of guilt. "I take it you accepted his invitation?" she'd added in a softer tone.

"Of course I accepted. Cambridge! It's like, when I

was studying nursing at UNH, people talked about Harvard like it was, you know, the pinnacle of something. Like you'd expect to see old guys in togas wandering around, spouting philosophy.''

"The only guys I ever saw in togas were undergrads and they were drunk," Erica said, recalling an *Animal House*–inspired party one of the houses had sponsored her junior year.

"Anyway, the main attraction isn't old buildings and Ethiopian restaurants. It's Avery." Fern released a wistful sigh.

Erica shook her head. "I thought you were setting your sights on Derrick Messinger. He certainly had his sights set on you."

"He did?" Fern sounded surprised. So much for Derrick's vaunted vibrations detector. "I suppose there's something to be said for fame and glamor, but Avery... God, Erica, I don't know why sometimes things click. Never in my wildest dreams would I have imagined clicking with a Harvard history professor. But this sort of thing isn't supposed to be logical, is it? It just is. You accept it."

"You celebrate it," Erica had said, genuinely happy for Fern, but unsettled for herself. Something had clicked between her and Jed. In her wildest dreams, she wouldn't have imagined clicking with him—except yes, she would have. He would have been the local man who could complete her fantasy about life in a small town. In her dreams, she'd have that life and the love of a man who shared her passion for nature and small-town society. They'd plant their roots and their garden together and live happily ever after, surrounded by verdant forests and pristine mountains, with deer roaming through their yard and devouring their garden.

But Jed wasn't the man to fulfill that dream with, and Erica didn't have his love. Just his amazing passion, which was nothing to sneeze at.

She hadn't seen him since he'd asked her to go to New York City with him. It had been such a bizarre idea, at odds with all her plans. New York would be like Boston to the tenth power: crowded, noisy, frenetic. A garden in New York would likely be a flower box on a fire escape. Apartment kitchens would be too small to bake in, if she ever mastered the art of baking.

But along with giving up everything she had in Rockwell, what would she gain by going to New York? Jed had been terribly vague on that score. He wasn't asking her to marry him, not that she was certain she'd have accepted if he did, but still. So why prolong things? Why torture herself by spending more time with him?

Because John Willetz had been her landlord, and her nearest neighbor for two years. She couldn't very well skip the service without arousing gossip.

Given the number of cars parked along the road, she figured the crowd would be significant. She and Jed wouldn't have to see each other, let alone talk.

She and Fern ambled down the center of the road to the open gates, then followed one of the winding paths up a hill to where a crowd had gathered. The instant Erica reached that crowd, her gaze collided with Jed's. So much for their not seeing each other. He wore a dark suit and a white shirt but no tie, which didn't surprise her. Jed Willetz in a tie would be as absurd as Pop Hackett in a dress.

Jed stood near the small hole that had been dug in front of a double-width stone of New Hampshire's finest granite, with his grandmother's and grandfather's

birth and death dates carved into it. There was no sign
of a box containing John Willetz's ashes; perhaps that
had already been lowered into the ground.

Next to Jed stood his father. Jed had a couple of
inches in height on Jack, and a good thirty pounds of
solid muscle. Erica had never realized how scrawny
Jack Willetz was, but beside his son he looked as if
his body had been constructed out of Tinkertoys. He
wore faded corduroy slacks and an even more faded
plaid shirt under a winter coat. It wasn't that cold, but
the sun had failed to burn through the layer of gray
clouds that spread above the graveyard.

Hands in pockets, Jack was chatting amiably with a
short, plump woman Erica recognized as Reena
Keefer, the maple syrup lady. Scanning the crowd,
Erica also spotted Hazel Nagy, who glowered at Fern,
and Myrna Gilhooley from town hall, and Butch We-
ber, who owned the Moosehead. Glenn Rideout was
also there, his arm around a mousy woman with brown
hair as fluffy as cotton balls. Was that Randy's mother?
Erica had never met her.

She noticed Meryl Hummer standing off to the side,
snapping photos. Just as unearthing the coin-filled box
had been last week's front-page story, the interment of
John Willetz's ashes was this week's front-page story.
Erica glimpsed Harriet Ettman in a thick, multicolored
cardigan that looked hand-knitted—maybe Erica ought
to take up knitting; it seemed like a wholesome, small-
town craft—and a chubby, balding man who kept tilting his head toward Glenn, cupping his ear and shouting, "Huh?" Potter Henley, Erica recalled.

At least fifty people were gathered around the grave
site, and Erica recognized just about all of them. Reverend Pith, of course, and Sewell McCormick. A few

teachers from the primary school; Dr. Hoyt, the pediatrician; Ostronkowicz from the gas station; Stuart Farnham, who worked for the state highway department and plowed the roads in the winter; Pop Hackett's wife, Elaine; Janelle from Rockwell Rx; Toad Regan, looking dazed and poking at a scraggly tuft of grass with his toe.

Erica knew *all* these people. She'd lived in Rockwell just under three years, and she knew *everyone.* And only one of them—*Fern Bernard*—did she consider a friend.

Silly thought. That she knew her fellow Rockwellians was enough. They were a community, neighbors, acquaintances. She could trust them all—well, no. She couldn't trust Toad. She couldn't trust Glenn Rideout. She couldn't trust Burt Johnson, the school principal, who was always meddling in her lesson plans and demanding that she put aside her big-city pedagogical concepts. Janelle had never screwed up a prescription for Erica, but she suspected that if she'd ever needed a drug for something more exotic than a flare-up of hay fever or strep throat, the entire town would be talking about it within an hour.

Of everyone gathered around the grave site, only Fern had any idea what Erica believed in, what she hoped for, what she cared about.

Only Fern and Jed.

Glancing back at him, she found him still staring at her. Why? What had she ever done to him, other than refuse to abandon her house and her job for a no-strings-attached romp with him in the Big Apple? Why did he look so…sad?

Because he was burying his grandfather's ashes, of course. The shadows veiling his eyes and the frown lines notching the bridge of his nose had nothing to do with her. He was in a mournful state because his beloved grandfather was truly dead and his father was a petty thief and all he wanted was to get away from this town where, like Erica, he knew everyone.

Reverend Pith began to speak: "Dearly Beloved..." and Erica's gaze slid to Jed again. If he was so damned sad about his grandfather, she thought, he ought to be staring at the hole in the ground, not at her. *She* wasn't his dearly beloved.

The minister droned on for a while and then turned to Jed. "Now we'll have a few words from the grandson of the dearly departed, John Edward Willetz III." Erica didn't care for Pith's profligate use of the word *dearly,* but she loved his use of Jed's full, formal name. It lent him a stature he hardly needed. Somehow, he seemed even taller when he was "the Third."

"Some of you may be here out of respect for my father and me," Jed said. He didn't shout, but his voice carried, cutting through the dank air. "But I'm sure all of you knew my grandfather. We said goodbye to him last January. Today all we're saying goodbye to is his remains. He's not here anymore. He left Rockwell a few months ago, when the ground was too frozen for us to bury him."

Jed paused. He took a deep breath and his eyes zeroed in on her again. She wished she could back up until she was hidden behind Darren Choate, who still had the build that had made him a standout defensive end on the high-school football team a few years back. But she couldn't very well recede into the crowd, not when Jed was watching her so intently.

"I don't know whether I believe in heaven," Jed

continued. "Sometimes I think heaven is where you go when you leave Rockwell."

A couple of people chuckled. The rest probably didn't get the joke.

"I will say this," Jed went on. "My grandfather was an ornery son of a bitch, but he was also one of the best people ever to call this town home. I miss him, and I'm sure you all do, too." With that he took a step back. His gaze still on Erica, he quirked one eyebrow, as if to ask how he'd done.

He'd done beautifully. His simple words were more eloquent than the Reverend Pith's long-winded bromides. Erica nodded, and Jed's mouth hinted at a smile.

She was touched that he wanted her approval, even though he had to know she wouldn't agree with his definition of heaven. It was *his* definition, though. Everyone was entitled to his or her own definition.

Hers was—not Rockwell. Heaven couldn't possibly have mud season. Heaven couldn't have pathetic creatures like Toad Regan breaking into people's houses and squeezing their wrists. Heaven couldn't have prigs and busybodies like Burt Johnson and Hazel Nagy interfering with the way Fern and Erica did their jobs.

Her heaven would have bountiful gardens, though. Fresh tomatoes ripe for picking, and not too many zucchini. Adequate sunshine and water and fresh air. Her heaven would abound in love.

The Reverend Pith asked Jed's father if he wanted to add anything. Jack ruminated for a moment, then cleared his throat and said, "Just that it don't matter how much you kiss up to someone—when they pass on, they're gonna leave you whatever the hell they feel like." Jed rolled his eyes. He could have been furious, but he seemed to have a sense of humor about his father's tastelessness. That sense of humor was just one more thing to love about him.

Not that Erica loved him. Heaven wasn't Jed Willetz—one night in bed with him notwithstanding.

The minister said a few more words, then dug a shovel into the small pile of dirt beside the hole and tossed some in. Jed took the shovel next, handed it to his father and strode through the crowd, barely stopping to shake hands and acknowledge the condolences people were uttering. He headed straight for her.

"What's this all about?" Fern muttered. "He's not going to fight you over the box, is he? I heard a rumor he was hiring a lawyer, but I didn't think it could be true."

"Jed started that rumor deliberately to get Glenn Rideout off my case," Erica whispered back, wondering if she could make a discreet departure before Jed reached her. Not possible. She was surrounded by Rockwellians, all of them swarming and chattering. What little she picked up from the din of conversation indicated that they weren't talking about the man whose ashes they'd just buried. They were analyzing Janelle's shocking-pink fleece jacket and Toad's bloodshot eyes, and commenting that, for all his poise, Jed Willetz was a scamp for having turned his back on his hometown. "What's he got in that big dirty city that he doesn't have here?" one person asked; another replied that what he had in that big dirty city was access to a lot more hot-to-trot women than what you might find in Rockwell.

The nearer he drew to Erica, the less she heard the voices around her. She smelled damp earth and Jed's minty fragrance, and she wanted to grab Fern's hand

and run for her life. But she held her ground, or, more accurately, the ground held her, its spongy consistency molding around her loafers.

"I'm leaving Rockwell tomorrow," he said.

She searched his words for a hint that he was asking her to join him. He'd already asked and she'd declined, and no, she didn't hear him asking again. "I'm sure you're needed back at your store." That sounded too cold and impersonal, so she added, "What you said about your grandfather was really nice."

"Much better than what old Pith had to say," Fern agreed.

Jed nodded briefly at her, then turned back to Erica. "I meant what I said the other day. And the weird thing is, I don't know why I said it."

"I figured as much."

"But I did mean it. And I can't shake the feeling that if I could have explained it, your answer would have been different."

Tears stung her eyes, and she lowered them so she wouldn't have to view his beautiful, bewildered face. "I don't know, Jed. I honestly don't."

"Well." He reached up and brushed a lock of hair back from her face. Then he placed a light kiss on her forehead. "Don't let this place chew you up and swallow you," he whispered. "It'll do that if you're not careful. It's got big teeth." He stepped back, gave her a heartbreaking smile and strode down the hill toward the gates.

"What was that all about?" Fern asked, staring after him.

Erica didn't answer. Staring at Jed's receding back, she felt a piercing pain in the vicinity of her heart, but she wasn't sure if Rockwell or Jed had bitten her. He'd never offered her a damn thing, he didn't know what he wanted or why—and he was walking out of her life.

This was not her definition of heaven.

CHAPTER SIXTEEN

JUNE IN MANHATTAN was usually hot and humid. The rich folks made their weekly escapes to the Hamptons or the Berkshires, leaving behind the teeming masses, whose tempers generally soared right along with the heat and humidity. When Derrick Messinger had been at the top of his game, he used to escape to the Hamptons, too. He'd never owned a beachfront estate, but he'd been able to rent a cottage about a mile north of the shoreline—not the most posh address, but worthy of a certain degree of prestige.

Then, of course, his career had fallen apart and the Hamptons had been out of the question.

They were in the question now. He was soaring once again. But if he wanted to flee the city for a weekend, he'd just as soon head north to, oh, say, the Moose Mountains of New Hampshire.

Rockwell might not have much going on, but if he was going to be a mile from the beach, anyway, what difference did it make? He'd enjoy better dining in the Hamptons, of course, but those restaurants were outrageously expensive, and there was always a chance someone famous would be seated at the next table just when you were knocking over your glass of wine or choking on your *pâté de foie gras*. Plus, in the Hamptons, there was always an A-list party going on, and if you weren't invited, you'd feel terribly un-A. A person didn't ever have to worry about anyone hosting an A-list party in Rockwell.

He hadn't been back to that hole-in-the-wall town since he'd hit the airwaves with his scoop on the antique box and its glittering contents. But he'd heard the tourist business continued to thrive there. In fact, he'd heard that from the owner of the silkscreen company that produced the town's commemorative T-shirts and, thanks to some clever negotiations, paid Derrick a ten-cent royalty on every shirt sold, that the town was planning to open a museum of some sort dedicated to the box. The box itself would not be featured at this museum, but photos of the box and its discovery would be on display for the numerous visitors who trooped through its doors. Derrick had suggested that Sonya look into a deal with the museum to show repeated broadcasts of the *I'm Just the Messenger* program he'd done on the subject. They could earn a fee for every showing. Money was money, after all.

Even without the subsidiary deals, that show had drawn a large enough audience in its original airing—especially when compared with Derrick's Jimmy Hoffa show, about which the less said the better—that Sonya had been able to jack up the price of his syndication contracts by a factor of three. Months after the broadcast, people were still coming up to him on the street and saying, "Hey, 'I'm Just the Messenger!' How about that box?"

Not just people—*women.* His failure to connect with that redheaded sprite—what was her name? Some plant. Heather, maybe—was all but forgotten. His vibes seemed to be back in full working order, detecting signals far and wide. There he was, after all, on a sunny brink-of-summer day, taking lunch in a pleasant midtown *trattoria* with a sparkling gem of a young lady named Adrienne, who had the most charming giggle and world-class knockers. He'd just wrapped up work on a new story, a bit of intense investigative journalism tracking down rumors that the Flatiron Building was haunted by the ghost of a dentist who'd lost his life's savings in the depression and somehow committed suicide with his pedal-powered drill. Derrick had brought a spiritualist into the building at night. They'd filmed auras with special cameras. Sonya had laid down a track of appropriately eerie music. Dr. Hufferspoin's ghost was not found, but the search had turned up some interesting objects, including a mangled Barbie doll jammed into an air-conditioning vent and a package of American cheese petrified to the consistency of Sheetrock in a storage room in the basement. The show was scheduled for broadcast next week. Predictions were that it would perform strongly, especially since June wasn't a ratings-sweep month and most of the network shows were in reruns.

Adrienne leaned across the table to spear a taste of his scampi. He didn't mind—she could eat the whole damn portion, as long as she kept leaning forward like that, affording him such a terrific view of her cleavage. His gaze followed her as she settled back in her chair, and then it slid past her to the window overlooking the sidewalk. "Excuse me," he blurted out, astonished to have noticed, strolling past the restaurant, a pedestrian wearing a Rockwell—the Town of Hidden Treasures T-shirt. One didn't expect to see that in midtown Manhattan. "I'll be right back, sweetheart."

He bolted from the table, leaving Adrienne chomping on his shrimp, and raced to the door. He hadn't caught the face of the person in the shirt, and now she was nearly to the corner, her back to him. She was tall, with a small, nicely curved butt and long, dark hair.

"Hey!" he shouted, charging after her.

West Forty-fourth Street was clogged with pedestrians, as usual, but either they recognized him and assumed he was chasing a major story or else they took him for a madman, because most of them hastily moved out of his way. Fortunately, the light at the corner was red, and he was able to catch up to her. Before she could step off the curb, he clamped a hand on her shoulder.

She screamed and spun around.

Erica Leitner! He couldn't remember her friend's name, but hers was emblazoned on his heart, since she'd done so much to salvage his professional reputation. "Well, hello!" he said in his smoothest interview voice. "Small world!"

"Derrick Messinger?"

"I was just having lunch," he said, refraining from air-kissing her. He was a TV personality, but she was a Harvard alum dwelling in a small Yankee town. He didn't think making kissy-kissy would go over well with her. "I glanced through the restaurant window and saw your T-shirt."

She peered down, as if to refresh her memory of the T-shirt she was wearing. It was tucked neatly into a straight, knee-length khaki skirt. A purse was slung over her shoulder, and simple sandals protected her feet. No pedicure, he noticed, but then, they probably didn't know what pedicures were in Rockwell. Her fingers curled around the handle of a wheeled overnight bag.

"Well," she finally said. "I succumbed and bought a T-shirt."

"I'm sure you made Glenn Rideout very happy." He remembered the bartender's name, too, for some reason.

She smiled and shook her head. "I bought it from Pop Hackett. After Glenn sicced his slimy lawyer on me, I wasn't going to give him any of my money."

"Really? He pursued a legal case against you?" Maybe there was a story in that. A juicy small-town-scandal follow-up.

"His lawyer sued for ownership of the box. A judge in Manchester told him he was too greedy for words and threw out the suit. I'm afraid there're some bad feelings between Glenn and me." She looked mildly troubled by this.

"So, what brings you to New York?" Derrick asked, tucking Erica's hand around his elbow and leading her back toward the restaurant. He still sensed potential for a follow-up show on Rockwell's most famous citizen. It wouldn't hurt to cultivate her.

She gently slid her hand free and drew to a halt. "I need to see Jed Willetz. I know he's got a store somewhere in the city—downtown, I think he said. I can't remember the name of it, though. And I don't know my way around Manhattan very well."

"You're a Boston girl. Of course you don't know Manhattan." He dug into an inner pocket on his silk-blend blazer, pulled out his cell phone and speed-dialed. "Let me buzz Sonya. She arranged to keep in touch with Mr. Willetz when we got back to New York. She thought he might serve as our liaison with Rockwell. I'm not sure I agreed to, but she might— Sonya!" he said brightly into the phone when she picked up. "I'm a block from Times Square. You'll never guess who's standing here next to me."

"A hooker?"

"Don't be silly. They've cleaned up the neighborhood. No, Sonya, I ran into Erica Leitner, of all people. She's in town, and she's trying to locate Jed Willetz. You wouldn't by any chance know the name of his store, would you?"

"Erica Leitner? Listen, Derrick," Sonya said, the words spitting out as fast as bullets from an Uzi. "You find out where she's staying and do anything you can for her. We want exclusive rights to her. I don't want anyone else getting their hands on her—*Today* or *Nightline* or *Letterman.* She's ours."

"Don't worry about it. Can we help her out?"

"Of course we can help her out. I'm going through my files even as we speak—okay, here it is—City Resale. The address is in SoHo. You got a pen?"

Derrick pulled a business card from the gold-plated card case he'd treated himself to as a Father's Day gift, since he had no children that he knew of and couldn't expect anyone to buy a gift for him. He plucked a pen from the pocket where he kept his good-luck rubber band and, on the back of the card, jotted down the address and phone number Sonya dictated. Then he handed the card to Erica.

"Escort her down there yourself," Sonya instructed him. "Treat her like a visiting dignitary. Flag down a cab and see her into the store, okay? I'm thinking part two, Derrick. 'Rockwell Box, the Sequel.'"

Picturing Adrienne and her bosom waiting for him back at the restaurant, Derrick winced. "Sonya, I can't. I was in the middle of something when I spotted Erica."

"Something more important than your career?"

He sighed. "All right. I'll do it." Before Sonya

could issue more orders, he disconnected the phone.
"I'll take you to Jed Willetz's store," he said, panto-
miming a gallant bow.

"That's not necessary."

"You're a visitor to my town. It's the least I can
do." He tucked her hand into the crook of his elbow
again and hustled her down the street toward the restaurant.

"This isn't downtown, is it?" she asked skeptically.

"We'll be taking a cab. I just have to do one thing."
He steered her into the restaurant's vestibule, then released her hand. "Wait here—I'll be right back." Before she could object, he darted into the dining room,
hurried over to the window table where Adrienne was
busy scarfing down his scampi and said, "I'm so sorry,
sweetheart, I've got to run."

"Why?" Adrienne asked, a buttery pink shrimp
curled over her lower lip.

"It could be the biggest scoop of my career. You
know how it is for us journalists. Here's fifty dollars."
He dropped a few bills onto the table. "That should
cover everything, including dessert. Try the *tiramisu.*
It's supposed to be incredible here." He kissed her on
the crown of her head to avoid the shrimp, then
sprinted back to the vestibule.

Erica was gone.

SHE DIDN'T NEED Derrick Messinger accompanying her
to Jed's store. More important, she didn't *want* him
accompanying her. That he'd glimpsed her while having his lunch had been pure coincidence. It was a huge,
crowded city, but he'd chosen to eat at a restaurant just
a block from the Port Authority Bus Terminal.

She hadn't driven to the city. Not knowing her way

around, she wouldn't risk navigating through such a traffic-clogged place, and she suspected that parking the car in a garage for any length of time would wind up costing more than the bus fare. She'd figured she would find a telephone directory somewhere, and in the Yellow Pages, under "Furniture, Used" she'd get Jed's store address. Or she'd try the White Pages and get his home address. She'd hoped to track down his address via the Web, but Internet service was iffy in Rockwell, and after she'd gotten disconnected six times she'd given up. She'd also tracked down his father at the Moosehead, but he'd insisted he didn't have Jed's address. "I got his cell phone number," Jack had offered between slurps of beer.

Erica had Jed's cell phone number, too. But she didn't want to phone him. If she did, he'd either beg her to come—not terribly likely—or ask her not to come—fifty-fifty odds, she calculated. If she came, it might be to spend a little time with him, or a lot. This trip to New York couldn't be just about him, though. If she was truly prepared to step into a new life, it was the *life* she had to evaluate, not a man who might or might not be a part of that life.

So she'd traveled to Manhattan to feel it swirling around her, to hear it, smell it, wander among the shadows of its towering buildings. She'd come to compare it with Rockwell. She'd come because a public school on the Upper West Side had been very impressed with her résumé and wanted to offer her a position on its faculty.

Why not? she'd thought. She could be impulsive. She could dream new dreams if the old ones weren't coming true.

She'd come to check out the job, the city, the environment. She'd come to find out if this was a place where her new dreams could take root. But for some reason, she couldn't concentrate on any of those reasons for this trip until she saw Jed.

As the cab swept her downtown to the address she'd read from the back of Derrick Messinger's business card, she closed her eyes and took deep breaths. She had no idea what to expect. He could have a girlfriend here, or several. He probably did. His invitation for her to join him in New York was more than two months old. He might not even remember her anymore.

Oh, but she remembered him. She remembered everything about him—his eyes, his smile, his chronically mussed hair, his low voice. His protectiveness, not just when she'd been fighting off Toad Regan but when she'd been inundated by reporters shoving microphones and cameras into her face. She remembered his humor, his blunt candor and his refusal to use his lousy relationship with his father as an excuse for everything that might be wrong in his life. She remembered his willingness to listen when she wanted to talk, and to kiss when she wanted to be kissed.

The more she'd remembered in the weeks since he'd left Rockwell, the more convinced she grew that she loved him.

It was crazy. She'd known him such a short time. He was a junk dealer who'd never been to college, while she'd earned herself two Ivy League degrees. He was a small-town boy who'd chosen the big city, and she was an urban girl who'd chosen the small town. She had no idea if he liked Dave Matthews or the films of Almodóvar.

The cab double-parked. "This is it," the driver called through the partition.

Erica passed him the fare plus a two-dollar tip and got out of the cab, dragging her suitcase behind her. Jed might panic when he saw the bag, but he didn't need to. She had a room reserved at the midtown Marriott. She'd intended to check in and wash up before attempting to track Jed down, but the instant Derrick had handed her his card with the address of Jed's store written on it, she hadn't been able to think about anything else but finding him, seeing him, forcing herself to acknowledge how crazy it was for her to be in love with him. Before she made any more life-altering decisions, she needed to find out whether she'd made the biggest mistake of her life by giving up on Rockwell and all her old dreams.

"You haven't given up," she whispered to herself as the cab drove away. "You've chosen something new."

She turned to survey the building. It was huge, occupying a corner, the first floor consisting of showcase windows filled with household furnishings—wood pieces, upholstered pieces, lamps and accessories, some apparently vintage and others merely tacky. She'd expected his store to be smaller and more modest. Actually, she'd expected it to be something along the lines of the town dump in Rockwell, where Jed's father worked.

This emporium was no town dump. Through the windows she saw the silhouettes of people moving around inside—customers and staff. City Resale was no one-man operation.

But one man had created it. Jed. He'd taken junk and turned it into something valuable.

Anxiety seized her. What if Jed was too busy to see

her? What if he *said* he was too busy because he didn't
want to see her?

"Stop it," she ordered herself. "You're strong. You
can handle this."

Reminding herself she wasn't the sweet, gentle earth
mother she'd once aspired to be, she squared her shoulders and steeled her spine. No matter how hard she'd
tried, she had never come close to that ideal. Her garden was a disaster, a war between weeds and extremely
militant zucchini vines. Her cooking skills remained
pathetic. Her last attempt at baking bread had nearly
set her house on fire. After that, a new cricket had
taken up residence in her oven. Whenever she'd turned
it on, the cricket had screeched. She'd viewed that as
a sign.

She would never be an earth mother. All the L.L.
Bean apparel in the world wouldn't turn her into a rural
native. She was what she was—a nice Jewish girl from
Brookline who'd earned degrees at Harvard and
Brown, who could take on a classroom filled with
eight- and nine-year-olds and emerge victorious—and
she might as well stop running from her identity.

Bracing herself with a deep breath, she wheeled her
bag around the corner to the front double doors. Above
them a sign read City Resale. She pulled the door open
and went inside.

The showroom resembled a cross between a furniture store and an antique shop. Sofas, chairs, tables and
armoires were arranged in semicoherent groupings
around rug remnants, then piled high with afghans,
vases, old leather-bound books, dinged and scratched
chess sets and assorted other tchotchkes. Framed mirrors, lithograph prints and portrait paintings of dreary,
forgettable ancestors hung on the walls.

Erica meandered through the showroom until she found an available clerk. A young, pretty blond clerk. Jed worked with this woman. He worked with lots of women and lived in a city filled with lots more. He'd slept with Erica only because she'd been the new girl in Rockwell, the most convenient female in that tiny town. In New York, every female was convenient.

Stop it, she silently scolded herself. If Jed didn't consider her convenient enough for his purposes anymore, well, she didn't want to be convenient, anyway. She wanted... She wanted to accept the life she was designed for, she wanted to accept herself, and she wanted, if possible, Jed to accept her.

"Excuse me," she said, claiming the cute blond clerk's attention. "I'm looking for Jed Willetz."

"He's upstairs," the clerk told her.

Erica surveyed the store in search of a stairway or elevator. "How do I get upstairs?"

"You're not allowed up there. It's not open to the public."

Erica wondered whether the clerk was being deliberately difficult or was merely dense. "Then how can we get Jed downstairs?" she asked.

Merely dense, she decided when the clerk frowned for a minute, then nodded enthusiastically, as if Erica had just come up with a brilliant idea. "I'll phone upstairs and ask him to come down," she said.

"Thank you." Erica followed her to a small office off the showroom, convinced that if she didn't walk the clerk through each step of this task, it wouldn't be successfully completed.

The blonde's ponytail swayed saucily as she reached across the desk for the phone, punched in three numbers and listened. "Hi, Jed? Some woman in the store wants to see you."

Some woman, Erica thought, pinching her lips. She'd never thought of herself as *some woman* before. Derrick had treated her like a returning hero, not just *some woman.*

The clerk listened for a minute, then hung up. "He'll be down in a couple of minutes," she reported.

Erica thanked her again and moved away from the office, wheeling her bag behind her. She paused to inspect a cherry sideboard, which wore a few nicks but looked warm and graceful, and a set of four ladder-back chairs with a dark walnut stain, and a Deco-style vanity table with a cloudy three-paned mirror. That people actually discarded such furniture astonished her. It was good solid stuff.

Maybe it hadn't been good solid stuff when Jed had obtained it. Maybe it had been splintered and teetering, and he'd repaired it like a surgeon mending a broken body. Maybe these pieces looked so good only because of Jed's talent and labor.

He would probably be friendly when he saw her, she prepped herself. He'd ask how she was doing, and he'd be surprised when she told him. Perhaps he'd ask her if she was free for dinner. Possibly he'd even invite her back to his bed. They'd had quite a spectacular time that one night.

But she cautioned herself to lower her expectations. He could be involved with someone, already claimed. He could be a whole lot different in the city than he was in his hometown. She'd come to New York to learn about herself, not because he was here.

Yeah, right.

"Hey," his familiar voice rolled over her from behind. She spun around and saw—a surgeon.

No, he wasn't a surgeon. He had a surgical mask dangling by its ties around his neck like a surgeon emerging from the operating room, but he was dressed in a T-shirt, jeans and a leather bib apron. Clear plastic goggles perched on the crown of his head and his shoes were covered in pale dust.

"Great T-shirt," he said.

She smiled hesitantly.

He lifted the neck strap of his apron over his head, managing not to dislodge the goggles, and let the bib fall to his waist. His T-shirt read, Rockwell—the Town of Hidden Treasures. "You got one, too?"

"Just before I left. Glenn Rideout was so scared of my supposed shark of a lawyer, he sold it to me for ten bucks."

"Ten? I paid eighteen for mine at the Superette!" She tried to muster the proper indignation at this gross injustice.

Jed chuckled, a deep, sexy sound. "What are you doing here?"

"It's a long story."

"I've got time." He motioned with his head toward a hallway near the office. "Leave your bag here and come on." The blond clerk stared at them, as if to object to Jed's taking some woman where customers weren't allowed to go, but she belatedly seemed to remember that Jed was the boss, and she fell back a step and let them pass.

The hallway led to a freight elevator. Jed pulled a key from the pocket of his jeans and used it to activate the elevator.

He still hadn't touched her. He hadn't kissed her

cheek, let alone her mouth. He hadn't even spoken her name. Maybe he couldn't remember it.

That was all right. She'd refresh his memory, tell an abridged version of her long story and catch a cab to the hotel. She would survive. She wouldn't fall apart until she was locked safely inside her hotel room, where she could wail and moan and curse his soul to hell.

The elevator rumbled to a halt and Jed shoved open the hinged metal grating. Not surprisingly, the car was enormous. He could fit an entire bedroom set inside it if he had to. In his line of work, he probably had to on a regular basis.

They stepped into the car. Jed shoved the door shut and yanked a lever to make the elevator rise. His eyes narrowed on her, silvery cool and beautiful. Abruptly, he shoved the lever to stop the car. "In case you were wondering," he said, "I'd be jumping your bones right now if I didn't have sawdust all over me."

Well. That had to mean something.

"Sawdust has its drawbacks," she said, feeling slightly more confident than she had minutes ago.

He reactivated the elevator, which crept up to the second floor and bumped to a stop. Pushing open the grating, he gestured for her to precede him into a vast, well-lit workshop jammed with merchandise in various stages of disrepair. Sofas with stuffing oozing from them stood side by side with Chippendale-style high-boys, butcher-block kitchen tables, three-legged chairs, tarnished silver trays and a carved wooden rocking horse in desperate need of a competent groom. Bright fluorescent lights stretched overhead, and the room smelled of raw wood, lacquer and solvent.

He led her down an aisle between piles of clutter to

an open area where a long trestle table stood on a canvas drop cloth, its finish sanded off in places and flaked and chipped in others. An electric sander rested on the table. A bench along one wall held an array of carpentry tools, paintbrushes and cans of paint, stains and varnish.

"This is where you perform magic," Erica said.

Jed snorted. "It's not magic. It's a sander." He lifted the bulky tool, then placed it back on the table and dropped his goggles next to it.

"Do you work here all alone?"

"Not usually. A guy who specializes in reupholstery is here three days a week, and some students come in after school for a couple of hours every day so they can learn some skills and make a little money. Then I've got experts like your professor friend, when I pick up a piece I think might be really old. They'll come in and appraise it, and if it needs work I'll hire a pro who can repair it without ruining its value as an antique." He shrugged, untied his apron and draped it over a hook on the wall by his tool bench.

Erica stared at his Rockwell T-shirt because it was easier than staring at his face. He looked a little tired, a little tousled, smudged here and there with sawdust. Even unkempt, he was absurdly attractive.

Did he really want to jump her bones, or was that just his idea of friendly small talk? Whichever it was, now wasn't the time to renew their sexual acquaintanceship. She wasn't the person she'd been when they'd last seen each other. He might not even recognize her bones by the time she was done telling him her long story.

Which wasn't all that long, really. "I've left Rockwell," she began, because he seemed to be waiting for her to say something.

"What do you mean?"

She suddenly felt weary, but she saw no place to sit. A gazillion pieces of furniture filled this workshop, but nowhere for a woman to rest her tired feet.

Jed must have sensed her fatigue, because he dragged over a frumpy armchair that his reupholstery specialist had obviously not gotten around to refurbishing yet. She settled into it, adjusting her bottom on the lumpy cushions, and waited while he hauled over a vinyl dinette chair. He straddled it backward, rested his hands on the back and his chin on his hands, and peered into her face. He looked curious, she decided. Not excited, not eager to jump her bones but willing to hear her out.

"The box turned out to be worth a lot," she began. "Well, not the box itself. That was worth something, of course. I donated it to Harvard. I also donated two of the coins, which will be included in the display they're arranging for the box. It's not as if I'm some sort of altruist—I got a tax break for making the donation."

Jed nodded slightly. His eyes glowed brighter than the overhead fixtures.

"The rest of the coins I sold to a rare-coin dealer. They were worth almost two hundred thousand dollars."

"Nice." Jed brushed the edge of his jaw with his knuckles, loosening some sawdust. "It must've made Rideout nuts, your making all that money off the coins."

"Well, I shared it with him." She cut off Jed's scowl by adding, "Actually, not with him. I shared it with Randy. I set up a trust fund so his father can't touch a penny of that money. It'll all be waiting for Randy when he's ready to go to college.''

Jed appeared mollified. "All right. Just as long as Rideout doesn't get his greedy paws on it.''

"In a way, he does get his greedy paws on the money, because now he won't have to pay for Randy's education out of his own pocket. But I had the feeling that if Randy got into college, his father wouldn't have paid for it anyway. I set things up so I'm the trustee of the fund. That way I can make sure it isn't mishandled.'' She smiled, still proud of how well she'd finessed Glenn Rideout. "Talk about making Glenn nuts! How could he sue me when I was so generous in sharing my bounty with his son?''

Jed chuckled appreciatively.

"Anyway, that's the story of the box. Maybe you heard about it from your father.''

"As if I talk to my father on a regular basis,'' Jed scoffed. "Every now and then he calls and asks me when I'm going to sell my grandfather's place and what I'm going to do with the money I make from the sale. That's about the sum of it.''

"I thought he was interested in the box. He certainly talked to me about it.''

"He probably offered to invest some of your profits for you.''

"He had some ideas. So did just about everybody else in town.'' Her smile grew pensive. All those people with their ideas had been her neighbors, her compatriots, the folks who'd populated her dream.

But that dream had died, and she'd buried it as effectively as Jed had buried his grandfather's ashes. Now she'd reached the hard part of her story, the part that still hurt, the part about her failures and the end of her dream. "My garden is a disaster."

Jed didn't seem startled by the abrupt change in subject. "No more treasures buried there, huh?"

"The zucchini is overgrowing everything in sight. Most of the tomato plants died. The peas are anemic. There are weeds everywhere. I was weeding every day, Jed, every single day, and the weeds just kept coming back. And I put some fencing in to keep the deer out, but something small kept burrowing under the fence and munching on the plants. Randy thought it might be a groundhog."

"They're known to do that."

"But it doesn't matter, because even if my garden produced a good crop, I wouldn't know what to do with the vegetables. I'm an awful cook, Jed."

His nod of agreement didn't flatter her.

"I studied everything I could about canning, but I knew I'd make a mess of it. I probably wouldn't get the jars sealed properly and everything would rot, and I'd poison myself with rancid tomato sauce next winter."

"You're not stupid, Erica. You could have figured it out."

"It has nothing to do with stupidity. We all have our strengths and weaknesses, Jed. My strengths are intellectual. I'm a scholar and a teacher—a damn good teacher. But I'm not an earth mother. I always wanted to be one, and I tried really hard—but it's not what I am."

To her chagrin, she felt a tear leak from her eye and skitter down her cheek.

Jed didn't comment on it or hand her a handkerchief.

She would have hated it if he had. She didn't want his pity.

"I wanted to belong in Rockwell, but I never did. So I sold my house."

"No kidding?" He leaned back in apparent shock. "Someone actually bought that old shack?"

"*I* bought that old shack not too long ago," she reminded him.

"Well, okay. Sorry." He appeared to be suppressing a grin. "What about your teaching job?"

"School districts all over the place are desperate for talented teachers. Especially teachers with credentials like mine. I've been offered a job at a primary school on the Upper West Side," she told him, watching him, searching for any sign of panic or dread in his face.

He maintained his poker face. "Where else have you applied?" he asked.

She should lie, but she didn't. "Just New York City."

Then she saw him relax, finally allowing a smile to claim him. "Good," he said. Just that one simple word.

"Jed, when you asked me to come to New York back in April, you were just, I don't know, caught up in the moment. I have no expectations here, no hopes beyond the fact that you're one of the very few people I know in the city. Your invitation was never about commitment or everlasting love or anything like that. I'm sure we both understand that." Which hardly explained why the first thing she'd done after disembarking from the bus was to track Jed down.

He reached out and pulled one of her hands from her lap. She hadn't been aware until that moment of how much her fingers had been fidgeting. "I'm glad you're so positive about what that invitation meant. Because I sure as hell never figured it out.''

She wished his hand didn't feel so warm and enveloping. He was telling her he had no idea why he'd even asked her to join him in New York. Why did his hand seem to say that he knew exactly why he'd asked?

"The few times I phoned my dad, I asked about you. He said you were rich and snooty and didn't give a damn about him or anybody else. Then he moved on to badgering me about my grandfather's place.''

"I *did* give a damn!'' Erica protested. "About him and *everybody* else! I would have probably given up on Rockwell a long time ago if I hadn't cared so much.''

"Hey, you don't have to convince me. I'm just saying, I wanted to hear about you. I wanted to know what you were doing. I wanted to know if you were missing me. Because I missed you—pretty much nonstop.''

She gaped at him. "Why didn't you call me? Why didn't you let me know?''

"Erica, I asked you to come with me and you said no. What am I, a masochist? One no got the job done.'' He stroked his thumb across the back of her hand, slowly, tenderly. "You chose Rockwell over me. It didn't matter how much I missed you. As long as you chose Rockwell, nothing would ever work between us.''

"It wasn't Rockwell I chose,'' she tried to explain. "It was a dream, this fantasy idea of myself that I didn't want to give up. Erica Leitner, the gardener, the baker, the small-town woman connected to the earth and the sky and the mountains.'' She sighed. "After you left, the dream just shriveled up and blew away.

So I told Burt Johnson I'd be resigning at the end of the school year and I put my house up for sale.''

"And you came to New York."

"I considered some openings in the Boston area. Fern Bernard was really pushing for those, since she goes down there practically every weekend to see Avery Gilman.''

"But you came to New York."

"Tell me I'm not making a mistake this time," she whispered. "Tell me this is a dream worth pursuing.''

His hand tightened around hers. "I don't have any fancy college degree," he reminded her. "I'm a junk dealer, just like my father.''

"You're not a junk dealer, Jed. I see what's up here, and I saw what's downstairs in your store. What you are is a miracle worker. You transform all this stuff—'' she gestured toward the jumble of items awaiting repair "—into beautiful things people would love to have in their homes. You see below the surface, below the dirt and the damage. You know how to tell the treasures from the junk. You know what's valuable.''

"You're what's valuable to me," he said. "You're incredible, Erica. You lose a dream, and you just pick yourself up and start dreaming something new. You've got so much courage, so much strength." He lifted her hand to his lips and pressed a kiss against her palm. "Take the job in New York. We'll dream something new together.''

For the first time since she'd gotten off the bus— for the first time since she'd gotten *on* it… For the first time since she'd told Jed, back in Rockwell, that she wouldn't go to New York with him, she felt her soul flower open and fill with light. She didn't need mud and a garden and an L.L. Bean sun hat to feel connected to something bigger than herself, something more important, more vital. She felt connected now.

This was who she was. Not an earth mother, not a small-town rustic but a woman who had found the man with whom she wanted to share her dreams.

He swung his leg over his chair and stood, then pulled her to her feet and wrapped his arms around her. His mouth met hers in a long, loving kiss. "Just tell me one thing," he murmured once they'd come up for air.

"Yes," she whispered. "Anything."

"Who the hell bought your house?"

She grinned. "The town did."

"What?"

"The town of Rockwell. They're going to turn it into a tourist destination—the house where the hidden treasure was found. They're calling it a museum, and they're going to charge admission. For an extra fee, a visitor will be permitted to shovel in the backyard for ten minutes, in case there are any other treasures buried there. Sewell McCormick predicts the town will make a fortune on it."

Jed threw back his head and let loose a laugh. "Oh, God, what a town," he roared.

She plucked at his shirt. "Rockwell is in your blood, Jed. Mine, too. Look at us, wearing these shirts."

"Well, they're true," he said before dropping a gentle kiss onto her mouth. "We found a treasure there, didn't we?" He kissed her again, a lot less gently, and she decided this new dream was going to turn out fine.

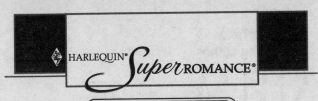

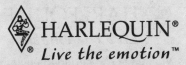

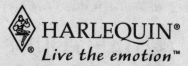

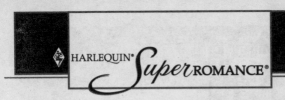

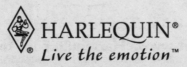

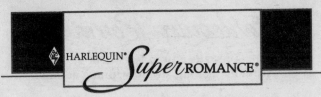

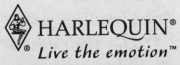

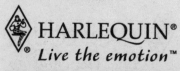

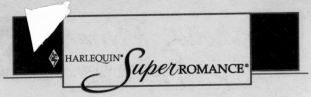

HARLEQUIN *Super*ROMANCE®

WHITE KNIGHT INVESTIGATIONS

A new series by M.J. Rodgers

Meet the Knight brothers, David, Jack, Richard and Jared— Silver Valley, Washington's finest detectives. They're ready and willing to help anyone who calls!

Baby by Chance
(#1116 March 2003)

Susan Carter needs to find the man who fathered her unborn child. In desperation she turns to David Knight. She knows she's going to look bad—she doesn't even know the man's last name— but she has no other choice.

For the Defense
(#1137 June 2003)

Jack Knight isn't used to having to justify himself to anyone, and that's exactly what lawyer Diana Mason is demanding he do. He's not the Knight she wants working for her, but he's the only one who can prove her client is innocent of murder.

Available wherever Harlequin books are sold.

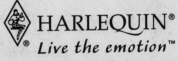

HARLEQUIN®
Live the emotion™

Visit us at www.eHarlequin.com

HSRWKI2T

Cowgirl, Say Yes
by Brenda Mott,
author of *Sarah's Legacy*

Widowed rancher Wade Darland and his children have never met a cowgirl like Tess Vega, who has just set up a horse sanctuary for abused and abandoned horses. They all want more of her in their lives. Now they have to get Tess to say yes!

On sale starting April 2003

Buffalo Summer
by Nadia Nichols,
author of *Montana Dreaming*

Caleb McCutcheon is living his dream—owning a large Rocky Mountain West ranch and a herd of magnificent buffalo. Now if only the woman he's beginning to love would agree to share his dream…

On sale starting June 2003

Heartwarming stories with a sense of humor, genuine charm and emotion and lots of family!

Available wherever Harlequin books are sold.

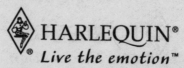

HARLEQUIN®
Live the emotion™

Visit us at www.eHarlequin.com

HSRHORAJ